HOOD

HOOD

SEASON ONE

LILITH SAINTCROW

SAINTCROW

For those who did not return.

History is a set of lies agreed upon.

- NAPOLEON BONAPARTE

NOTE_

Several generation ships left Old Terra in pairs, carrying many cultural influences. Anglene was settled by one of those pairs; the discerning Reader is invited to search for the provenance of several terms that, while scientific when the ships were sent, have long since passed into common usage.

Readers are also invited to remember that the legends this particular story is built upon served many different purposes, from the personal to the social to the cultural. True legends are shapeshifting mirrors; we see in them what we wish.

If this tale does not suit, you are more than free to write your own.

PART 1
LANDFALL_

HOME FRONT_

"Peacetime has different demands," the general with yellowed teeth—definitely not implants—said through bloodless lips, every pore on his sagging face visible at the head of the transport's long, dimly lit alley. Even if you didn't have your earfillers in or your audio jacked you knew what he was yammering about, because the text-scroll at the bottom jumped out in flashing noro-red, the color they trained you to take seriously.

The Corps joke was only corpses didn't snap to attention when noro popped. Three-dimensional, the words throbbed like a bad tooth, a speech about transitioning to what every soldat longed for if they had any sense robbed of its enticement by the readipak appeals to patriotism.

The only time they started talking about Greater Anglene was when they wanted some idiots to "volunteer" for shit duty. You learned that quick in the Corps, but some didn't learn quick *enough* and ended up gutshot, whisped, choked by kanno-gassa, or pounded into rags of flesh by a barrage they could have avoided by simply staying home.

"Gonna get *laaaid*," the clipped-bald serjeant at the end of Hood's row said for the fiftieth time since they jumped atmo. Hood's stomach turned over, but he didn't move. It was best to stay still when motion wasn't absolutely required. "Oh, man," the serjeant continued, "I am gonna get so *laaaid*."

"Good for you," a caporal with new teeth-buds filling in her bottom jaw and the pink of reconstructive flesh on her cheeks barked across the aisle. "Shut up about it, some of us are tryna sleep."

The serje caressed his X-lock, staring straight ahead. Bare scalp gleamed under a thin screen of dark fuzz; he shut up, but Hood was sure it was a mercy of short duration. At least this wasn't transpo to a combat drop; you could—technically—smack your X-lock and get up, fumble down the central aisle with boots grabbing tacfloor and every muscle fighting standard transport grav, and make it to the head.

It wasn't worth it; Corps transport grav was notoriously tricky, given to small bubbles. If you took a header on the metal grating made for grab-boots, you could land hard, flay uniform and flesh both, and get a bunch of assholes laughing at you in the bargain.

So Hood lowered his eyelids another fraction, trying not to stare at flashing red text. Fighting the training meant to keep you alive was only acceptable in short doses and extraordinary situations; Logic take it all, Hood looked forward to being a civilian again.

At least now the rebellion was over and *civilian* wasn't just another word for *casualty*. Or even worse, *insurgent*—a redband wrapped up in rags, ready to thump a thermal 'nade or shoot a dumbass soldat just trying to do their job. Hood exhaled, slowly, passing the midpoint where the trigger should be squeezed.

No targets in range. Except that stupid sex-starved serje, who inhaled like he was going to start in again.

"Don't," someone muttered in the row behind them, a harsh throat-cut combat whisper. "Don't do it, ya moonie logicfucker."

Maybe the serje heard, or maybe he just decided talking about it was no use when he could fantasize quietly. In any case, he shut up and Hood's fingers fell away from the hilt tucked along his left hip. Slim, razor-edged, and entirely illegal, part of any old-timer's kit, the whisp was a redband's preferred assassination tool, easy to make and practically undetectable even on morascans. Get close in a crowd, slide the whisp between barely perceptible seams of wrap-armor, vanish into the confusion. More than one officer learned about the whisps too late, bled dry on dust-filthy streets between billets. Settlements crowded with sullen faces, readipak food and the chaos of combat drops, waiting in a filthy hide with only his own stink and the ryfl to keep him company—and all the while, not a single word from home.

What a word. *Home.* As if all planets, all mining moons or asteroids, all settlements, all cities weren't the fucking same. Interchangeable, like soldats on the firing line. Getting into long-range training just made you lonelier, it didn't make you any less...what was the word?

Marah would know. She'd used it once in primary school, for a history report. *Fungible*, that was it. Like a fungus, only not. Double meanings in the same sounds like a good hide, one you could use more than once. Variation kept you safe, but sometimes they wouldn't expect you to strike again from the same spot.

Hood took a deep breath. Sweat, oil, uniform cloth, the slight hot smell of primed 'nades and cryon. Boots worn so long the feet felt naked without them, uniforms clean and pressed as if you were on R&R, hair and faces freshly shaved since it was peacetime now and regulations that meant nothing in the field must be adhered to, so help you Logic and pray a *polis-militaire* didn't show up.

The tethered shimscreen at the head of the transport flickered. The general's face vanished; a ripple of interest went through caged soldats. But it was only footage of another Victory Parade, this one on Capricorn Prime. Evanescent flutters filling the air, flymsytape that would disappear when the humidity rose, bright dots raining on an apathetic crowd watching dress-uniformed Corpsmen march in blue-clad lockstep. Black with blue stripe was for the polis, blue dress was for the Corps, noro-red for *watch your shit, swabbie.*

Hood shut his eyes. As soon as they docked he'd be put on a smaller transport, one with actual seats instead of cradles and X-locks. He might even achieve a fitful sleep before landing on Sagittarius Prime. He'd be processed out, given a slap on the back, and as soon as his boots touched the street outside the rectangular black CPC in Sharud he would be plain old Robb Locke again. He could hire a khibi to take him out to Lamóre, and even if his father wouldn't see him there would be the hay-fragrant loft to sleep in. Shit, he'd done it before when Father was mad. And if the barn was locked or he didn't feel like it, he could hoof out to Madán, and there...

Hood closed his eyes, and saw that clearing in the woods near Lamór Slee, the water turned to a trickle under fierce summer heat. The afternoon before he left, Marah's arms crossed and the light on her long, curling blue-black hair. *You don't have to, Robb. Nobody will think any less of you, and who cares what your father says?*

Of course his progenitor hadn't written. But even in his dreams, Hood wondered why *she* hadn't.

It didn't matter. Once he got home, he'd pick up where he let off. That was the promise, right? *Join Parl Jun, and do your duty!* All the holos had adoring girls beaming at uniformed shapes, and everyone who came back from leave talked about getting laid by chieweed pretties.

Well, he'd done everything that could be considered duty, maybe he'd even get something like a reward. Hood dropped into sleep with a soldat's ease, and if his dreaming hands twitched, feeling the jolt of the ryfl, that was all right. At least dreams couldn't hurt you.

Or so he thought then.

ONE-A-PENNY, TWO-A-PENNY_

IN SPACE, NOBODY COULD HEAR YOU CURSE WHEN YOU SKINNED your knuckles.

At least, so Marah Madán told herself, sucking on her knuckles and tasting blood. The warning light flicker-faded, and a steady row of blue and green was her reward for guesswork and hope, not to mention a generous helping of her own flesh left on unforgiving metal. "Try it again," she yelled through the hatch, even though she knew they would hear her over the intercom, snugging herself into the standing cradle and X-harness near the door. "Yes, I'm clipped in." She shoved the catch closed, hurriedly, since Will wouldn't engage until he got the harness feedback.

"*Now* you are clipped in. All Terrans are safely stowed." Will's disembodied, static-spike voice floated from at least three speakers. "Mistress, all readings are within acceptable limits. Standby for gravsat in three...two..."

Marah braced herself. If this didn't work, she was going to have to get creative.

"One," Will finished, and a deep, happy thrumming added itself to the rest of the engine noises. A familiar dragging along all her limbs settled into an ache on her bruised left hip as well as the smaller pain of her knuckles throbbing. The voice changed, spilled through the grating nearest her with far less interference. "Grav engaged at ninety-three percent standard. Terran vitals holding steady. Mistress, are you all right?"

"Fine." She ached all over, but that was usual after a few days collecting and stacking salvage. "Just had to hit it kind of hard. Jorah? How we doing?"

"Ready to jump as soon as you're on deck, boss lady." Her pilot's cheerful, deep baritone lost only a little of its warmth through the intercom's electronic throat. "Will, start crunching gate numbers."

"The navsat has already begun," Will replied, equably. After a while, you started inferring emotion onto skarls, an operational hazard. Even the latex-skinned Wi3+ series the Corps used for limited trauma support got names and imputed personalities. "Mistress, the closest first-aid cabinet is fully stocked. It is located—"

"—in the next chuteway, Will, yes, thank you." Marah suppressed the urge to grind her teeth. Her head-cover had slipped, her Corps-shorn hair in the most awkward phase of growing-out. Too long to stay out of her way, too short to tie back, and enough to make her grimly swear she would *never* cut it again, Mother Moon witness her vow. A few minutes with a keratin spinner would solve it, but she preferred the old way. "I'm *fine*. Just some skinned knuckles. I'm a medic, not a mechanic."

"You have aptitude." A little red eye across the under-engine bay blinked, right over the tiny fisheye lens Will was probably using to watch her right now. Of course, a synthetic could sync with just about any tech advanced or open enough; you'd have to have something low on the Erdmann Scale or military highgrade to keep them out. Their ethical programming was stringent enough to keep skarls from peering where they shouldn't, but it always permitted safety checks while outside a planet's gravwell.

"Aptitude my ass," Marah muttered. "Usually when a male says that, he wants something from me."

Jorah's laugh crackled through the comm grating, cut off midway by Will's reply, placid and undisturbed. "You must be careful, mistress. Infection can compromise a Terran system in very little time."

"Thanks, Will," Jorah cut in. "Give the lady some privacy, huh?"

The red light flickered off, but it was a safe bet Will was monitoring in other ways. Dad should have named him Spye like the HSS agent in the old flat-talkies. Unfortunately, First Echelon Aethelstan Rotherwood Madán had seen no need to give Will anything other than a utilitarian pun of a callsign, and by the time Marah was eight, she'd taken to calling him Will too. It was too late to change now.

When Marah reached the bridge, the lean iron-haired skarl turned in the navigator's seat and examined her. The retainer had a weathered face, almost parental in its changelessness; not a single line on it had moved since her childhood. Will's consciousness resided in the Terran-looking frame as a matter of course, since you couldn't expect a WiII retainer to let its Terran wander unprotected; his secondary consciousness often resided in Madán alcazar's stone walls and seamless tech. When he retired to his upgrade cabinet, the two synced; degradation of the secondary would set in after a couple tendays without the catch-up.

Outside the bridge's bubble, stars glittered in hard blackness. Much closer, Sagg Prime glowed, a blue jewel with two habitable moons glittering sharply as well. The salvage belt past the uninhabited Sagg-Roque 4, stuffed with cruiser remains and cubes of compressed, unscreened rubbish that nevertheless might hold traces of minerals or tech worth stripping, moved with deceptive slowness. It took a light touch and one eye always on the scanners to avoid being caught between interlocking fields of trash. The further in you went, the better the pickings were—and the more dangerous it was when the thrusters decided they were going to stop taking overflow and demand most of the available power instead.

Jorah stretched out his legs, his beefy paws steady and delicate as he tapped, got returns, ran them again. "How bad is it?"

Normally she would have assumed he was talking about the grav shunted from the core, but he jabbed a meaty finger at her bandaged hand.

"I'm *fine*," Marah checked the line of tolerances on the secondary board—all green or yellow, safe enough. "I know how to apply antiseptic and skintape. What gate are we aiming for?" A tiny starsteal hop would get them across the empty space between the edge of the belt and home, and she was almost looking forward to real grav instead of the facsimile.

Almost.

"The usual. Sagg P, A-1." Jorah shrugged, and his careful nonchalance was a sign of deep relief. The A-1 gate was busy enough to slip through without a search, not like either of the moon-gates. "If there's anyone really on-spot around we'll have to, you know, just fly casual."

"All our flymsywork's in order." Marah resettled her head-cover and glanced at Will before settling in the captain's cradle, running her gaze along the primary readouts. "Right?"

"Yes, mistress." Will's murmur was barely audible, since he would suspect the question was rhetorical.

"Uh-huh. Sure." Jorah grinned. His left canine gleamed under a scarred lip, freshly budded in with his fraction of the last load's sellworth. After a couple days out, he lost the miserable look he had planetside, unbuttoning his violently patterned shirts and scratching luxuriously at a Corps surplus under while on night watch, singing old chieweed songs while the smears or pinpricks of stars went on their cold, impersonal way outside. He wasn't really fat, just *big*, long thick heavyworlder bones, muscles used to hauling, a bushy gingerish head, and palms that Marah could use as a scalp-warmer if she was still fully Corps-cropped.

"The gate is set, our queue order fixed," Will recited. "Awaiting your mark, mistress."

For probably the thousandth time that day, Marah buckled in. She flicked a few toggles, glanced at Jorah, and watched the lights all turn green, a sweet sight indeed. "One-a-penny, two-a-penny," she said, softly. Then, in her usual crisp captain's voice, "Hit it."

The stars turned to greasy, random-swirling streaks, and she exhaled.

"We'll make it." Jorah hunched in the refitted pilot's cradle. They'd had to cut part of the console away and rewire it, he was just so huge. "But I'm tellin' you, Marah, we need servicing."

"I know." She was lucky to have a good pilot who didn't refuse to take an elderly transport out of atmo, really. The wrights would have a field day with the *Retreat* as soon as they touched down. "Soon as we hit the ground. I shouldn't have pushed it."

"Well, *I* told you it was safe." Jorah was unwilling to impute a bad call to a capitaine he respected; it was a pilot's courtesy, and one she rather cherished.

A jolt, the star-smears turning over, and she watched the countdown. The clinic could use everything she brought and more, since Madán's liquidity was hedged with the trust fund restrictions to keep a First Echelon's birthright from being frittered away.

Well, where there was Discipline there was a way, as the saying went. They taught you triage in the Corps, allocating resources for maximum efficiency. The Wi3s could help and calculate, but the final decision was Terran; on that, the Triad Laws were quite clear. They taught you in school it was for the best; besides, synthetics couldn't be sued or punished.

A derelict or malicious medical worker could.

So, they gave you triage drills all through your residency until you learned your limits. Fatigue was a brain-killer, rest strictly enjoined and enforced except under the worst combat conditions. It was dinned into medics over and over—*you can't help anyone if you're dead on your feet*. Burnout and fatigue aided the enemy.

The best thing about being out of the Corps was the luxury of deciding what she was going to burn herself out *on*. A lot of people chose korprene or eating a white rail. Slow overdose on the one hand, a quick venting on the other; either road led you away into the black between stars.

So much space, and only slivers of it habitable by Terrans.

Fighting over those slices, ostensibly for living space or resources, was really just sheer madness. "Resources" as a concept lost all meaning when you were talking about infinity.

Except there was the difference between those who wrested the resources free and those who profited. Even on the ships fleeing Old Terra, the division was sharp and uncrossable.

Thinking about history put Marah in a bad mood, and she had other worries now.

"Beginning gate countdown." Will's hatchet profile was serene, contemplative. Colored light flashed over his cheeks, and he turned his head slightly, glancing at her. The faint silvery sheen over his eyes gleamed, whites, iris, and pupil all refracting differently than a born Terran's; he must be worried for it to show. "Mistress, there is official activity around the gate point."

"Great," Jorah muttered. It was too late to change course now.

Starstreaks spun counterclockwise, the bubble briefly darkening to shield Terran eyes from a possibly insanity-producing sight. *Ivanhoe's Retreat* popped out of starseal much closer to Sagg Prime's familiar bluegreen bulk. The planet filled the entire view, scanners fuzzing for a moment before untangling skeins of data. Much closer, a great suborbital transport ring glittered with a move-along pattern. The Aegis cruisers weren't doing spot checks, but the *Retreat*'s tingler lit up a fraction of a second before Will spoke. "They are scanning, mistress."

"That's fine," she murmured. Jorah brought the ship around, clearing their landing quadrant, and began muttering his usual song of nerves.

Will would make sure their scans didn't show anything...unusual. Offmarket mods on a retainer weren't *quite* legal, but Marah was First Echelon, and would only get a fine.

Or so she hoped.

Comms lit up, a watch-me pattern in blue. "It's official," Jorah said. "Ugh."

"Shh." Marah touched the proper dial, leaned forward, and the hailer dropped from overhead. She caught it, wincing a little when her palm smacked against metal—grav was at half while syncing with Sagg Prime's well and setting up their landing angle, and it made her proprioception slightly off. "This is Marah Madán of House Madán Mizar, capitaine of the *Ivanhoe's Retreat*. Our registration is in order and our cargo secure. What is your query?"

A familiar voice drifted through the comms. "Another mission of mercy, Mads?"

"Hi, Giz." She didn't have to work to sound tired. Still, a thin thread of warmth curled through the bottom of her chest; she quashed it sternly. "What are you doing out of the well?"

"Orders." Which was all he ever said; you could drop a secret into Ged Gizabón and never even hear it hit the water. Even in secondary he'd been like that, let alone tertiary school. "What are you bringing in, dare I ask?"

"Medical supplies and salvage." Marah restrained the urge to add more. Unnecessary details were a dead giveaway. "As usual, and as our transmitted manifest says."

"I suppose if we came and looked, that's exactly what we'd find?" There was even a note of amusement in his voice, but that didn't mean anything.

"You want to?" Marah closed her eyes; she wasn't a Discipline or even a fullblown Lunacer, but a little prayer never hurt. "I'll make you a cup of tai. Instant, but still hot." That was the joke in tertiary; even Echelons were on tiny stipends during higher schooling.

Giz laughed, the acid bark he'd come back from the war with. "No fraternizing on duty, they tell me. Pass by, Lady of Madán." Lights turned blue on the cronkboard, and Jorah nudged the ship forward, not waiting for Marah's glance. "I'll take that tai later, when I'm off-shift."

"Certainly." *And I'll pick that time to be very, very busy.* Or maybe she wouldn't, but she had to ration the attention she gave any man, Echelon or peasant. It was an old, familiar calculation, comforting like any threadbare habit. "Over and out." She hit the toggle and exhaled, hard.

"He knows," Jorah muttered, darkly, his broad face flushing.

"Not necessarily." She rubbed at her temples; her right hand stung with antibiotic and skintape around her abraded knuckles. "He just acts like he does and watches for people getting nervous."

"Huh." Jorah considered this, popped the grav-tuner, and oriented them for entry, waiting for the navsat to clear a route. "He makes *me* nervous."

Well, they didn't call Ged Gizabón *Noth's Ryfl* for nothing, she supposed. "He does that to a lot of people."

"But not you?" Jorah very deliberately didn't sneak a glance at her, but he obviously *wanted* to.

It was hard to be nervous when you remembered a scab-kneed transfer kid with a shy smile, a high-prowed nose, bright blue bad-luck eyes, and a shock of dark hair. Or when you had stopped, mouth ajar in shock, at a young soldat's cot in a trauma tent, artillery shaking the earth into liquefaction less than three miles away away, and snapped *get the fuck away with that, he's fine.*

"Not me." Her side-screen lit, showing the starboard buffers were heating up before they touched more than a fringe of atmo. "But the buffers do make me a little concerned. Will, route that overflow."

"Yes, mistress," Will said, and from there it was like every other landing.

They were almost home.

OLD WARHORSES_

"You just let them through?" Captain Parmecy was an oiled, black-haired weasel with a seamed scar down the left side of his face—it looked like a corefrag, and his left eye was a standard issue ocular implant instead of a bud—and affected astonishment. His new black-and-blue thermaseal polis uniform, creased precisely at every regulation fold, probably still smelled of distribution center moth-repellant, or maybe it was just his expression that made it seem that way. "It's a hunk of junk, it's barely spaceworthy. That's a smuggler's ship."

"That's our Lady of Madán," Ged Gizabón replied, calmly. His gloved hands, fingertips pressing together, didn't move; the sleek console in front of him already had the next five ships in line shimmering in the holo field, scan-symbols popping under each glowing 3D representation. "She's First Echelon, she can fly what she wants, and the Sharl will be displeased if she's interfered with." It wasn't quite a lie; Noth knew Marah dabbled in quasi-legal salvage to keep the clinic open, but moving against a First Echelon, even one whose lone representative was a single female, was unprofitable.

Especially since after the old lord's death, Marah had been a ward of Parl Riccar himself. Besides, she charmed even grasping, flat-eyed Noth. She flat-out charmed *everyone*.

Or maybe that was just Giz's personal opinion. Noth really wouldn't give two shits if she was interfered with, but Giz himself would, and that was good enough. He was endlessly glad this was his last stint on gate duty.

"Oh." Parmecy's thin, scraped-clean cheek jumped, a tiny tic. Next he'd look for someone else to blame for his *faux pas*. "Sounded pretty chummy."

Yes, right on time. The only thing worse than arrogance was predictability. "She runs a Free Clinic for non-cits in the Saur. Goes out picking up salvage to buy supplies." Ged strung out the words one by one. "She's also a decorated Corps veteran."

"What, a pink star?" Parmecy decided to laugh, but the sound died halfway as Ged stared at him, bad-luck blue eyes cold as an arctic moon. The bridge was dead silent, every shipman, mate, or officer bending to their duties. They knew, even if this transfer fuckwad didn't, who could be stopped and who could not; the asshole wasn't making any friends by insisting on by-the-book *or* assuming Marah had been rear-echelon comfort staff.

"Valor, at the Battle of Galvesto. Combat medic." Ged watched the color leave Parmecy's face, turning the weasel the exact shade of Corps-ration *fromage gris*. He glanced at the outgoing capitain, Simur Haldane, who shook his head fractionally. Haldane's crisp white cap glowed under bridge lighting, and his big rangy frame filled the capitain's chair comfortably. He looked like he was enjoying this, or maybe he was just constipated. Hard to tell with good old Grab-'em Haldane. "Decorated four times, as a matter of fact. The big G was only her third."

"Galvesto." Haldane made a slight *tsk*ing sound, shaking his head. "That was a bad show, wasn't it, Giz?"

That was one way of putting it. The stink, the shaking, the noise, the filth, the screaming...a pitched battle, one of the bigger ones, and a near thing. The redbands had won that one, but victory had ripped their guts out, and the second phase of the rebellion had been well and truly finished.

You couldn't tell that until later, though. Or if you could, the word didn't reach the soldats or the insurgents on the ground for a long while.

"The worst," Giz muttered, as he tapped an actual smuggler's ship an Aegis civil security detail was going to have to board and search. Thinking of Galvesto was never pleasant, even if the memory included Marah's pale face hovering like a gift over his blood-damp cot.

She'd stopped the other medic from loading Giz's veins with oblivion to ease his passing. At the time, writhing in pain, he'd been ready for anything to take the agony away. But later, when they fished the bits out of his belly, back, and legs to find out he was miraculously uninfected, clear of nerve agent, and not paralyzed either, plain old Third Echelon Ged Gizabón of Tabor—not yet a Second—knew what he owed, and where.

It was the only debt in his life Ged actually *liked* paying on.

"Decorated *you* for that one too," Haldane said. He was enjoying this; his retirement was starting out with twitting a rearward rank-climber, always one of his favourite things.

"And gave you a silver for Belheim, Simur." Another bad show, that one. Giz didn't glance at Parmecy, but the message was clear. Being in a supply depot when a redband infiltrated tossing grenades and getting sent home after the explosion was not at *all* like meritorious frontline service. "A couple of old warhorses, that's us."

"Ah." Parmecy cleared his throat. "I apologize, Capitain Gizabón." Staggering over the accent syllable that meant Echelon, just a little, just enough to make it an insult. Apparently he hadn't known Giz was a decorated vet, either. What the fuck had he been doing with his first two tendays planetside, if not finding out who the players actually were? The man was an idiot, but Noth was sure he'd be a *useful* one on gate duty, and Giz didn't necessarily disagree.

He was just unwilling to let said idiot put his filthy mouth on Marah's name.

"Good." Giz also did not quite accept the apology. The temperature of the bridge dropped a few degrees, and icy politeness settled in every corner. "There's traffic to clear, Parmecy. Let's get to it."

By the time the expected military transport came, a big black blot in the orbital ring like a chokfish caught in a net, Parmecy's uniform armpits were suspiciously dark. Getting a plum appointment like Transport Commissioner Capitain for the jewel of Anglene was a step up for him, but now he'd insulted a Second Echelon—even if just a newly minted one yanked up from Third for meritorious service—who just happened to be Shar Notheim's intelligence head.

Giz let Parmecy anticipate the worst, personally clearing the military transport to bring yet another load of Sagittarius Prime's sons and daughters fully home from pacification duty. Then he smiled, that sharklike grin he reserved for those on the thinnest of puddle-ice, and left the bridge for his own jump back to planetside.

"Parmecy," he heard Capitain Haldane say, genially, "you done fucked up, son." The door to the bridgelift whisked shut, cutting off the rest of the conversation, and Giz let out a soft, unamused laugh.

He wouldn't tell Marah she caused trouble everywhere. And he wouldn't tell Noth that she was going out more regularly on smuggling runs. There was only so much trouble Sharl Notheim would let even a First Echelon cause, after all.

Now that the war was over, Noth's feathered nest was about to become a little less comfortable. Ged watched the stripes of light on either side of the door, horizontal bands passing through in rapid succession—another psychological ploy, to give a Terran a sensation of relative movement even in near-low grav so they didn't go sprawling or vomiting when the hatch opened.

At least Parl Regnant Riccar Planetegan was still on his exploratory crusade. If Hinri and Ileanor's eldest son himself ever wandered home, who could tell what he'd think of the Redband Rebellion *or* his little brother's handling of it? Parl Regent Jun had a lock on any means of communicating with his wandering elder star, and the rebellion's slow, bloody death was sure proof Riccar hadn't bothered to leave other, less official intel routes in place.

Either that or he just didn't care. Still, Riccar should come back if Anglene's ship was drifting, right? The Helm and First Echelon families had awakened periodically to steer the great generations ships while other echelons and steerage slept in serried ranks of ova-sperm cryo, drifting through space to bring Terra's children to safe harbor.

The Firsts' duty was to guide, even planetside.

But apparently Discipline had spoken and the Parl Regnant was searching for new worlds. As if Anglene wasn't enough for *anyone* to handle.

Well, Parl Jun was the ruler in practice, and Sharl Noth, with his squeezing of maximum cryon for the war effort—and maximum profit for other items as well—was in very good odor with his royal Helm patron. Which meant Ged Gizabón was too, since favour, like shit, flowed downhill. Even in space, trash found the nearest well and circled it, incrementally closer and closer until it fell in.

It was enough to give anyone vertigo, Ged decided, and the lift made a soft sound as it delivered him to the giant echoing cavern of a transport bay, busy with shuttles, pinnaces, and coracles to be deployed about a fleet's business. There were more pleasant things to think about, to be sure. He couldn't wait to get planetside again.

Marah had agreed to tai.

SOMEWHERE TO GO_

IT WAS AN ARTICLE OF SOLDAT FAITH THAT ANY TRANSPORT taking you on leave went half the speed of one hauling you to the front, and Hood had expected demobilization to be no different. But after scrubdown and vaccinations, exit flymsywork and papierwork, issuance of this, that, and the other, standing in line though thankfully not at attention, civilian ID issued, rechecked, verified, Corpsoldat ID processed into demob, and before he knew it he was outside the front door of the rectangular black Corpsoldat Processing Centre, blinking in a golden Sagittarius sunset, his dit-bag on his shoulder and no ryfl in easy reach. He was plain old Robbhan Locke of House Lamóre again, a proud Second Echelon boy home from the war.

He could spend the night in the centre, but he wanted to go... home? Was that *really* the word? His Corps-issued lunch had even included fruit, and it had been metric months since he'd tasted small green Sagg Prime pitfruit.

Outside of a readipak, that was.

Newly demobbed soldats milled around, and the better pickpockets were probably having a fine day. Civvie fleecers kept their distance from the guards at the wide silica doors. The career-stripers on guard gazed jealously and pitilessly at the soldats-now-veterans, and Robb's heart lodged in his throat like the idiot chunk of meat it was. He couldn't swallow to get it into its proper place, and his entire skin itched at being out in the open without a ryfl or wrap-armor. Most of the demobbed had chosen dress blues to walk out in, but he'd opted for broken-in fatigues and the grab-boots that had seen him through the last eight metric months, glove-soft and familiar. Probably still with desert dust worked into the grabbers, despite a zipher bath to shake off any contamination.

Go home, the red-nosed colonel said at the end of the final exit interview. *Try to forget everything.*

Easy for *him* to say.

"Move it, soldat," someone barked behind him, and his hand itched for a whisp-hilt. "Keep the stairs clear."

Hood sank his boots into the stairs as the swabbie who wanted the steps clear just barely avoided a collision. It was a squat heavy-worlder who had a mouthful of new teeth from buds, an ocular bud covered with the regulation blue and white dressing-eyepatch, and a dark blue, ill-fitting civvie suit with a placket, two pockets, and a mech driver's loop on either side of the knees. He looked about to say something else, too, but one of the *polis-militaires* yelled something from the top of the flight and the heavyworlder visibly decided it wasn't worth getting into a scuffle during his first few moments of demob.

"Lot of blues." A tall, rangy fellow caporal halted next to Hood, his long nose twitching. He wasn't in dress blues either, but in fatigues that showed just as much hard wear as Hood's own. "They should just put a few bars across the street and let us sort it out that way."

"Yeah," Hood managed—no, he was *Locke* now, plain old Robbhan again—through dry lips. A jolt of something alcoholic would go down really well at the moment. Lipwalking wasn't good in the field, but back at base, what else was there to do?

"You got somewhere to go?" The caporal didn't look concerned, but he still eyed Robb sideways with burning dark eyes, much like

Ged Gizabón's despite the color. This guy looked vaguely familiar, too, though his hair was dirty sand instead of Giz's shock of unruly red-black. "I mean, uh, you from Sagg Prime? Of course you are, but—"

"I'm from Lamóre. Out near the Forest Preserve." Robb examined the caporal's nametag. *Oh. So that's who you are, but you're not Robard.* "Muchson? As in, Robard Muchson?"

"His little brother." A tentative smile bloomed on his coppery face, youth peeping out through a soldat's detached, calculating gaze. "Milar. You're...?"

Hood. But there was no need for callsign or company name here. "Locke. Robb Locke." He offered his hand; they were demobilized now. No salutes, no more surrenders, and he was just a plain old fellow whose father had bought a Second Echelon estate and hated the son who was supposed to inherit it and claw even further up the ladder.

"Hey, I remember him talking about you." Milar's grasp was firm, warm, and callused as his own. "You went to primary and secondary together, right?" The caporal grinned, an easy expression, but a shadow darkened his bloodshot gaze.

Now Robb remembered little Milar, knob-kneed and with a perpetual scab on his nose. Big dark-haired Robard had tormented his younger siblings mercilessly, not to mention anyone else unlucky enough to be smaller or weaker whenever he could get away with it. "Yeah, we got into a lot of trouble together. You were five standards behind, right? Damn, time flies." A few shakes later—at least he wasn't a squeezer like his bâtard brother—they were acquaintances. "Robard demobbed too?"

Milar shook his finely modeled head. Short, sandy-wooly curls held his hair very close to the scalp. "Nope, he got sent home in a case. Chiron, one of the moons. Long-ranger got him."

Now that was news. "Shit, I'm sorry." But not overly so. Robard had been an asshole, and war was unlikely to change that.

Still, you mourned every soldat, because replacements were bad for unit cohesiveness and tended to get their asses, not to mention someone else's, shot off at the slightest provocation. You wanted a tight group of buddies, and you wanted *them* to stay alive first and foremost, but you also wanted them to stay put instead of being transferred to some other meatgrinder.

"Yeah, well." A moment of silence, under heavy golden afternoon light. Milar glanced away, rolled his shoulders once, an easy movement, bracing himself for the rest of the day. "You got somewhere to go, Locke?"

"Out to the old homestead, I guess." Thank Discipline his name didn't bear one of those telltale accents; Lamóre wasn't a hereditary estate. Robb had been expected to turn administrator and get a commission to stay in control of what Father considered his due. "But maybe not right away."

That earned another grin from Milar Muchson's ready store. Looked like the kid was easygoing, but you couldn't really tell until the firing started. "You want to catch a drink?"

It was both a relief and a fresh terror to be free of the Corp's control. When all you had to do was wait for orders, you didn't have to choose. Now, a dizzying array of options threatened to drown them both.

Robb Locke's cheeks felt strange, because they had bunched up. He was, of all things, smiling. "I thought you'd never ask."

FALSE 3D_

In a large, very comfortable study on a planet in the Capricorn system, upon a heavy, almost antique wooden desk scattered with permasheaves, temporary sheaves, and quite a few notes scrawled on loose flymsy, the encrypto-dish glowed. Between its paired flat circles, one invisibly tethered atop a column of unsteady air, light and sound was distorted to provide a rendering of a man with dark hair and honey highlights, his cheeks shaven clean but still shadowed—the Parl Regnant stubbled earlier than most.

He did *everything* earlier, faster, better.

"Well, little brother, that finishes all the business." The holograph smiled, a familiar, easy expression captured in false 3D. Spackles and noise ran through the image before it firmed, transmission across the gulf of space fraying the edges of every word. "It was good to get your fittles, all of them. I was beginning to think you'd forgotten all about me." A short pause, expressions flittering over Parl Regnant Riccar's handsome coppery face. Probably wondering whether to say *that was a joke, Jun.* "We just cleared the edge of the Ring. They're programming the starsteal now, soon we'll know if this crazy idea will work or not. Just imagine, coming out without a gate. We'll either be famous or dead." A quick grin, familiar from coinage and credit flymsy notes as if the ruler of Great Anglene could be anything *other* than famous. "The succession package is really clear, you shouldn't have any trouble."

It was, Parl Regent Jun thought a trifle bitterly, just like the jackass to mention it. Whenever he felt a twinge of conscience, getting out this old recording and playing it provided a salutary sting.

Had Riccar really, honestly thought about what he was doing? Or had his own mortality just become apparent to him halfway through his little venture?

It would become even more so before long, Jun knew. Everything was almost, *almost* ready.

"You might not hear from us for a while," Riccar said. Another thin thread of silvery static ran from the top of the image to the bottom, fractional data-loss instantly bridged by Terran eyes and brain working simultaneously, erasing gaps in what it was coded to recognize as another human face. "If that while ends up being forever, well...I love you, little brother."

"Liar," Parl Jun muttered, the corners of his generous, mobile mouth drawing down. Even the double sisters and tech-heavy but finger-thin fillet meant to clasp a Parl's head and shout his status had been laid aside for the moment, and he was in a shabby brown jumpsuit with padding at mechanic-necessary places, comfortable and completely un-royal. For at least a quarter-standard he could be completely alone, and he was wasting it listening to this drek.

Again.

The holograph was almost as expressive as Riccar in person, but not nearly as suffocating. Raw charisma didn't leak out of its every pixel, and there was no feeling dwarfed by a tall broad-shouldered man whose laugh filled an entire Star Chamber. Jun settled in the chair behind the desk, his grab-boot's soles pointed at the Great Helmsman.

It was unexpectedly satisfying.

"Well." Riccar stared intently at whatever bead was capturing this message to be fittle-beamed like a ryfl bolt for Anglene—the entire galaxy must have been a dim thread of light from the bridge of Riccar's great exploratory armada. It was a gamble—the three old Ark-class ships available hadn't had starsteal yet, the great advance in interstellar travel only a theoretical skeleton in great sheaves of painstaking data by the scientists who loaded Terra's chosen-frozen few onto the paired, massive quasi-sentient ships and consigned them to the Helm and First Echelon families to lead and guide.

Chapter and verse, historical worsts. A few other Arks might have reached their intended target galaxies; there was no way of knowing even with fittle and starsteal. More genships could be built, really— they had the blueprints, the tech was right there, but why bother with such a resource-intensive gamble? Plenty of room on Anglene's planets and moons, especially since the terraforming had gone better than even the ancient best-case projections even if the fleet had been pared down to half-size. The only problem nowadays was a great mass of transplanted Terrans refusing to uphold their end of the social bargain.

The hands who would not obey a capitain's order were mutinous deadweight, and should be set adrift. It was only proper.

"They're calling for me," Riccar continued, as if he hadn't reached the end of any subject that could conceivably be about *him* and gotten bored of reciting platitudes. "I do love you, little brother. I know we haven't always seen eye to eye, but out here, well, things like that get small. Hopefully I'll see you again someday. For family, brother, and for Anglene."

"For Anglene," Jun murmured reflexively, and watched the holograph fold itself down. Had Riccar been drunk? Not on anything alcoholic, but maybe on his vision of himself as the Great Helmsman swinging into the Deeps? Even complete control over a clutch of inhabited star-systems wasn't enough for his brother's pride.

No, Riccar wanted more, and set out to grab it from the cold reaches of space. History, both Old Terran and Anglene, was full of men like him.

Jun made himself even more comfortable, eyeing the encrypted fittle player's flat, hovering black topdisc as if it would light up with a hurried postscript. Of course Riccar's transmissions could be replayed in entirety before an adoring crowd, even the recital of coordinates and governmental folderol each started with. Playing to the captures, both Free Network and chieweed, was a Planetagen family duty.

One of the many.

Outside the great wraparound window, Capricorn Tertius glowed in the dusk. Most of the planet was a preserve held in common by the First Echelon of Anglene, but significant tracts were reserved for House Planetagen, a prerogative of the Helm for summering or resource management. Tropical greenery, mostly blue-tinted in the lowlands but shading purple-to-blush in higher elevations, moved gently under seasonable winds. Jun wouldn't have another planetside vacation in a while, even a working on; the rest of his plans required being in orbit.

Still, he was going through Riccar's old messages one by one. Perhaps he was even saying farewell, in his own way.

This was, after all, the alcazar they had both largely grown up in, watched over by tech and by hand as their parents governed the galaxy. Jun had taken refuge in this room more than once, fleeing the rough camaraderie of Jun's loud, broad-shouldered, hunt-crazed friends.

Now, it was converted to a Parl Regent's private study.

Very few of the Three Echelons had bothered with Jun, especially since Mother's partiality was fixed at an early age. She was probably watching from one of Logic's many hells, if the Discipline was right, or was a restless ghost on the dark side of some cold satellite if the Moon was. And how Gran Marl Ileanor would be gnashing her teeth to find Riccar on a wild chase and Jun with the wheel in his hands.

It wasn't quite that she had disdained her younger son. It was just that everything, to Mother, had its use, and she intended to see that use embarked upon posthaste. *Enter the Discipline, Jun. It's what you're fit for.*

Well, he hadn't taken orders but the Discipline's seminary schools had taught him plenty. Most importantly, how to wait. How to revisit this very room periodically, closing his eyes and hearing the laughter, the brittle snap of a bone breaking, his own sniveling cries, and Riccar's fury.

How dare you touch a Planetagen!

Parl Regent Jun rubbed at his left arm, a slow, meditative movement he indulged in nowhere but here. No scan would show the break, of course. Setting and re-matrix was even fairly noninvasive, as modern medical tech went. Still, sometimes it ached, for no other reason than his father Hinri's cold, remembered glare.

Stop whining, Jun. You are Planetagen.

Father was no doubt in one of Logic's heavens, being firmly Discipline. He was probably fuming over anything being left in Jun's hands at all, much less the entire galaxy. At least their neglect had been benign instead of malevolent. Once they had what they wanted —and what parent would have wanted more than Riccar, indeed— they were disposed to be absent but relatively kind.

Jun smiled, a rather sweet expression on a long-nosed, drowsy-eyed face. He thumbed the encrypto-dish off and stood, crossing to the large window and gazing unseeing on fleshy leaves, giant trunks, hanging vines, the vivid splashes of bird-flickers in the canopy, steam rising from the forest floor in lazy curls as the day's heat released itself from Capricorn loam. The entire system was a heat-trap. His chair spun lazily, borrowed movement imparting a simulacrum of life.

Well, the redband rebellion was finished. The Planetagen name and primacy was even more firmly assured. Even the ghosts of his cursed family would have to admit as much.

When he was finished contemplating the seethe outside, he turned on his heel and strode for the double doors, snapping the double rosters on both left and right arms, settling the fillet upon his brow and feeling the slight tingle as it scanned for biometrics and alerted the security net that the alcazar's sole important inhabitant was on the move. It was time to wash off sweat from épfée practice and allow the chamber presence to dress him, then the smaller Star Chamber would activate when he stepped inside, holograms crowding him. Clients, Aegis bureaucrats, Corps officers, and ministers were waiting for direction, the hive of Anglene needing its brooding intelligence stirred, massaged, and sometimes stung in order to move in any direction—least of all forward.

Now that he had practiced his stinging, Parl Regent Jun was certain he could do everything else. Especially since Riccar had thoughtfully removed his big brainless self from the entire game. After a decent interval, it would be Parl Regnant Jun instead of merely Regent, and the sound of it suited him—though he would refuse the Senatus Prime the first time it brought such a title to him.

It wouldn't do to seem *too* eager.

Really, all Jun hoped for was a maintenance of the new status quo. A galaxy at rest, with his hands upon the rudder.

He was even, he found as he approached the doors, smiling without sarcasm.

For once.

INVITATION_

GO WHERE THE CLIENTS ARE WAS A RULE OF BUSINESS, SURE. IT was also a rule of healthcare, which meant the Madán Free Clinic sat, barred windows under heavy metallic stat-shielding and outer doors scanlocked, on the border between the Saur and downtown Sharud. The slum proper boiled to the northeast, baking under hard midday glare that shimmered over the scraped bedrock dishes and glittering machinery of the port in the distance. Heat soaked into concrete and silica, settled on the bare straining shoulders of khibi-drivers, gleamed from pavement, bounced between high tenements or attempted to tiptoe into alleys full of rancid shade. Varied pops and crackles of illegal weapons echoed through the great north-eastern sink, and in the distance a polis siren rose as some poor sap with a thin blue stripe on his uniform had to descend and bring unwelcome outside law upon whoever was silly enough to call the law in that part of the city.

At least it wasn't the hiss-blur of ryfl fire or the thump of projectile mortars, *or* the thunder of artillery. So Marah told the shakes and the uncomfortable fullness in her bladder they were *both* going to have to wait. Her body understood very well there was a possibility of having to dump cargo and run, because both kids standing in front of her were likely armed.

"No," she repeated, patiently, her hands dangling loose and easy, and wished she'd grabbed her head-cover before coming outside. It was difficult to look severe while a mop of waves tried to eat your face. "Not inside, soldats. You know the rules."

The older of the two young men—not boys, but still too young for Corps service, not that it mattered now with the war done—leaned forward on his grab-boot's heavy mag-clicking toes. The ends of the green handkerchief knotted around his left jacket sleeve swayed in the hot breeze, and behind Marah, Pannelore the new clinic guard loomed. He was a slab of heavyworlder muscle, but his calm and absolute lack of testosterone-fueled ego-kicking worked wonders where his size didn't.

"I got a pain," the younger kid—the sandy-haired one—repeated somewhat uncertainly, and Marah restrained the urge to roll her eyes.

"Today is a Brot day, yes." Dark curls fell in her eyes but she did *not* brush them away, because the older kid had his right hand suspiciously close to his hip and any sudden movement might make him even more nervous. "I'm well aware; I was there when the truce was negotiated. And in a few minutes you can go in."

"If it's a Brot day, why ent we goin in right now?" The older one was trying to play moderator to the young one's aggressiveness, but Marah had been good-pol-bad-pol'd before.

These kids had nothing on Robb and Giz in secondary school. And why was she thinking of Robb? He'd never answered a single letter; there was no use in wondering.

I might as well just tell them the truth. It might even work. "Because you're both armed," she said, softly, a simple statement of fact. It was exactly the same tone she would use with a battle-mad soldat. "And nothing's seriously wrong with either of you. I don't mind being lied to unless the lies are stupid, fellows. You know Smiling Hal's here because he was stabbed this morning, and you're looking to finish him off."

They stared at her, a pair of hazel eyes and a pair of dark brown, and the older one's scar-knuckled hand tensed, touching what was no doubt the butt of a cheap matterbeam repeater. Marah held his gaze in particular. *You don't want to shoot me, kid. That's too much trouble even for a Saur ganglander.*

"Lady Madán." Pann's quiet tone matched hers. At least he wasn't the type to spin a wad of bluster; that would have been dropping a lit flare into a damp kanno mine. "Why don't you go on inside and let me finish parlaying these young gentlemen?"

Because if it's me, they can back down with no honour lost. "I think we understand each other now," she said, steadily. The older boy didn't disagree, but he didn't break eye contact, either. His boots were held together with dull grey choktape and that jacket of his, though worn proudly, was probably hot as the slice of Great Under several varieties of Discipline sinners ended up in.

Wilbert, that's his name. She couldn't remember it before, but now she had it too late to use.

She didn't even precisely *like* Smiling Hall the second lieutenant of the Merries, but nobody—Logic *or* Lunacer— needed to be shot in her clinic. Doctor Tamarl was on duty today, and her natural punctiliousness would not allow her to let Hal leave until she was certain he wasn't bleeding internally anymore and the infection risk was minimal. Nobody had pinged the Sharl's black-and-blues about the boy's wounds despite Aegis law requiring all matterbeam or projectile wounds to be reported because this was the Saur and polis were barely a step above the perennial scuttling of blattaria; if Marah simply delayed these two Brots long enough, Sibby the receptionist would get Hal out the side entrance.

Not the back, which would almost certainly be watched. And they could avoid a Saur gang war neatly, if everyone would just cooperate.

"I got me a pain," the younger Brot said again, half uncertainly, and glanced at the older boy. A stint in the Corps might have done both of them some good.

At the very least, it would have fixed the older one's teeth; buds were part of the standard medical package. Normally dental care was only for citizens, and those attached to Echelon estates or corporate concerns. "We'll take a look at you in a few minutes," Marah repeated. "And you, too. I'll bet that pains you."

"What?" Wilbert blinked. He was relaxing, obviously deciding that he could afford to tell whoever sent him—probably the new lieutenant Keno, since the head of the Brots would want deniability—that they'd missed Hal and spoken to the Lady of Madán herself about it. "You, uh, what?"

Now was the time for Marah to raise her hand, slowly, and point at her cheek right where the small angry bulge rested on his. Her sleek silver rister gave a haptic buzz, but she ignored it. "Right there, looks like an abscess. We can probably get that cleaned and sealed for you. Once we get you in the door, we'll do the papierwork."

"Uh...Lady Madán..." Pann, behind her, sounded alarmed.

Just stay pax, Pannelore. She couldn't say it, sensing that if she broke contact now, the younger kid might get impatient, and *that* was a bad prospect because Wilbert would be forced to save his honour. Gang rules aped Old Terran warlord stories, at least in the Saur, and it showed.

Were there slums on other planets, now? The war had changed everything, and dispossessed large swathes of the population.

"That'd be nice, I guess." Wilbert nodded, his shoulders relaxing a critical few fractions, and things would have been fine if someone hadn't locked the teenager's wrist and twisted the arm away, a familiar face rising over his shoulder.

It was Ged Gizabón, his red-black Corps-sheared hair grown out to a far lesser degree than Marah's, his long nose and knife-sharp mouth matching bladed cheekbones, and his black thermasealed coat bearing the Sharl's governance sigil high on the left breast right where a Corps nametag and barcode would go. A thin blue stripe ran down from his left shoulder too, the sign of civil law enforcement's iron fist, enforcing Aegis decisions but without any part in setting policy. "Easy," he muttered Wilbert's ear. His eyes were paler than the blue stripe, and burned like pieces of summer sky on first-class planets, the ones that had enough oxygen. "Be very easy right now, you little shit."

Oh, for Logic's sake. "Giz." Marah tried not to sound surprised. Of course Pann, being taller, had seen Noth's Ryfl easing through the crowd, and attempted to warn her. "There's no need for that. We're just having a conversation."

"He doesn't need *this* to talk." Muscle flickered in Giz's wrist as he cast a single blue glance at the younger kid, who had frozen from either good sense or pure bewilderment. He stripped a low-end matterbeam repeater, its butt wrapped with a strand of silvery chok-tape, from the older kid with a contemptuous little jerk. "Do you?"

The younger one tensed and Marah stepped forward. Getting shot while doing charity work was not high on anyone's list of desires, even if those of the First Echelon were required to show a certain disdain for physical danger and likewise display a certain *noblesse oblige*. Still, if the Brots thought they'd been insulted, they might stop coming or embargo the clinic from their territory, which would halt a whole slice of the Saur from coming for care. "Ged. Please. Let go of him."

"Oh, man." The younger kid was having trouble processing. "Oh, *man.*"

"Lovvi." Wilbert stood stiff and straight, almost at attention. So that was the younger one's name—traditional, as traditional as Wilbert's own. "Lovvi, back up."

"Stay where you are." Giz even sounded amused. He glanced at Marah. The faint lavender lines in his irises almost glowed in certain lights, giving his gaze an eerie intensity. That was why they called blues bad luck; still, the recessives couldn't be ironed out because the overall genetic health of the population had to be taken into account. "Except you, Marah. You should go inside, I'll handle this."

No, thank you. "This is *my* clinic, Giz. And these are *my* patients. I'll thank you not to manhandle them."

Pann stepped forward too, looming over Marah. "We're clear," he said, conversationally. Sibby must have pinged him through the small audio bead in his right ear. "Lady Madán? We're clear."

That meant Smiling Hal was both treated and bundled out the hidden side entrance. "Come on in." She tried to smile too, and perhaps even managed a normal expression. "Lovvi, is it? And you're Wilbert, and—"

"We're leaving." The older kid tried to slide sideways, away from Giz, and stopped dead, a curious look spreading over his face.

Marah couldn't see what the polis had in his other hand to enforce such stillness. Probably Wilbert's own matterbeam repeater; Giz was a great believer in using what was lying about instead of bemoaning a lack of supplies. He also looked maddeningly cool in his long black polis thermaseal with the thin blue stripe running down over heart, hip, and knee.

"You need a deportment lesson, young swabbie," Ged said, mildy, in Wilbert's ear. "When our Lady of Madán invites, you attend." He even smiled, a rather thoughtful expression. "Let's go."

NOTHING GOOD_

THE HANGOVER WAS A LIVING THING, TWISTING AND TURNING inside Hood's skull. It pounded in time to the khibi's bumps and whining rattles, filled his stomach with sour heat, and turned his eyes into dry silica marbles. Milar would have accompanied him for this, except the other caporal's condition was even worse than his own.

There was one good thing about pouring down rotgut in a ramshackle pub-hole on the west fringe of the Saur. The resultant physical misery made each increasingly familiar curve of Via Oldbow less painful than it could have been, if only because he was grimly holding onto the runny eggs and flatcakes with lumps of sting-leavening he'd swallowed at a food-khibi outside the sleephole he and Milar had collapsed in. They'd exchanged numbers, too; both of them had civilian risters, flatbands covering the tiny scar on the back of the wrist where the Corpsoldat glimchip had been excised. Both of them wore the dead-black bands with the reflective face on the inside of the wrist, no betraying gleam to give away their position, and the observation had filled Robb's throat with another bubble of hot sourness.

Bump-whine-screech, the khibi's narrow nose riding on a bed of screaming air and its twin-swelling hind end lifting and dropping as its own tethers and repellers struggled to keep up, the driver's lean muscled back hunching over the steering bolts, dust rising in a plume —all a redband had to do was draw a bead. Khibis were cheap and easy to steer, but a ryfl bolt in a repeller field or even at the juncture between driver and passenger and bang-pow-zip, all you had to do was comb the wreckage for salvage.

In the shimmering distance, a great grey stone bulk rose in piercing spires—Madán's great alcazar, Marah's home, its needles and walls stuffed with glowing or invisible security tech. *A pile of shit for a king turd*, Father always said, but bowed and scraped every time old Aethelstan visited the holder of his largesse at spring and harvest. Lamóre wasn't *quite* enfeoffed to Madán, but no administrator would hold it unless Madán signed off on the appointment. So it was *play nice* when Aethelstan visited, and Father's oily smile whenever Marah knocked at the front door was almost enough to turn Robb's stomach.

She didn't knock often, preferring to toss pebbles at his bedroom window—probably because that was what Robb did at hers—but when old Aethelstan showed up at Festival times it was protocol all the way.

Each time at the festival gathering, Marah and Robb would slip away, sometimes with a group of other kids, most often with Ged, sometimes alone, fleeing to the woods to play banda or Old Terra, sparring with long willow switches. Later, of course, there were other games to play, but never the one he really wanted.

Not that he minded, really; Marah was more than worth waiting for. Better to keep his hands off until he was sure he could do something right for a change. If that day came, he'd probably take up praying with gratitude.

The khibi crested the last rise, dropping to rattle over a small stone bridge that had probably been built right after terraforming. Fields stretched fallow on either side, and that was the first indication of...well, not exactly trouble. Maybe Father had simply been unable to care for the fringes without a son to help.

Hood had little time to follow *that* unappetizing line of thought further, because the khibi rattled to a stop and the driver thumbed its drive down, the conveyance settling on a bed of colorless, frictionless tether. She unwound her wrap helmet and turned her head, her profile glowing, pomme-bright cheeks and a bold bright red-painted mouth. Her hair was glossy brown, like a ripe castanea, and dark with sweat close to her head where the wrap-helmet pressed. "This is far as I go."

Great. Now he had to argue. Robb settled himself a little more firmly in the passenger cradle. His sweat was full of metabolized liquor and an unsteady metallic smell that was probably waste from adrenaline and cortisol flooding him. He was ready for an attack, he just couldn't tell from what quarter. "I paid you to take me to Lamóre." There. A simple, reasonable statement. Marah would be proud.

The driver continued to stare sideways, her long narrow nose and thrust-forward chin turning her into a serviceable prow for an old Terran timbership. "Ent nobody goin out that way." Her accent shouted *Saur*, but that was to be expected.

"Then give me a third back." Robb's own speech-rhythm was unbearably precise. Not quite Echelon, with its second-to-last stress making everything a singsong and each syllable clipped for maximum enunciation, but not quite the thivvy-cant of the dispossessed or estate-less either.

The driver did him the vast honour of considering his point before shaking her head. "Naw." Her broad back stiffened, and her gloved hand was on the switch that would dump the khibi's cargo if said cargo became a nuisance.

Hood felt every thread on the crushed, faded cloth cushioning of the passenger cradle, his right palm itching for a whisp-hilt. A khibi-licker wouldn't dare dump a Corpsoldat out on a mining moon or asteroid; the reprisals would be absolute and terrifying. Here in civilization, though, it was a different story.

Still, he supposed he could give the woman one last chance at fair play. "You really want to do this?" Thank Discipline he didn't sound like his father; no, Robbhan Locke just sounded tired, though Hood was painfully, completely alert inside the camouflage carapace of a real, living, breathing man.

A *civilian*, for Logic's sake.

"Fine." Grudgingly, the castanea-haired khibi driver produced a handful of crumpled handful of credit bills, Parl Jun's heavy jaw on newer papier—heavier than flymsy—issuance turned into an amorphous blob. She held them up, fanning slightly in the hot breeze. "You ent gon find nothin good out there."

"There never was." Not even when Madán had held Lamóre as part of a fellow Echelon's gambling debt. Old Locke had been cunning and crafty indeed to gain it as a boon—and with it, a position as Second Echelon, allowing his heir to be born into rights and privileges the elder couldn't dream of.

Or just enough of those rights and privileges to make joining the Corps a way to keep them, once the war started. Father's insistence on a tertiary degree in civil administration to hold the damn place had been kicked right in the crotch.

The driver shook her head, the darkest bits close to the scalp beginning to dry. Under a wrap, you got soaked quickly. "You're young Locke, you are."

For my sins, then. "That I am." No reason to deny it. She wasn't one of the tenants—he didn't even know who was tenanting out here now, and none of them would be picking up extra cash as a khibi driver. She might have been one of the many Father's administrative and business deals had choked, and if so, she might be looking to get a little of her own back.

Always making friends, the Lockes. It was a Logic-be-damned talent.

"Ah." The driver considered this, her gloved thumb stroking one of the drive-bars. The other was still on the button, and Hood surfaced inside Robb's head, vaguely interested in keeping them both from being dumped. "Back from the war." It wasn't a question.

"The Corps called." A traditional answer. As a veteran, Robb's status as a Second Echelon was secure, and he hadn't had to take a single Administration Capability Test to cement it. No, he'd bought it with a ryfl, the old-fashioned Terran way.

"Young men off fighting, and paying no nevermind to their folk." The woman made a soft *tch* sound, clicking her tongue.

"Folk paid no nevermind to us in the Corps, either." He hadn't gotten a single letter, fittle, or rister-pop, despite promises and concern. Which was, after all, the reason he hadn't gone to the edge of the Saur looking for a certain clinic.

Why bother? She'd made it exquisitely clear. That morning by the Slee, her hair warm with blue highlights, pleading with him. *Robb, don't. Just take the tests and get posted somewhere he can't get to you. I could even—*

And his own terrible, reflexive reply. *Some trouble even you can't buy off, Madán.*

Why the fuck had he said it? It was true, but since when was *that* a consideration when he opened his mouth?

The khibi driver shrugged, an easy rolling movement. "Look, it ent healthy to go out this way. Bad luck, all right?" The bills fluttered again as she fanned them, but her right hand was still on the eject button.

"It always was." So Robb—instead of Hood—got out, hefted his bag, and snatched the wad of credits from her hand. "Thanks." *For nothing.*

Maybe that touched the driver's poverty-atrophied heart. In any case, she eyed him sidelong, knees clamping on the khibi-saddle and both hands returning to basic quickstart-and-drive position. "Take you back to town for free."

"Nope." He shouldered the bag to give his refusal the proper weight, and in a few minutes the khibi was rattling into the distance, taking the bridge with a bump and a sideways wallow controlled with quick grace by the driver, who rose out of the saddle like a caballiene on a fine Gemini equine.

Robb Locke put his head down and walked for home. It wasn't until he rounded the last corner that everything became clear.

Lamór's ancient alcazar was exponentially smaller than Madán, with a single squat tower providing a defensive vantage for tech shielding. It was also mostly timber instead of stone, at least for the interior walls. The foundation and load-bearers were terraform-lifted rock, scorch marks spattering along their sides. None of the marks bore the coruscations of ryfl fire, and there was no blast detritus from artillery or matterbeam chipping.

It was extremely old-fashioned, to burn a compound with accelerant instead.

Only the timber skeleton of the first floor remained, heavy beams charred black. The barn was still standing, though its large doors were torn open and whatever forage, fodder, or livestock remained was long gone.

No wonder the roadside fields had been fallow.

Something hung from the main midbeam, swaying gently. A sodden, shapeless mass, rotting on a rope. Robb knew what it was, but, miserably impelled, he approached, step by step, as if it was a patrol and some jacknape general or IntSec bobblehead wanted helmcam visuals.

Winter rains had pooled among the burning, and summer-yellowed weeds forced their way up through paving and flagstone. The hanging thing's steady, slow motion was just the wind pushing a desiccated, picked-clean corpse, bone showing discolored through rags of flesh and clothing. One of the lower legs had fallen free, meat and marrow probably carried off by an enterprising predator.

He would not limp, or complain about the damp, anymore.

Robbhan Locke stood in the shattered remains of his childhood home, staring at the hanged man. Of course he knew who it was. Who else could it be?

His conniving, genius father was never going to lecture—or beat —him again.

GREATER SAFETY_

"Prices are falling." Sharl Notheim, the military governeur of wartime Sagittarius Prime, settled more firmly in his cushioned black Xomo chair. He was not exactly corpulent, though a visitor might have been forgiven the thought upon seeing him in his habitual long black padded polis thermaseal with its lapels, cuffs, and hem holding the blue stripe of polis along with the buff of civil magistracy service. It wasn't quite time for the Aegis to take over administration of the jewel of both Anglene and Parl Jun's munitions plans, and when it was, only one of the stripes would remain. "It's becoming difficult, now that Your Grace's genius has rid us of rebels."

"*Mostly* rid." The tethered shimmerscreen held Parl Jun's familiar face with its blondish goatee, and the Regent's expression was thoughtful but not, at least, *disappointed* as it has been once or twice. "There's still ongoing pacification in the outlying areas. Demand will hold steady for a few months, at least."

In other words, the Parl Regent expected his cut. Noth's teeth showed, a serene bud-grown smile glowing between thick cheeks patted with expensive lotion after every morning scraping. "That is welcome news indeed. I trust the last shipment was satisfactory?" It had better be; Noth scraped the bottom of every barrel for the war effort as a matter of course. His appointment to this station was a matter of results gained and retained; his predecessor had not grasped as much.

Which made him, in Noth's view, an idiot. Still, he'd been a useful one before the inevitable occurred.

"Very." Parl Jun's brow held a wrinkle or two, visible like a chie-weed's aesthetic mods. The image translator was Aegis-level tech, but there was still slight digital noise, the encryption meaning loss of quality visuals. And the parl would never be a kulturworker star of high gloss and uncompressed definition, genetics had put paid to *that*. "There are one or two items I was hoping to see, however."

Now was the time to play dumb. Notheim allowed his eyebrows to raise as if he was both surprised and worried. "Oh?" Behind him, a floor-to-ceiling window, dialed to maximum opacity to not blind the screen, looked out over Sharud. The capital's spires were beautiful; it was a shame the Saur hugged them so closely.

"Zeroes, Noth." Parl Jun's tone, bounced over lightyears by the technological wonder of fittlestream, was crystal clear. "I was expecting a few more zeroes."

"That's very abstract." Noth decided it probably wasn't wise to make any further jest and kept his hands flat on the smooth black desktop. Raising them now would be overacting, so he simply regarded the disembodied head floating on a tether-held rectangle. "I told you, prices are falling."

"They haven't fallen by *that* much." During the first half of the war Jun might have scowled to make his point. He'd learned to keep his expression a little smoother, probably during the dark days when it looked like Anglene might well shatter into small jealously guarded polities like Old Terra. The fracturing was bad enough on a single planet, but several star systems with current tech all jostling each other might put an end to the entire species, or bomb it back into a pre-Shiptime blur.

"Market forces move with more fluidity down here on the ground, Your Grace." Noth wasn't *quite* ready for the postwar scouring yet, so it was time to smooth the Helm's royal temper. "If I am not performing as well as Your Grace would desire, I will happily make way for a replacement." A dangerous offer—and one he would not have made if he suspected there was any chance at all of it being accepted.

Noth's canniness, brutality, and knowledge of how to extract Sagg Prime's resources was indispensable at this particular point.

Consequently, Jun's smile was a small, pained curve, and his tone shifted a few degrees. "Oh, that's not even a consideration. Which you well know." Nevertheless, the royal brow-wrinkling was far more pronounced now. "You do have, I presume, other methods for making up the shortfall?"

"Not with Sagittarius Prime resources, Your Grace." Notheim had no control over other planets in the system, just this largest and most remunerative one. As if Jun didn't have more credits and privileges than he could ever spend, even if he replaced all his organs at intervals like the cautionary tale of Old Midas. "This planet is Prime. All we have is agriculture, kultur, and cryon mines. The latter were the source of our recent good fortune." No cryon meant no ryfls, no hedgebomb mortars, and no wrap-armor. A faint dewing of sweat had begun at the small of Noth's back, and under his arms too. Fortunately, his uniform under the coat was the black of governance, a circle-cross Aegis badge high on his left chest with Jun's personal sigil dangling underneath. He was Jun's creature, but he didn't hand his brains over when his patron offered a palm for greasing.

If the greedy Helm fuck wanted to squeeze more out of the jewel of Anglene, not to mention its rapidly obsolescent in peacetime munitions-making system, he needed Noth, and what was more, he knew it. The Sharl's Needle, a massive black spike at the heart of Sharud, was a good vantage point, but it was also slippery as fuck, and wouldn't forgive a bumbler at its apex.

"Well," Parl Jun murmured, the tetherscreen's convexity waxing and waning at the edges as the signal was bounced through FTL relays. Its edges gleamed wetly, just like Jun's beady little eyes. Not like Riccar; the Parl Regnant's good looks were all but programmed. "I suppose it can't be helped."

That was the sound of baffled Helm greed, and if the connection hadn't been visual Noth would have made a face. "If it could, Your Grace, I would personally attend to the helping. Your service is my good fortune." *Now* was the moment to raise his gloved hands and spread them, a placatory gesture. Thank Logic and Discipline—and the Lunacer's Mother Moon too—his office was deserted.

Having Arthe or Gizabón witness this would be...indelicate.

"And yours is mine, Noth." Jun probably suspected much in the way of skimming but there was little he could *prove*, and that was a fine state of affairs. "Very well. Send me a complete forecast report for the next two standard orbits, with quarterly mapping."

"Yes, Your Grace." The numbers weren't going to change no matter how many times the Parl Regent requested them. But when the Helm demanded, those below *did*, if they wanted to keep their heads attached, not to mention their comfortable sinecures. The desperate and the ambitious both found it worthwhile to keep on the baby Planetagen's good side, ever since the *real* helmsman had decided to sail off the map.

Riccar was a well-muscled, blundering idiot and Jun a highly intelligent, ruthless, and avaricious mustelidae, but if a man wished to dance, he had to follow the music. A powerful patron was necessary, especially for those not born into Echelon.

"Very good. Oh, before I go." Parl Jun's brow smoothed, and he finally arrived at his entire reason for this normally unnecessary call. "There are distressing rumors of smuggling in your system. Over-stated, I'm sure." In other words, he suspected Noth of digging into the profit margins even more than usual.

"Very." The sweat was a heavy mist instead of a dew, now. How did the little swabbie *know*? He had to be simply trailing a salvage-line, but Noth couldn't afford to take any chances. "The penalties for such behavior are severe, and applied conscientiously." In other words, Sagittarius Prime's military governeur and chief polis official had things well under control, and wasn't siphoning off more than the usual pittance. "Your Grace's orders are *quite* clear." After all, summary executions were only legally possible with Jun's approval, even if said approval was issued after the fact.

At least, the ones Noth's troops had to put on permasheave were.

"I'm glad we understand each other," Jun said silkily, his dark gaze glinting. "Fair winds, Sharl Notheim."

"Following stars, Your Grace."

The tetherscreen darkened; the eye of royalty closed. Noth sagged in his very ergonomic chair, its own tethers humming as his weight shifted, and let out a sharp breath.

So. Jun suspected Notheim had been feathering his own nest to a more-than-natural degree. He'd be a fool not to, really; the only change in the situation was that Jun had bothered to mention the matter, a clear warning. It was time for Noth to wind up some of his more profitable concerns and seek greater safety, possibly in liquidity. He really should have retired last standard after the Lamóre affair, but with the war still going on, who could abandon his post?

Noth reached for the handset on his desk and remembered Ged Gizabón was off-duty after his very last gate stint. It probably wouldn't help to have the sardonic Corps intel-grabber in the office right now, either. There probably wasn't a problem in the Sagg system the Logic-cold man couldn't solve, but some were best left outside his capable hands, indeed.

Noth rubbed at his temples, swinging the chair back and around so he could look over sweltering, glittering summertime Sharud and the smoke-shimmer of the Saur clinging between it and the port's headache-sharp glitter. Headaches loomed on every horizon now. Fortunately, his sainted mother Magara Notheim's son was no fool, and he had made plans.

It was time to put a few of them into action.

ABLE TO DECIDE_

HER DOORLESS OFFICE WAS TINY—IT HAD ONCE BEEN A CLOSET; space was at a premium at the Clinic. Two doctors and one Corps-trained medic, all three requiring exam rooms with fully equipped homeostasis tables, took up a lot of estate. There were supply rooms, the waiting room, and the administrator's desk, cabinets, and other ephemera to account for as well.

Marah dropped into her sprung-spring bargain caster-chair and sighed, stretching her neck with short, efficient movements held just long enough to make the muscles relax a fraction. "Well, you just ruined *that*." She didn't sound angry, at least, only faintly disappointed. "Ged, this our new clinic security, Pannelore Cooke. Pann, meet Ged Gizabón, lately of Tabor." The formality of the introduction didn't even sting; it was just Marah's etiquette, habitual and kind. A true First Echelon did not let anyone stand in darkness wondering the proper form of address.

"Oh." The slab of brainless heavyworld muscle who had almost let a couple of skinny Saur kids point a repeater at Marah blinked, examining Giz in the hallway's dark, close confines. There was only room for one of them in the doorway, and Marah apparently had instructions to give the swabbie. "*That's* Gizabón? I mean, er, pleasure, sir, smooth sailing."

"Charmed, I'm sure, and steer well." Giz tried a smile, making sure his thermaseal-clad shoulder claimed a little more than half the door-space. Any amusement or politeness probably wasn't reaching his eyes, but at least he was making the effort.

"He doesn't usually slither in the front door. It sets a bad example." Marah's grin was a shadow of its usual self, but at least it wasn't the pained half-curve that meant she was a few ticks away from attempting a polite escape. So she was annoyed, but not *angry*.

That was a good sign.

"I couldn't wait in the alley to waylay you, now could I?" Ged turned his gaze on the walls, festooned with reminders scrawled on flymsy or papier scraps as well as pictures torn from an all-system calendar. The moons of Gemini Prime, a shot of low-grav waterfalls on Capricorn Quattrus with the iridescence of failed terraforming rippling the sky, a kuotta bird from Virgo Secundus in full flight with its lacy wings spread. "You should be more careful."

"Giz." *No lectures today*, her tone said, a clear warning also turning her dark eyes solemn; the difference between pupil and iris was barely a few shades, which gave her gaze a piercing quality old Aethelstan's had shared. At least she wasn't pale under her copper coloring, though she probably should have been.

"I know." He took care to make the words conciliatory. It was enough that she knew he *could* lecture her. She would probably even stand still for it, before giving that forced smile and vanishing like synthetic baccasmoke. "Where's Will?" The skarl should have been attending his mistress.

"At home." Marah's expression did not invite further questioning. She leaned back in the chair, which squeaked a protest. It looked like someone had fished it out of a salvage-pot; choktape, that cheapest and most effective of materials, bloomed silvery over the seat and two of the casters. "What do you want, Giz? It's been a long day, and I have work to do."

"Mh. You promised me tai." Ged glanced at thickset, dark-eyed Pann, who at least had the sense not to crowd his betters. The heavy-worlder's gaze was locked on the floor at some indeterminate point approaching Marah's sensible cushioned boot-toes; Giz understood. You couldn't look directly at a sun-star and keep your eyes, after all. "Not only that, but I have news."

"Marah?" The Clinic's main receptionist, a round woman with a short orange-dyed ruff standing straight up from her skull, peered between the two men, sliding a plump arm into the gap and moving Pannelore aside. A faint sheen of sweat showed on the heavyworlder security's corded neck, too; that was interesting. "Doctor Tamarl wants to know if you seriously want to seal that kid's mouth. It'll take most of our remaining plasmir stock."

"Plasmir?" Marah blinked, half-turned to the ancient console taking up half her cluttered desk, and shook her head, turning back when she realized she didn't need it to answer this question. "Oh, yes. We're getting a shipment tomorrow, including cryo-held buds. Tell her I *am* serious, and to please do so."

"The doors are still shut." The receptionist didn't glance at Giz, but she held herself very stiffly away from his black-clad shoulder. Maybe she knew enough not to crowd her betters too, or perhaps she just wanted to be on the safe side. Either was acceptable; Giz disliked being elbowed.

"Yes." Marah nodded, reaching for a pale-blue headscarf set next to an arthritic, almost antique sheave-binder. Her hair had gone wild, a cloud of soft waves begging for attention. "Pann, will you?"

"Of course." Pann bowed, somewhat stiffly, a truncated motion since he had less than a third of the doorway to perform it in. Still, the movement mollified Giz somewhat; at least the swabbie had some manners. "Close to time anyway." He meant clinic cutoff time, handing out slips to those who hadn't been seen yet to give them primacy the next day—if triage didn't bump them even further down the line.

At least Marah kept mostly to regular hours. She'd pour herself into the black hole of need without reservation if tradition and her skarl would let her.

"Thank you both." Marah waited until the door was clear again, and turned her full attention to Ged, rain on a thirsty plant. She turned the head-cover in her slim, pretty fingers, not quite a Lunacer's turban, but it would keep her hair in check. "News?"

"In a moment." Ged stayed on the threshold. He was sore from this morning's punishing épfée practice at Korovo Salle, the clatter of practice blades and harsh sounds of effort still ringing inside his skull. He *did* have news, but first on the agenda was registering just how foolish she'd been. "That kid could have shot you." *And then I would have had to kill him.*

Adding that would only lead to trouble, but he *had* to say something. Maybe it would even sink in, if he repeated it patiently and often enough, water wearing at terraform slot-crypts.

Marah's lips firmed. "No *lectures*, Giz."

"Just noting." He tried a slight, lopsided smile, very carefully not staring at her mouth. "So. Noth has an idea."

"Great." Marah made a face, stretching her arms as if pained, the headwrap dangling from her right fist. Papier tucked into folders made henges on her desk, stacked tree-fiber keeping its utility even in this day and age. She belonged in her alcazar, in a long flowing costume of the Old Shiptime, or at a gathering of the Echelons with her hair dressed high and bangles on her pretty wrists. "Spare me his brainwaves. They make me feel dirty."

If she only knew half of what Giz did to keep Noth's ideas in check, it might change a thing or two between them. "Well, this is a good one, or I wouldn't have bothered to bring it." Then again, she didn't *need* to know. The filth could stay safely locked in his skull, and she could stay clean. "He wants a commission on easing Corpsoldat back into civilian life, and he wants you to oversee it."

She gave the idea at least three full metric seconds of consideration before shaking her head and gathering her hair for covering. The tumbled cloud was very fetching, and watching her corral it was pleasant in its own way as well. "I don't want to be a figurehead for one of Noth's little morality plays."

So Giz lobbed the better part of the offer over her ramparts. "He's prepared to fully fund the clinic for as long as you do so."

"Blood money." Her mouth drew down at the corners, and those dark eyes narrowed. She could stop a man's heart with that expression; on old Aethelstan it might have been a scowl, but Marah just looked thoughtful, disbelieving, and just the tiniest bit severe.

"Lump sums, disbursed straight into a trust under the control of you or your representative." Suggesting that bit to Noth had made the Sharl roll his eyes, but Giz had shrugged in the particular way that told the Sharl he'd end up offering it anyways, so why didn't they cut out the dancing? "I told him you wouldn't even consider it otherwise."

She finished knotting the head-cover and leaned back in the ancient, creaking chair before making an irritable little movement to beckon him further inside. Giz took the invitation, his own mouth wanting to curve into a satisfied smile. He denied it—why let her see the happiness even moving a few feet closer caused?

Showing anything like that was a good way to get stamped on. Or, more likely, provoke Marah into politely vanishing. A First Echelon girl had to be careful where she expressed affection; offers for heir-breeding or uniting Houses would inevitably pile at her doorstep. The fact that she was easy on the eyes and kind as well would just intensify the hunt.

Plenty of Echelons, not to mention steerage, confused mercy with weakness. It was up to Ged to insulate her, as far as she'd let him. So Giz kept his usual sardonic expression, and folded his arms. Looming over her, but of course she didn't look fazed, tucking a few curls lengthening into ripples under sky-blue cloth.

The Corps barbers deserved a *chateau-dif* term under cachet for what they'd done to that hair. Giz remembered its long raven flow, blue highlights in sunshine, a girl running fleet and flushed on the track during Physical Conditioning. Or the night of the Shipbuilder

Dance their second cycle of tertiary school, Marah's black dress starred with small crystals, her hair piled high and threaded with the same pseudo-gems on fine filaments.

A long time ago, but he was cursed with a good memory.

Marah studied him from top to toe. "I sense a caveat."

Being under her gaze was the most pleasant kind of pressure possible. "He thinks it'll keep you out of trouble." That much was true; Giz happened to agree. Keeping her busy with do-gooding on the Sharl's terms was a neat solution, and one he hoped she'd go for.

"Me?" Mock-innocence looked good on her, she spread her hands with an amused twinkle in her eyes and a slight shake of her chin. The rag turned her head into a statue's, a clean profile balanced upon a slim column. "And why on earth would Sharl Notheim think I'm ever in any trouble?"

"He's corrupt, Marah. Not stupid." There was a difference, and one Giz himself was mindful of. It would be immensely satisfying to cut the man loose, but then he might have to take Notheim's place.

And that would rob him of a certain necessary latitude of action.

"Fair point." She spread her hands, a stain of antiseptic across her right palm. Her knuckles were skinned too, and skintaped, but it still made his own hand twinge to see. Had she been in a fight? Unlikely, the scrapes looked mechanical rather than brawl-made. Which was a blessings since he'd have to hunt down her opponent. "He can send a proposal to Will, then."

Good enough. The synthetic might even add his own voice to the chorus, and he had a better chance of being listened to than anyone. Ged contented himself with a simple, "He'll be pleased."

"Mph." Her expression suggested she didn't much care if Notheim was pleased or not. It was all right, really—with Giz at Noth's right hand, Marah could do largely as *she* pleased.

If only she realized as much. Or, Giz thought, maybe she did; he couldn't decide. He hadn't been able to decide whether she was oblivious or perfectly aware of his feelings since secondary school.

Not that it mattered. He was in the habit; besides, what other star did he have to steer by? It was easier, when he became...confused, to ask himself what she'd do. Or Robb, though that answer was always depressingly direct, not to mention violent. "In any case," Ged continued, "I've carried the message, and delivered it. Where would you like tai?"

Was she going to turn him down? She hesitated, and Giz held himself very still. Patience had grown into a habit, too. There was little that wouldn't fall in your lap if you just arranged things and waited.

"Would you think me an airheaded Echelon chieweed if I said *somewhere nice*?" Marah rubbed delicately at her temples, a fingertip massage that apparently did nothing for whatever headache was stalking her. "It's been a day."

Anywhere you like. "I would never think you an airhead chieweed, Marah." It was a day for unmitigated truth, or at least, as much as she'd accept in that quarter. Giz leaned against the doorframe, watching as she half-turned to gaze at the floating, dark-dormant touchscreen tethered to the cluttered desktop, obviously weighing going back to work.

Thankfully, she turned back, losing the battle. "Thanks, Giz."

"Anything for you." *If you only knew, m'enfante.* An old Corps song, one whose lyrics mutated from tender to pornographic at will— as any soldier's ditty did, when passed from mouth to mouth.

Marah's smile became natural, and her shoulders relaxed. Sky-blue cloth brought home how burnished her skin was, and the two tails of the wrap nestled against the side of her neck, the lucky little bâtards. "Well, go sit in the waiting room. I'll be done in a few minutes."

It would probably take an hour or so. But waiting for her was never a chore, especially when he'd made the tension weighing her back diminish. Giz tipped her a brief Corps salute, bathed in the balm of her half-unwilling laugh, and went to settle in an uncomfortable plastic chair.

For as long as it took.

CHANGE_

THE RIBBON-VIA FROM THE NORTH EDGE OF SHARUD WAS PAVED; a shadow of summer drought brushed over tawny and forested hills alike. The khibi, piloted by a lean morose teenager with a scarred mouth, halted in a cloud of pallid dust just outside Madán's gates; Marah leaned from the cradle so the wall-sensors could verify her biometrics as well as security hardware in her rister, and the two massive leaves modeled after a generation ship's bay-seals swung open with a theatrical, though subtle, groan.

She couldn't blame them, or Will, who thought that any visitor to the great hall of Madán should be appropriately impressed by the house's age and valor. Third Echelon held no terraform-age properties and it was rare for a Second Echelon's alcazar to be in the hands of the original line instead of a junior branch, but the First endured. Their lines were given primacy when heir-breeding applications were processed, and Marah herself would probably have to undergo in-vitro if Madán was to continue.

Deciding exactly when to subject herself to that inevitability was a complex process. The Corps had taken her, but only after a few of her eggs were safely stored in Aegis Codex. Given the number of Echelons professing preference for the Moon who had gone over to the redbands either implicitly or explicitly, she was lucky to have been accepted into the Corps, and doubly lucky that her estate wasn't entailed and she hadn't been scooped up into "protective custody."

The khibi rattled to a stop. She could have pinged Will to pick her up in one of Madán's sleek dark needles, but getting out of the city's crowded, seething bowl had become an overwhelming necessity in the middle of their second cup of tai, when Giz's sleek silver rister buzzed and he glanced at its face on the inside of his wrist instead of the back—a Corps habit. Ged was called again to the black atmo-piercing spire of the Shar's Needle; it was a faint guilty relief to witness an emergency that demanded nothing from her personally.

Sorry, Marah. We can finish later. Giz's mournful, half-hopeful look, blue eyes darkening slightly. All she could give him was a *maybe* and a bright smile in response, and he'd flagged a khibi despite her perfect capability for performing that little chore. He even held out his hand for hers as she climbed into the passenger cradle, the small motion of a skarl or bodyservant instead of a fellow Echelon.

Or a spouse, making certain his other legal half was well stabilized.

Marah's fingers still tingled at the memory of his palm, warm skin and reined strength. Now, though, the khibi was rattle-whining up the long, curving, sealed-stone drive, and the driver was probably making plans to add a few credits to his fee when he dropped her off. She pinched the bridge of her nose, the day's heat and irritations almost, *almost* ready to be sloughed from her shoulders once she stepped inside the massive front doors and Madán folded around her.

The alcazar was a burden even at the best of times, but it was also refuge.

Gathering dusk folded itself into every crevice and crease, bedrock terraformed up to make thick walls and piercing, only partly aesthetic towers with pinprick points. Sagittarius Prime was the jewel of Anglene despite being the third of the settled systems, and its Great Alcazars had been designed with an equal mix of aesthetics

and defensibility, not like Capricorn's domes or Virgo's purely func-
tional bunkers.

Her home's front doors should have been sealed tight, but a
vertical line of golden light widened as the right-hand leaf opened. At
least those didn't speak, squeak, or groan; Marah had attended to
programming that bit of household upkeep herself.

A familiar lean shadow in the glow was Will, grey hair glinting
and his utilitarian coverall perhaps blackened with engine-grease. He
would apologize for his appearance, Marah would tell him not to
worry about it, and she could spend at least an hour losing herself in
work on the khibiCAT while the day settled inside her and tension
drained away.

Or so she thought. Will stepped outside and hurried down the
stairs, the very picture of a faithful retainer in a fresh dark-grey jumpsuit, and Marah's headache threatened to return.

Clean clothes and that expression on her synthetic could only
mean one thing. She had a guest, or perhaps more than one; it wasn't
a formal visit or her rister would have buzzed. She often turned its
reflective face to the inside of her wrist as well, a habitual move when
she forgot she was no longer in the Corps.

I should have stayed at tai. Marah tensed in the indifferently
cushioned passenger cradle, bracing herself for unpleasantness.

"I took the liberty of putting him in the drawing room," Will fretted,
the words echoing in the receiving hall's wide stone expanse. Stairs
rose on either side, grand sweeping arms rising into gloom, and the
great basalt chandelier overhead, carved to look like tangled
grapevines, was dark and dead since the glare from it would only
make Marah's headache worse.

At least there was that.

"And you're sure?" She couldn't help herself; it wasn't like Will
could be mistaken. "You're *sure* it's him?"

"Of course." Will's eyes were sheer silver from lid to lid, a sign of internal struggle. The older a synthetic became, the more it could develop antipathies. The Triads didn't allow for them to endanger a Terran even if the antipathy was pronounced, and there was a school of Artificial Thought that held a skarl's dislike was the result of several lightning-fast calculations too subtle to be conscious—if they could be said to be truly conscious instead of semi-sentient—akin to a Terran's gut reaction.

Instinct could be bred into beasts and data-loaded into synthetics; it was solely Terran to ignore your impulses.

Marah's palms were damp. She took a deep breath, and Will glided before her. The second smaller drawing room, for an heir's private guests, was just past the heavy static-sealed doorway of her father's study, and each time she used this hall she held in a lungful while going past *that* piece of real estate. The habit was so deep as to be completely unconscious, and when she spoke it was in on a long exhale that was only partly relieved. "You're *sure?*"

"Yes, mistress." Will indicated the door. The hall-lamps glowed, familiar golden light perfectly engineered to clarify without glaring or robbing decorations of color. "Shall I accompany you?"

Oh, that would just make this even *worse.* "No." Her skin crawled; she would have liked a shower and some formal wear. "Thank you."

Will did not press that particular issue. He was, however, not quite done. "I would remind you, mistress—"

"I need no reminder, Will." *Of anything. Anyway, Father is dead, and can't disapprove.* Even if she did tiptoe past the sealed door of the room that was hers by right now. Sooner or later she'd have to open the main study. She made a quick gesture; the sensor-bars on either side of the study door flushed a deep welcoming pink. Her chin set, and she swept into the room, very aware she was in her clinic scrubs instead of anything even remotely fashionable.

Good clothes were better than wrap-armor. On the other hand, maybe she could have suited up a mech; very little could hurt you inside one of those mobile metal cages.

The blond man turned from an empty, painfully clean fireplace; maybe he had been studying the tchotchkes on the mantel. He'd never been in *this* room before, usually preferring to toss pebbles at her window when she lived in the gardener's cottage near Madán's ancient, lichen-starred garden walls.

Taller. Broader in the shoulder, like Giz after his own Corps service; this man was in fatigues creased with hard use. A short mat of golden hair, freshly cropped to keep the intransigent cowlick above his nape tamed. Dark eyes, with new fans of wrinkles at their corners, and his strong jawline. Solar radiation had lightened his hair and weathered his skin a bit; the light patina took away the pretty Echelon heir-boy, returning a man.

His gaze flickered down to her toes and back up, a soldat's measuring a replacement or a new commander, making his judgments in a hurry to be repented at leisure. "Hullo, Mads." The old nickname, curiously hoarse, and his voice hadn't changed at all.

Marah's heart climbed into her throat. She halted just inside the door, barely aware of Will's tension behind her. The synthetic wouldn't retreat down the hall until he was sure there wasn't going to be any...unpleasantness.

"Robb?" she managed, and felt like a moonshot fool all over again. Of course it was, Will had said as much, but the fact of his presence still pushed the breath out of her in a wondering sigh.

"In the flesh." A sardonic twist to his mouth, new and unwelcome cynicism, a slight hitching lift of one muscular shoulder before it dropped. "Despite everyone's best attempts."

Marah hurled herself across the room, threw her arms around him, and Robb Locke winced. He smelled of fresh air, an edge of acrid military male sweat, and underneath it, a breath of the leggy, smiling boy she'd known all her life—or so close it made no difference. "You *asshole!*" she all but yelled into his chest. Was he taller, or did she simply feel small? The words bounced off paneling, the priceless antique Virgo throw rugs, the heavy curtains drawn against nightfall over the large bay windows. "You complete, utter *asshole.*"

"What'd I do now?" A familiar exchange, but Robb held himself stiff and straight, no attempt to hold her in return. The leashed strength married to ironspine stillness made it like hugging Will right after he came out of the upgrade cabinet, before he'd finished protocol flushes. "Hey. Wow. You cut your hair."

"The Corps won't take you with a mop." She stepped back, held him at arm's length with her fists knotted in his shirt-front. Familiar fatigue material, with no strange fluid-moving layer underneath saying *wrap-armor*. His eyes glowed, fallen meteors slowly cooling. *I could still burn you plenty*, the brown irises said, and the pupils were compressed, smoldering carbon.

"You went..." Now Robb moved, a little, his hands coming up to bracelet her wrists. But gently, calluses scraping a little. He didn't squeeze or try to twist her grasp free, and his skin was warm as Giz's. "When did you join?"

Great Logic, you didn't know? "Second standard of the war." Marah peered at his face. "I thought...well, it was stupid. I thought somehow I'd find you if I joined up." She'd further thought that in the Corps her Echelon might not matter. That was the great promise— service as a leveling factor, doing your duty by comrades of all different stations, steerage to Helm itself.

It was a pleasant lie, but a lie nonetheless. The Corps simply settled itself into the same strata as the outside world, making only lip service to progress *or* leveling.

Robb absorbed this. He watched her face, his own going through several small cascading changes at once. "Find me?"

She might have suspected anyone else of playing at incomprehension, but never him. Robb, while sometimes painfully intransigent, preferred silence to mendacity. At least, he had before he left, and the war couldn't change that.

Or could it?

"You promised to write." Old hurt, still sharp and fresh, turned Marah's tone a little more bitter than she liked. "Remember? I mean, you probably didn't have a lot of time, what with getting into trouble all through intro-camp. Or that's what I told myself. *He's probably being disciplined, I'll hear from him sooner or later.*" Her mouth twisted; she wasn't doing very well at keeping the solid mask of polite indifference. Still, this was *Robb*, he would dislike the mask more than the implied judgment. "But I never did."

"I wrote every tenday." Robb's fingers tensed slightly on her wrists, just a twitch. "Except a few that were too busy, what with combat drops and all." The same flat, matter-of-fact tone you heard from any exhausted soldat giving an after-action report, stinking of battle and standing in whatever approximation of at ease could be found.

"I wrote every tenday too. Like I promised." Marah's hands were numb, and her knees felt suspiciously soft as well. She leaned into him, the touch sending a hot flood of what could be strength down her arms, spreading into her chest. He was *alive*, and right in front of her. "You mean to tell me...well, of course. Couldn't take the risk Echelons would pass coded news. But when the surrender..." She realized the absurdity even as she said it.

"There's not a lot of surrender going on." Robb glanced past her at the door, probably weighing an escape route. How many times had Giz done that, or Marah herself, gauging the distance in case the firing started? You never lost the habit of tracking cover after your first brush with live fire. Not if you wanted to survive, anyway. "Murder, yeah, but not a lot of redbands *surrendered*."

"You were on IP." Her shiver wasn't dramatic in the slightest, nor was it distaste. It was a far more basic—and entirely reasonable— sensation. Insurgency Patrol was the absolute worst duty, especially on planets or mining moons where the terraforming had just barely managed to make a breathable atmosphere. Even if the entire population was sullen villeins, swabbies, and criminals, no wonder they wished for better; with the mineral and other riches to be extracted, no wonder Jun Planetagen was unwilling to entertain even a ghost of ease for what he considered dregs. And then there were the great corporation combines, and Echelons with estates as large as her own. "Wounded?"

"Couple scars." Another half-hitching shrug. There was a faint well-healed scar on his chin, just a thin white line, but she knew it was from Physical Conditioning in primary school. He studied her face, gaze skittering from directly meeting hers and likewise unwilling to settle on her mouth. "You?"

"The same." Her arm twinged, and the scar on her thigh—oh, she could get it erased, to be sure, but had only taken muscle and bone repair—gave a heatless twinge. She'd been bare minutes from bleeding out in the final moments of Second Galvesto, the last-ditch defense of her medical station and its all but helpless patients almost, *almost* failing before the counterattack thundered out of a violet sky, a full combat drop of infantry mechs supported by hedgebomb artillery and pinpoint mortars.

And just before that terrible incident, Ged Gizabón's face, blood-less, blue eyes alight, staring at her from the aid station cot. The other medic—Castirióne, arrived barely ten days before the battle—had approached Marah afterwards. *I triaged wrong*, he'd said, and Marah had been put in the uncomfortable, squirming position of admitting she hadn't triaged, she *knew* the soldat, and had made an emotional call instead of a logical one.

Well, it was the right one anyway, Casti had said, and gone on his way looking relieved. Marah, however, had stood in her tent, the shivers going all through her like they threatened to now.

"Infantry?" Robb's raised eyebrows said he didn't think she'd go into that branch of the Corps, and damn him, he was right, but not because she hadn't tried.

"Corps Medical." They had not, after all, been willing to risk a First Echelon without a live, of-age heir on the front lines. Marah had appealed the decision.

It had done exactly no good at all.

"Of course. You're smart enough." His shoulders relaxed a little more, and his arms dropped too. He still held her wrists, but an onlooker would assume he was clasping her hands, a pretty picture of returning soldats. His fatigues had seen hard use, the dusty Corpscroix on the right breast fading. There were worn spots where equipment straps would rest, too.

"You've been to Lamóre?" Marah's throat was dry. It was a thorny relief to find out she could still read him, watching his mouth and the corners of his eyes. Dead giveaways, even though the Corps taught an infantryman to make his face a wall. "I'm so sorry, Robb."

Which wasn't *quite* an untruth. She'd often wished, especially when younger, that old Locke would somehow disappear and leave his son free from the sharp suffocating weight of expectation and abuse. But she was sorry, because even if you hated your progenitor... well, she loved her own father, but then again, he had never beaten her.

Not even emotionally.

"I don't suppose you know..." The old Robb wouldn't have sounded so tentative.

Marah's heart couldn't decide whether to stay in her throat or splash into her guts. "Treason. Or so Notheim said. I didn't know until Giz went on leave and fittled me halfway through my last tour." Bad news always arrived at the worst time, or so the Corps said, and she'd read Giz's letter three times in a row, her eyebrows knotting together and the sound of faraway artillery underscoring each character.

"Giz." Robb's face changed a few degrees and he dropped her wrists.

"Yes." Was he jealous? Marah shifted her weight slightly, leaning away from the prospect. The same old habit, rationing her affection, letting her hands fall to her sides and smoothing her expression. "He went into the Corps too, right after you. Decorated for bravery a few times, both frontline and intel work." Why goad him? Oh, she knew —if Robb was going to be an ass, she would needle him, just as she always had. "He's back, and working for Notheim."

"The Sharl, yes?" Of course, it would be a new name to him.

Noth had arrived after the trial of the former Sharl for treason. Old Gannecke had been hung too; Giz's and subtle mentions after demobilization had left enough unsaid that Marah could guess at what he *really* wanted to tell her about that whole affair. "I see. Figures."

"It wasn't his choice. He does his service just like the rest of us." It was time for a subject change, as usual when one of them was angry at the other. Sometimes she felt like a tether between two tugs, each straining to snap an invisible cord. "I've got a ship now, we do salvage runs. Sell everything we can for my clinic near the Saur."

"That's just like you." It could have been admiring or sarcastic, his half-smile a flash of the old Robb again.

At least that was the same. Precious little was these days. "So I'm told. Are you hungry?" Kamany was visiting his mother in Capricorn; it was a shame, since he would have liked to feed one of what he considered his own.

The kitchen belonged to Madán, but it was Kam's all the same.

"No." Robb dismissed the Terran need for nourishment with a slight jerk of his chin. "They hung my father." A fine trembling slid through him, communicating through the air between them to settle in her own hands, her aching wrists, her tense shoulders. "Nobody bothered to cut him down?"

"The Treason Laws. The Senatus..." Didn't he *know*? But of course, Robb had his own peculiar ideas about what was and wasn't expected, and woe to anyone who set a foot on the wrong side of them. It was one more way he was just like his father, and he would have hated to hear her say it, so Marah didn't. "Anyone who tried would get strung up next to him."

"If they got caught, sure." His perennial refrain, from primary school to the day he left. He must have come straight from the demob; he was rumpled and more than a little dirty, and that was new. His father had always been on him to scrub like a proper Echelon was expected to. "In any case, we'll see."

"You cut him down." It wasn't even a difficult guess. Her heart thumped into her throat again and decided to stay there, a hammering obstruction like a road-repair mech. How was she going to smooth *this* over? At least the rebellion was done; she could make the case that treason wasn't applicable anymore. The only question was whether to break this news to Giz before he found out from someone else.

Assuming anyone went out to Lamóre anymore; the tenants there were probably glad to khibi into Sharud instead of dealing with Old Locke.

Robb's jaw settled in its usual sullen hardness, and his eyelids dropped a fraction as if she'd started lecturing him. "How could I *not?*"

"I don't know, Robb. The way he treated you, I'm just surprised." Now she felt faintly ridiculous, and longed to clutch at his fatigue jacket again. If she held hard enough, it might even matter.

"Me too." He leaned back fractionally, as if he wanted to shake her off too, but not enough to truly loosen a tether-grip. Sometimes, after his father had been at him, Robb didn't want to be touched. "You wrote to me?"

"Every damn tenday." *Did you think I wouldn't?* All of a sudden it was that afternoon in the Preserve near the Slee again, cold even in bright sunshine, cupping her elbows and hugging herself, her pulse high and thready, nervous sweat all over her when he'd told her he was joining the Corps. When the rebellion took more than a few second-class, incompletely terraformed worlds, it crossed from insurgency into flat-out war, and whoever wasn't already signed up to the Corps was encouraged to do their duty—and turn in anyone whose sympathies weren't of the accepted sort as well. "Except Galvesto."

Robb's dark gaze lost some of its burning. Maybe she'd said the right thing, for once, and managed to soothe him. You could never tell which way he'd explode when you dropped the 'nade in—and sometimes, you didn't even know it was live until the blast bloomed. "You were at Galvesto?"

"Both times." Another shiver. The night wasn't cold and neither was the drawing room, but her skin roughened with gooseflesh anyway. She never wanted to think of that fucking mining moon ever again, even if its position *had* made it a linchpin of redband defense in the Aquarius system. "I wasn't this rude before the war. Let's get you some tai, and something to eat. I'm sure you're tired."

"I'm not one of your patients." The same prickly pride, a Second Echelon's defense against both those above and below. At least Robb had been born into Echelon schooling, not bought like his father; Robb could have an Aegis career and solidify into a hereditary position if he cared to.

Maybe that was why Old Locke had hated his heir so much.

"Good." Marah made her fingers loosen from curled fists. They ached with unsaid things, just like the rest of her. "Because I'd like to thump you on the head for being difficult, just like usual." It was time for a subject change. "Your letters didn't get through to me either, then. I wonder where they're sitting now?"

Robb snorted. "Probably in some censor's rocket-stroker."

At least he wasn't angry at *her* over it, for once. A laugh jolted free; halfway through, it turned into a shaking inhale as the news caught up with her. Robb was here. He was *alive*. "It's good to see you."

"Is it?" He sounded only mildly interested, and scratched at the side of his neck. The old Robb would have hugged her, a brief excruciating moment of contact proving he wasn't upset. "I should head back to town."

"Great Under, why?" She smoothed her clinic scrubs, settled her rister with the reflective face on the inside of her wrist like a Corps mass-issued one with chip support instead of a whisper-thin new model, and took a few steps back to put them on even footing again. "Will will be overjoyed to have someone else to fuss over."

"Sure he will." Robb's grin was a shadow of its old self, since he knew very well what the skarl thought of the Lockes and their station well below the Madáns'. He sobered quickly, glancing at the curtained window as if he expected a mortar strike at any moment, and what he was *really* worried about escaped in a breathy rush. "I cut him down, Marah. If they find me here it won't be good for you."

Did he honestly think she cared? He was here, and *alive*, and that was all she could scrape up the energy to worry about. "We'll take care of it, Giz and I."

"Giz." Robb's mouth thinned, and the old banked fire filled his dark gaze again. It used to take longer to stoke that glow.

Marah suppressed a sigh. "He's not the same, Robb."

"Neither am I." He stepped back, away from the mantel and the clean, summer-unused fireplace, perhaps unwilling to be touched again. "I really should go."

"And what, spend all your muster-out pay in a fleabitten hole in the Saur?" She knew this game; Robb wanted her to protest, so he could give in. At least that hadn't changed. "Come on, Robb. Don't be ridiculous."

In the end, he agreed semi-grudgingly to dinner but no evening tai, and further agreed to stay in the gardener's cottage. It was anyone's guess whether he'd be there in the morning, though, and she knew as much even as she lifted her rister to formally tap for Will, waiting in the hall like an Old Terran ghost.

Some things changed, Marah thought...and some did not. But at least he was home.

NO SHORTAGE_

Two days later a beautiful early summer afternoon folded over Sharud, the promise of dust-choked heat later ameliorated by a rare cool night. In a metric month or two the rains would sweep in, the northern half of Sagittarius Prime showering before the harvest festivals—First, Great, and Last— and the celebratory break during winter's long chill slumber. But for now it was bright gold sunshine, the freshness of Sharud Forest Preserve full of birdsong and the creeping crepitation of terraform-spurred life in the underbrush... and a single plume of dark smoke lifting its shaggy head to announce *someone's having a bad day*.

Notheim held a folded square of heavy cloth mouchoir to his nose. Nasal filters were undignified for a man of his station when dealing with this offal, and a pocket-rag was a sign of Echelon breeding, much in demand among the lower orders. "What kind of contraband?"

"Cryon." Ged Gizabón, straight and black in his uniform, was at his patron's shoulder with a couth murmur, giving information when necessary or wanted, holding his peace otherwise. That particular, limited recalcitrance was a rarity, and it was one reason Noth kept him, despite the blue-eyed bâtard knowing where certain things were buried.

Having a Corps intel officer in your empty was hardly comfortable or advisable, despite said service being politely called as honourable as any other.

The smugglers, their arms cuffed tightly behind their backs and sensahoods pulled down to their shoulders, had been forced to their knees in a straggling line. Dust swirled choking-dry on the edge of autumn, painting every surface matte gold. Noth almost envied the unbroken rest these sad sacks were about to receive.

This chain of smugglers, however, was a mystery, and Noth did not like such things. "How odd," he murmured. His pomade was beginning to soften outside the cool of climate control; only chie-weeds sealed their hairdos. "With prices about to go down, why bother?"

"Quick profit, perhaps? It's fresh product, too." Giz didn't sound unsettled, merely thoughtful. He was fresh as a bellis-flower in thermaseal, and his black hair's glistening was probably the result of good genetics instead of oil. It was enough to make you despise the man; his calm was a comfort and irritant all at once as well.

Noth was unsettled enough for both of them. Besides, he hated being out of the office, though he knew its frequent necessity. The personal touch wasn't simply for protocol-bound Echelons. "Whose property is this?"

"Tabit. Both sons dead in the war, father dead two standards before, mother who knows?" The chief of Noth's unofficial intelligence gathering also admitted when lacunae existed, which alone made him well worth retaining. Subordinates who didn't try to papier over the unknown to soothe their master's ego were rare and useful; Noth did his best not to commit the ancient kingly sin of killing the messenger.

"I see." After all, taking your troubles out on a fittle-carrier was only momentarily satisfying, and had no long-term utility. Noth indicated the hooded smugglers. "No treasonous connections?" Of course, if there had been one, Giz would have already told him. But it never hurt to be sure.

"Not yet. They're Saur flotsam." Gizabón's shrug was more sensed than seen; his shadow, cast before them and lengthening, moved on dry dirt and yellowed weeds. He'd come back from the war Second Echelon instead of Third, but it didn't seem to have inflated his ego past bearing. "In any case, the Tabits were freeholders, not tenants *or* Echelon."

Not villeins, and not people of consequence either. The class between those two shores was full of troublemakers, though Parl Jun worried more about Echelon traitors. To each their own, certainly. "Simple theft," Noth murmured. A summary execution was not called for.

That was a bother. You didn't want to give little swabbies the idea that the captain was merciful. Or worse, weak.

"Sir?" One of the officers, his helmet's faceshield modulating his voice into a weird muffled hiss, approached with a heavy step, polis grab-boots crushing drought-dead weeds and loosing a cargo of bright white floating seeds that would find no purchase on uniforms or needles. "We found this in the barn." A sheaf of flyers fluttered in his gauntleted fist, brightly colored scrap flymsy-fylm.

Giz stepped forward, accepting the mess. He flicked through, and his long nose wrinkled once. His mouth moved, as if to shape a vulgar syllable, but he compressed his lips and glanced at Noth. "Propaganda, sir."

RISE UP, one said in screaming high-simple Anglene. And another: *KILL A POLIS, THE MOON WILL FORGIVE.* Typo-ridden and full of muddy pictures of so-called atrocities, it was standard rebellious fare.

Noth's cheeks swelled; a grin lit his cold brown eyes. "I see." He motioned for the squad serjeants, two interchangeable figures in black polis gear with blue piping, their own faceshields glittering hard and anonymous. Male, female, the armor was the same and blurred every outline. True leveling, the kind they said happened in the Corps. "We have a nest of traitors here, soldats."

Gizabón said nothing, just gazed over the line of kneeling figures. His information, as usual, was solid, and the potential of netting significant contraband high enough that Noth had decided to come along on this little excursion as well. Normally, one of the lesser lieutenants would be in charge, the entire operation a well-tuned ship.

The contraband would go for a nice profit on the open market or the black one, wherever prices were better. A percentage would go to Noth, of course, a smaller percentage to Gizabón, and an even smaller fraction shared among the squads.

The lion's share, of course, was Parl Jun's. It was an unexpected gift, a few more zeroes to whet that appetite. Noth could even ration it out over a few metric months and gain some breathing room.

"Orders, sir?" The squad serjeant on the left—they were a matched set, like Brick and Bat in the old literacy primers—bobbed his head, showing willingness. He was the more eager of the two; the right-hand serje was a former Saur brat content to let others take the risks while she did cleanup. They worked well together, especially under Noth's Ryfl.

"I think an example must be made." Noth glanced at Giz, squinting. The glare was hideous; he much preferred to see the giant nuclear reactors that powered all Terran life from behind smoked silica. "Giz?"

"You're right." There was never any other answer from Gizabón's direction, unless it was silence. Which made the man even more useful; if the Ryfl thought Noth was making a fool of himself, he'd generally let the quiet do all the speaking needed, saving his patron's ego but still making his feelings known. "What kind of example?"

Noth pointed at the barn. "There's good timbers in there. Take a few and hammer them up, then fire the place. Load the contraband, I'll expect a manifest in two hours."

"Sir." Two crisp salutes from Brick and Bat, strict about-faces since the Sharl ran his service along Corps lines, and orders began to crackle downward like flak. It took so little to set the cleansing in motion, but that was no comfort. If only the shaggoshit clinging to shoes knew better than to get in the way, all the unpleasantness could be avoided entirely.

But the ordure just had to go and place itself in the traffic lanes, making for splatter. Logic knew how much Notheim hated the stink and untidiness, and all of it so *useless*.

"Hammering?" Giz probably didn't raise an eyebrow, but it sounded close. The shadow of his coat-hem moved slightly, but just from the breeze, not any flinching. "Making martyrs might be unwise."

"Saur flotsam," Noth quoted back at him, turning to face his Ryfl. Giz's superiors in the Corps had been extremely generous in their estimations, not to mention their analysis, of his capability; it was pleasant to find out they had, if anything, understated the fellow's quality. "You worry too much. Come on, let's go before they get started. I don't want to hear it."

Giz didn't quite hesitate, but he did remember his duty. "You don't want me to stay and check the manifest?"

"I've eyeballed it." Noth's smile still did not reach his cold brown gaze. It was more a predator's grimace than an expression of amusement, and he turned on one dress-booted heel. The lower ranks could wear grab-boots, but he was expected to set a certain *tone*. "If it's short of thirty thousand I'll have the squad serjeants put to the chain."

There was, after all, no shortage of applicants for the polis. Not with the flood of Corps veterans returning to every first-class planet, and quite a few of the second and third classes as well. The commission to ease them back into civilian life would be a nice tax sink, if Giz could induce the Madán girl to lend her name.

A First Echelon bitch had her uses, even if she ran quasi-legal salvage through Saur middlemen. If Noth had to, he could make life uncomfortable for such a creature, but there was no need. Not when she could be used in other ways, not least to provide Notheim some cover if Parl Jun came to stick his Helm-royal nose into affairs. And if Giz acquired ideas above his pay grade, a little pressure on a childhood friend might throttle his core.

Noth strode for his sleek black personal polis cruiser, Gizabón in his wake. The Sharl did not see the taller, black-clad man glance over his shoulder with a tightmouth grimace of distaste; nor did he suspect it.

It was just as well. After all, even the most discreet tool in a military governeur's hand could be replaced.

LUXURY_

The Sharud Forest Preserve ran through Madán's lands, shimmering green under a summer Sagittarius sun. Bushes thrashed several klicks away from an afternoon of routine polis work; a tall, slim woman half-fell through their clutching arms. At least she hadn't been caught outright, and at least the alcazar's perimeter and other defenses still recognized her.

Marah couldn't be too angry if she hadn't revoked safe harbor for one of her more troublesome clients. And at least the Lady of Madán didn't have roaming packs of half-synthetic canids as part of her alcazar defense matrix.

Or worse, anatidae. Those feathered nuisances were *smart*. There were even Terran legends of the non-synthetic versions used as watchmen, lost in the mists of pre-Shiptime.

Tall, pale-haired Alladal pressed her hand to her side and exhaled, hard. Scoreburns were painful but not immediately life-threatening; she'd been able to lie low in the woods for a little while. If there were internal injuries, well, she was *kind of shaggo'd*, as the chieweeds had taken to saying lately. But bringing polis bâtards here wasn't good manners even if Marah probably wouldn't be thrown in stockade for harboring a stray.

Probably.

Alladal's face was crusted with dried blood; a scab was matting up nicely under her dun Lunacer's headwrap. She scratched at the red door with two broken fingernails, a cat looking for safety.

The sensor-glows on either side of painted wood rippled. The door was unlocked, and she was invited in. Alladal twisted the knob, half-fell through. Getting over Madán's curtaining wall had been the hard part, but now, so close to her goal, she was rubber-kneed and gossypium-headed.

Iron-haired Will Skarl caught her shoulder and set her on her feet, his synthetic oculars shining flatly with a random reflection of overhead light. The small mudroom off the kitchen—*small* for Madán, it would fetch a fine rent for a family of five in the Saur—was just the same, wooden slats for mud-scraping over ancient stone flooring and a humming electrostatic shimmer to shake drier particles away, the kitchen shining golden through a wide, stone-framed doorway at the other end.

"Shhh." Will laid a finger upon his thin lips. "Don't say anything."

Of course. What he didn't hear he couldn't be forced to testify to, or replay from steno-recco capture. Not that a First Echelon's skarl would be made to testify anyway, but it was better safe than sorry.

Al's ribs twinged, and she coughed. At least the tail end of the explosion didn't carry cargo, so to speak; she wasn't bringing up blood. Will half-carried her into the kitchen's familiar glow, the air held at a steady temperature no matter how hard the oven was going inside *or* out.

Marah turned from the stove, caught in the act of measuring high-grade spice-tai into a saucepan. Looked as if she was going to boil it with lac and sweetener like a common laborer—probably a comment on any prospective guests at this hour, Moon and Logic both knew the Lady of Madán was above such common things as *moonshot* tai, indeed.

"I shall fetch medical supplies," Will announced, more to alert his mistress than to impart the information to one of said mistress's clients.

"Mother Moon." Marah turned from the silver stove. Her dark eyes widened, and even shaken from bed by the soft beeping of *someone's come over the fence* in her chambers—if she hadn't already been up—she looked impossibly *finished*, as if each messy curl was planned, her too-big Corps undershirt and loose-laced linen pants worn like high fashion instead of pyjamas. Chieweeds wished they could look that effortlessly Echelon; there was a whole industry of genebrush and etiquette handlers to burnish the less-deserving into faking a room above steerage. Marah indicated the usual wooden stool at the breakfast bar, and Will hurried Alladal over stone flags to settle her upon it. "Yes, go fetch the kit, Will. Get extra skintape, too."

"Yes, mistress." He hurried away, safely out of earshot within a few moments. The door to the hall swung in decreasing arcs from his passage as Marah flicked the heat on under the tai kettle, heading for the sink to wash her hands, that perennial medical first step.

Alladal held onto both sides of the stool and sagged with relief. Safe harbor achieved once more, and if she could just *breathe* for a few seconds she might believe she'd survived.

"Hi, Al." Water ran. Marah scrubbed at her hands like she wanted to take the skin off. "You look like a rough salvage. What happened?"

"Do you really want to know?" Al closed her eyes. Letting go of the stool's platform was chancy, but she managed, one finger at a time. It wouldn't do to show weakness.

At least Marah didn't take offense. "Guess not. Let's get that jacket off." No sooner had she said it than heavy, dirty canvas hit the floor; the Echelon also grabbed the hem of Al's shirt with the thoughtless, impersonal gentleness of one female technician working on another. "This too, unless you want me to cut it."

Alladal made a short plosive noise, denying any attachment to something so small. "It's shredded anyway." She'd gone through a hillside's worth of thrashvines, across a summer-choked streamlet more mud than water, and barely evaded the second patrol ring. "Don't worry, the clinic stuff's fine."

"I'm worried about you, not the materials." Maybe it was even true. Marah finished peeling off Alladal's shirt and began examining, her fingers soft and neutral. "Oh, Al. Ouch." Did she have to sound so goddamn disappointed? It must be so *easy* to live in this huge alcazar humming with tech and not have to scramble for rent, for food, for a pot to piss in.

Alladal fought the urge to close her eyes and slide off the stool. It would be so easy to collapse, but what would happen then? "Looks worse than it is."

"Scoreburns are tricky." Marah stiffened slightly, and the slight rustling of another creature in the room was Will, returning with a silver tray of med supplies and a float-tether that hummed into life. "Thank you. I think the khibiCAT needs some attention, Will. I'll call when I need you."

"Yes, mistress." And he was gone again, but the tray remained, drifting closer to Marah, who made a little beckoning movement, pointing where she wanted it. Easy, seamless tech, the alcazar moving to aid its inhabitant.

Mistress. Al's face was already contorted with discomfort; mockery wouldn't matter. "It must be so nice to be you."

"I'm not so sure." Marah's standard reply. She subtracted two stackable metal trays from the float, settled them on the counter, and picked up a shiny silver tube of painkiller antiseptic. Looked like Corps surplus; there was no shortage of it swilling around the port now. "Lift your arm...there." An indrawn breath, soft and pained. "How close were you to the blast?"

"Close *enough*." Al's irritability was a sign the worst was over, too. If you noticed your nerves were raw, it was because you weren't dancing at high speed to escape death's cold bony grasp—or worse, the little games polis played when they caught a noncitizen. "I almost got scooped in, too. They popped scores first and nets later."

"Well, yeah, that's standard when you want to take a position without risking a lot of casualties. On your own side, at least." Marah glanced up, measuring Alladal's expression while she palpated for internal injury. The kitchen looked like a gloss-holo Gracious Living chieweed illustration, even the chips and cracks in stone countertop and wax-rubbed wooden cabinets speaking softly of ease and comfort rather than poverty and displacement.

Alladal had reserved the more important question for last. "Am I going to scar?"

"Can't tell yet." To her credit, Marah visibly didn't consider the prospect likely *or* too small to warrant inspection. "You've clotted up. How long ago was this?"

"I had to lie over in the woods a bit." She had to be cagey, and not just to protect herself. On the other hand, the Lady of Madán didn't need protection. She was *Echelon*, and First at that. "They were cleaning up a raid out at the Tabit place. I tripped a sentry, they probably think it was a cervidae or something."

"Good." The line between Marah's eyebrows was familiar; the tai-pot on the stove began to send up fragrant steam as the appliance continued the steady work of stirring and heating. Lovely, stainless, useful tech, the birthright of any Echelon. Steerage villeins had to pay, make do, and pay again for a fraction of that ease. "Want to say you were here all night?"

Nice of her to offer an alibi. Really *noble*. "That'd make more problems than it solved." Let the lady think what she wanted of that statement. Al's conscience pricked her, a faint sting but still uncomfortable. "Thanks, though."

"Mh." Another glance, measuring damage, her almost-black gaze oddly directionless; Marah's impersonal fingertips tested a sore spot, Alladal flinched, and the Echelon reached for a handheld scanner. "I'd give you something to wash your face, but I want it to stay sealed while I work on this."

"Just get it over with. I'm tired." Alladal peeked between her thick, heavy lashes. Cool air was a balm against her naked torso and high shallow breasts. "You still haven't asked about the clinic's cut." If the woman would just act like a greedy Echelon pig, Al could disdain her and be done with it. But no, Marah kept being as decent as possible.

It was probably really nice to have that luxury, too. Mother Moon knew the rest of them couldn't afford it.

"Why?" Right now, Marah's expression was somewhat blank as she concentrated on assessing damage and applying antiseptic. "Do you have bad news?"

"Well, no." The last shipment of salvage had fetched a fine price, and Alladal's cut would be good too. The Lady of Madán didn't lower herself to hard bargaining in order to keep a middleman's cash.

"Then why even mention it?" Marah shook her head, curls stretching softly into ripples. Even her hair behaved, a sleek, glossy cloud. "It might be better if you don't talk."

"My lady Echelon, when have you ever known that to be an option?" Weary amusement filled Alladal as gooseflesh spilled down her back. If everyone thought she was a flighty little songbird, they wouldn't suspect the rest, and that kept Al safe.

Not to mention keeping those who depended on her safer.

"Hm." Marah made a soft noise of concentration and reached for a fresh pod of antiseptic, the kind with lowgrade analgesic included. No expense spared. "You *are* capable of keeping a few secrets."

The quiet observation shouldn't have made panic wriggle behind her breastbone, but Alladal's nerves were as raw as a villein's back after an old-fashioned lashing. Such things weren't the norm on first-class worlds anymore, but Al was from a different quarter of Anglene. She'd also bothered to read some history. "Only because I don't keep anyone else's."

"That's not quite true either." Marah's profile was serene and severe at once. If the statues of the Moon in her white temples ever pushed back her shadowing hood, she might look very much like the Lady of Madán. Al couldn't decide whether Marah cultivated the image or ignored it.

Or maybe it was just Alladal's personal opinion, finding fault in anything nice the way Sana always said her cousin did. "You know, if you weren't an Echelon, I might almost like you." That was as close to the truth as they'd get this morning. Keeping the other woman at bay with careful insults and a show of distrust was a habit by now; why change?

"And if you weren't so prickly, I might almost let you. Now shush, I need to listen to this." Marah popped in a silvery earfiller and began scanning with a handheld bone-wand, frowning slightly. "Just breathe, nice deep inhales, if you can."

Alladal took a deep breath, her ribs aching with expansion. For a moment she almost wanted to say something silly, like *you're not bad for an Echelon* or even *I don't really dislike you*, but Marah had told her to be quiet.

So she was.

MISTAKE GOING AROUND_

It was the first good night's sleep he'd had in a long while, even though the bed was too soft and Hood had to stretch out on the floor with two ancient comforters and his ditbag for a pillow. He woke in mellow grey predawn and lay still, listening intently, his breathing still the long imperceptible inhales and equally slow exhales of deep sleep.

You learned not to give any sign of waking. If the danger wasn't redbands it was a noncom looking to roust someone for an incidental, most likely unpleasant, duty. They tended to go for the ones already awake, following the very human habit of the easiest path.

Hood—and Robb inside him—took stock. He was on his back, a bar of early mornlight falling across his face. Quiet, very quiet, only the stealthy sounds of a structure expanding as a summer night's late-arriving coolness faded into a hot morning. He smelled the scorch of dust-eaters hurriedly brought out of their charging stations to make a room fit for a Terran guest's habitation, the staleness of a rarely opened space.

It was Marah's old bedroom in Madán's gardener's cottage, still with the ancient, beloved iron bedframe and a few plastyfylm posters of holo stars and chieweeds popular several standards ago on the walls. Looked like she'd left them hanging, maybe unwilling to let go of prewar innocence. There was the window he'd thrown pebbles at to invite her out for nightly rambles, now full of pearly filtered glow, and the white and yellow comforters were shabby because she'd used them, sleeping sprawled or curled.

She was just as beautiful as ever. Short hair suited her, blue-black curls in a triangular mass. He tried to imagine her in uniform, doing push-ups in basic intro-camp while a serjeant yelled, and failed completely. She'd probably been on easy circuit and straight into officer training. They wouldn't do less for a First Echelon.

It was no use. He wasn't going to sleep longer. The tyranny of consciousness had Hood in its claws, and he had to pretend to be Robb Locke now.

The "cottage" was a snug little house, stone turned plastic by terraform and drawn up to make foundation and half-walls, its roof newly repaired. The main alcazar would be self-healing to a certain degree, of course, tech under a synthetic's direction seamlessly performing maintenance. It spoke well of Madán family fortunes that the outbuildings were in good repair too. Of course, First Echelons got a tech stipend from the government; everyone owed a debt to the families who awoke on paired generation ships to deal with emergencies and corrections while the other echelons and the *hoi Pauloi* slept in egg-and-sperm form. The alcazars were only part of that payment for those who were born and died on the ships, trapped by their ancestors' generosity and their descendants' promised good living.

The Helm, of course, and other prerogatives and perquisites.

Hood left his bag on the floor of Marah's old bedroom, partly to see if habit would let him and partly to give himself an excuse to come back. The old Robb would have been over the the terraform-ancient skirting wall as soon as dawn began to whisper, or sooner. Getting caught here by Marah's father would be mortifying, but the worst would be if his own found out about it.

I told you to stay away from that girl. You think a cuckoo like you has a chance? And then, reversing himself the next day, *If you're going to put cargo in that girl, do it fast before she finds out what you really are.*

The tiny bathroom, the sitting room with its wide, ugly orange couch and cup-shaped chairs, the kitchenette and breakfast bar, all the same. But there were new lamps, and the kitchenette's window over the sink wasn't full of potted, carefully watered green. The sink was dry as a bone and the empty counters blazed free of dust by hurried housekeeping tech; Marah's old silver tai-kettle was nowhere in evidence.

Hood let himself out the front door and walked up the gravel path between garden beds, some lying fallow, others tended by small zipping silvery drones turning a shade less than noro-red when he passed, sensing the nearness of a Terran and retracting anything likely to cause even the least harm to one of its august owners or Terran guests. Cropleaf, globefruit, sannon fruit, brassicas—robust, dense foodstuffs ideal for smaller plots. Did she sell them? Keep them in the pantry for a rainy day? She probably distributed them in the Saur. Madán largesse, and most of the people she offered it to probably hated her for it.

The world was like that. It was a good thing she had that skarl watching over her. The custom Wɪɪɪ model was a butler-bodyguard build with several custom enhancements, a present from Gran Marl Ileanor to Marah's own progenitors on their heir-contracting day. Marah had idly wondered aloud sometimes if the gift was meant to keep an eye on her father's ambition, too, but never very loudly and only deep in the woods between Madán and Lamóre.

The drones went back to their work as soon as he was clear. He climbed the steps to the red-painted kitchen door, wondering if he should be clutching a hat and tugging his forelock to boot. It was a ridiculous feeling, where else would the small pathway from the gardener's house go? Still, it lingered.

You bâtard brat, you're not fit for the Second Echelon. His father's voice, deep, resonant, and coated with ice. Well, he would never again be disappointed by his too tall, too blond, too athletic, too stupid son.

Even though those qualities were, after all, what Locke senior had stipulated when he went through the heir approval process. With no spouse or available heir-carrier, he'd had to surrogate, and often stared at Robb during dinner, his gaze growing more and more fixed until he finally said, softly each time, *They made a mistake in the surrogate room, didn't they.*

It wasn't a question, and Hood had no answer. Each time, he simply hunched his shoulders and kept eating, because the price for stopping was one of the beatings. Today, though, he kept striding along, and when he realized he was scanning for tripwires, he hunched his shoulders, took a deep breath, and lengthened his stride. The war was over, or it had never reached here.

Hood still flinched every time he thought he sensed a trap.

The kitchen door was propped open and a faint draft of spicy good tai-smell tiptoed out. Marah was boiling it with sweetened lac and spices; they called it *moonshot* because it would keep a mechanic or shipwright awake and conscious enough to keep working on long shifts. There was even a low of hum voices. Maybe Kameny was cooking breakfast, but the voices were entirely too light to be his grumbling.

Maybe someone else had dropped in?

Hood had gotten them both moving but it was Robb who slid through the door, its sensors glowing steadily. He was in the wrong mood to meet Ged, if that lean dark canid was hanging around. Not to mention Robb was unshaven, with his eyes sleep-crusted and his mouth full of night-egg reek.

It was best to never show Gizabón—or anyone else—any weakness. Still, it would be good to see him again. Right?

It wasn't Giz. A rangy woman with a dun turban atop a kittenish face winced, balanced precariously on a familiar three-legged wooden stool as Marah bent, applying what looked like analgesic to a flour-pale face. Thin sweat-streaks in dermaspray makeup said this girl both cared for her appearance and had been out all night doing hard labor, and the easy way she sat in baggy commercial fatigue pants as well as a heavy, dust-colored canvas jacket said the job might have involved a shovel and something to bury. Under the jacket, her chest was smooth copper skin plastered with glaring-white bandages as well as a bandeau around her breasts; a rag of T-shirt material lay neatly in a medical waste tray. The biggest bandages lingered on the right side of her slightly-ridged stomach, and the bruising around it said *score-burn*.

"Oh, hello," the newcomer said, conversationally, in a light, well-modulated alto. It was a voice made for singing, and the way she talked said she knew as much. If she wanted to do a chieweed show, she was well set up for it. "Did you get a new household villein, Mads?"

"Hm? No, that's another friend of mine. We grew up together." Marah barely glanced at him, focused on her work. It was good to see her so calm and focused. A man could watch all he wanted if she was distracted. "Tai's on the stove, Robb. I forgot to tell you Kameny's offplanet."

The other woman measured him up and down. Platinum hair with dark roots feathered at her temples, vanished into her turban, and her eyes were very wide, pupils dilated with exhaustion or pain. "A bit thick for me," she said, and the tip of a pale tongue touched her lips. "But in good shape."

"Be nice." Marah frowned, her fingertips holding a long thin cut closed. She wore the same expression while playing lingo-chess. "If you want me to finish sealing this, stop wriggling."

"Looking's free." Hood studied the shape of the new woman's chin, then the bridge of her nose. If you stared there, people thought you were digging through their eye-holes to find the back of their skull. He even attempted an easy smile, baring his teeth in the socially accepted manner. "Let me guess, if anyone asks, you were never here, right? That's what they all say."

"You be nice too," Marah said, turning her chin slightly to toss the words over her shoulder. "Or I'll throw you *both* out. Which would please Will, but it would also waste some good tai." Her nubby linen pants were slipping at the waist, showing a smooth copper slice of her lower back when she bent.

"I couldn't bear to do that." The woman's smile broadened, and Hood hoped she was copying him. It would mean his own expression looked natural, that he was impersonating a civilian with some success. "It's Alladal, sir." Mischievous weight on the last word.

"Robb." That was all he'd give for free. Lunacers weren't *automatically* redbands, but better safe than sorry, loose lips sank dreadnoughts, and all that.

Besides, Marah wouldn't be silly enough to have a redband, or anyone redband-adjacent, at her alcazar, right? Wrong. Robb knew she might, the same way young Marah took in young avians with wing issues or an injured thamnophis. *Overactive empathy*, old Aethelstan had called it; Giz and Robb would just glance at each other and shrug when she brought another broken creature along.

"Pleasure, I'm sure." Alladal winked, a quick cheeky flicker of long lashes. Her cheekbones were high and wide, and her cheeks were slightly rough. Looked like she'd transitioned mid-puberty, without blockers despite them being an inalienable right. Some, especially on smaller planets and moons, didn't like the chance of even nominal side effects. "You can tell whoever you like I was here. Everyone knows I'm in love with Marah."

"Mm-hmm." Marah spared the girl a quick look, her mouth soft. It was a medic's distracted but kind expression, and Hood could suddenly imagine her in medipost, attending a shaking soldat still high on adrenaline and clutching his cleared-and-chained ryfl like a kid with a softie ursus. "Sure you are. Mostly because I'm a reliable audience."

"I have *sold out* the Camyron," Alladal returned, haughtily. Her chin twitched as if she wanted to toss her head, the motion instantly checked with a dancer's control. Her fingers moved too, tiny flicks like she felt a keyboard underneath them. "I don't need more *audience.*"

Marah clicked her tongue and reached for more skintape. "What you need is to be still and let me finish this if you don't want a scar. Or two."

"I'll look positively barbaric." Alladal settled into a watchful stillness, a little less disciplined than a soldat's but much more than a civilian's.

Interesting. Hood settled equally watchfully inside Robb's head, a borderline-unpleasant feeling only because it meant Robb was missing something—or his instincts said trouble was at hand.

But all that happened was Marah's smile widening a little as she sponged a slice on the other woman's hairline, a delicate, butterfly touch. "Well, I've seen you in green." It had the timbre of a private joke.

"Bitch." But Alladal gave a tight flicker of a grin. Her fingers kept moving, tapping invisible time, beautiful hands with cupped palms and the trained flexibility of a musician.

Hood headed for the sleek new crimson stove. The old silver one had predated Marah's father, and he suddenly missed its familiar presence and even its habit of scorching unattended kettles or saucepans, making Kameny curse. The cabinets were the same, and watched him like old, quiet friends. Will was nowhere in sight, which was unusual indeed; the synthetic probably thought young Robb had been aiming to steal the cutlery or something.

"What did they do?" Marah asked, suddenly. "I'll hear anyway."

Alladal's glance flickered to Robb, though her head stayed perfectly motionless. Apparently she trusted Marah's judgment, or the information wasn't expensive enough to keep back. "Hammered them."

Marah's hands stilled. Her entire body did, bracing itself like a soldat ready for shrapnel to be pulled free. "Mother Moon," she whispered. "Grant them rest."

Hood almost flinched, too. "Careful with that." There weren't a lot of Lunacers in the Corps—not openly, anyway, not anymore. It was better to thump a little Logic. He flicked open a cabinet and his face felt strange again, a half-pained smile rising. The mugs were where they'd always been when Kameny ran the kitchen with an iron fist and a mock-snarl that turned into sudden, cooing warmth when Marah had a scraped knee or a new busted-down animal friend. "Where did you say Kam went?"

"Visiting his mother." Marah exhaled softly and returned to her work. "Travel restrictions just loosened up, and I had to fill out eight forms as well as invent something for him to courier to Capricorn Quattrus." She checked Alladal's face, a swift neutral tactician's glance, then bent to applying the analgesic afresh. A few more swipes, each one for maximum saturation with minimum drip. But she was pale, and there were dark smudges under her eyes.

Looked like she wasn't sleeping well. If she was on call for assholes like this, no wonder. Hood busied himself with straining and pouring moonshot, careful not to splash the counter.

It would clean itself, but you didn't waste tai.

"Marah." Alladal's voice softened. She reached up as if to clasp Marah's hands, but the other woman swung away, almost angrily, tossing empty analgesic tubes into a flat metal pan with a clatter. "I'm sorry."

"For what?" The Lady of Madán selected a roll of chameleon skintape and opened it with the practiced twist of a professional. "Were they contacts?"

"No." The woman's mouth drew down, and she shifted uncomfortably on the stool. "Completely oblivious, garden-variety smugglers. Just...Noth's chacals found a trove of...stuff."

"Oh." Marah's charcoal eyebrows raised. "So smugglers just *happen* to squat over a trove of, what? Certainly not clinic supplies, so..." She halted, bit her lower lip, and turned even paler, visibly realizing what they must have come across. Her hands kept going, measuring and tearing bits of skintape, applying it fingertip-lightly.

She must have attended to a lot of flesh wounds. Her nails were trimmed or bitten all the way down, another change.

"That's why they hammered them, *enfante*." Alladal swayed slightly. She wasn't as careless as she appeared; sharp as a redband's whisp, this girl. But she was exhausted and her pupils were very swollen indeed. How long had Marah been working on her? That torn rag that had once been a shirt lay at the stool's feet, under a drift of used sponge and skintape-ends the house tech would sweep up and incinerate or put through a matrix unraveler. "It certainly wasn't for the cryon."

"Someone's moving cryon again?" Marah made a soft sound, perhaps of disappointment in shortsighted children. She had an artist's touch with the skintape. They probably took one look at her psych profile after Corps swear-in and decided the medical arm was the safest place to stick her and get high-grade effort; the woman would throw herself into an active terraform spiral to save a wounded pebble.

Did anyone ever change, or did they just become more what they were? It was a question that occurred to many a soldat in the middle of trying desperately to stay awake on night watch, or to a drunk, philosophical swabbie like old Seconfidle in the Shiptime stories.

"I guess. I thought they were rockthieves or tech runners." Alladal's eyelids lowered a fraction. If she was lying, that was a tell. Hood, finished with tai-pouring, watched her profile. "It looked like an idiot operation, all right? Then all of a sudden Sharl Noth comes along—no joke, he came out himself for this one."

"That's odd. I suppose Gizabón was with him?" Marah said it like it didn't matter.

That's right, he's working for the Sharl. Typical. Hood leaned against the stove, blowing across the top of his old, heavy blue mug. Spice-heavy steam filled his nose, scraped through his skull and turned him into a kid again. It didn't have the bite of Kameny's moonshot, but it was still good. How many times had he swallowed tai in this kitchen?

Alladal's generous mouth pulled down, and her dark eyes flashed. "Why you even talk to that bâtard—"

"For the same reasons I talk to smugglers, gang members, demobilized Corps, polis, and Sharl Notheim himself, Al." Marah's tone was quiet and firm. "Besides, I grew up with him. Do we really need to have this discussion again?"

"No." Alladal stilled. "Not today."

Which meant Robb wasn't going to hear the replay, but he could guess at its dimensions well enough.

"Good." Marah finished smoothing skintape, stepping back to view her work critically. Thin strands of platinum hair escaped Alladal's deftly wrapped headcover; maybe she *had* been a Crescent. Some of the more orthodox of the Moon's worshippers hid their hair from any sun, which was just as strange as the Discipline's heavens or hells of logic and cold rationality, when you thought about it. No god worth following would have thoughts on solar radiation *or* Terran peccadilloes.

Hammered. There was only one punishment the woman could be talking about. The only surprise was that they were doing cruxes here on one of the rich primary planets instead of out at the edges or on lower-rate worlds.

Hood stood slump-shouldered, contemplating his tai and trying to look smaller. Before the surrender, this conversation would have been mild treason at the very least, and a Corpsoldat would have to report it. Not just that, but any Anglene citizen of the Second Echelon was duty-bound to do the same.

Good thing the war was over, right? One day he might even believe it, though he already suspected Hood never would.

Marah nodded sharply, clearing a soldat for duty or rest, and began tidying the detritus of first aid with measured efficiency. "Pour her some tai, Robb."

"Already done." He picked up one of the guest mugs—a heavy

square red-glazed clonker—and approached the newcomer as he might any of Marah's other strays. "How many did they crux?"

"I stopped counting at six." Alladal's shoulders hunched too. She was tall and spare, but in that moment a child's fear peered through her wide dark eyes. "I can tell you where, though, if you're so curious."

Hood shook his head, held the mug with its handle politely jutting forward. "Was Giz there?"

"If you're going to put together an *I hate Gizabón* club, do it outside." Marah's back was stiff, and the metal tray of non-bio medical effluvia made a sharp sound as she set it on the counter. Another tray, hovering on an alcazar wall-tether, drifted uncertainly until she gestured at it, sending it out into the hall. "You don't know what he does behind the scenes."

"And you do, of course." Alladal's lip lifted. Either she'd gotten buds after transition or she'd been blessed with good dental genes and a near-religious attention to mouth-cleaning. "Looks like we're having that discussion after all. Again."

That irked him. "No," Hood said, and fixed the woman with a stare, still offering the mug. Running down Ged was one thing, but fucking with Marah was quite another. "We're not."

"Echelons stick together." Alladal slid stiffly from her perch and straightened, taking a few experimental steps for the door.

Hood tensed. Marah glanced at him and shook her head a fraction, her lips compressing. "You're welcome," she said, quietly. "See you next Tenday. Or before."

The woman's only farewell was a shipwright's pungent curse before she vanished through the mudroom, and Robb's throat was dry. "She always like that?"

"Only when provoked." Marah's steady movement didn't cease. Looked like she could clear up medical litter in her sleep, and probably had at one point or another. "She was in the hôpital when the war started. Her entire family...I gather it was a Corps response near a polis armory."

The first wave of insurrection had gone after supplies and communication nexuses; civilian casualties had been high. It was just shitty all over, and nobody knew that better than the infantry. "Lot of that going around." He searched for something useful to do, and found it, setting the spurned tai carefully on the counter and shaking out scorched fingertips. "Want me to make you breakfast?"

"Sure." But her tension didn't diminish, and nothing in the kitchen was quite where it had been before he left for the Corps. Even the cabinets were sudden strangers despite their solemn, unchanged wooden faces. "And thank you, Robb." *For not being an asshole*, she probably wanted to add, or maybe it was just the familiar, comforting roil of self-hatred inside his own head.

It wasn't until he found the lac in its usual place in the fridge that he realized he was completely Robb Locke again, and for once, it didn't hurt. It was, rather, a comfort.

And like any mercy, it was of short duration.

BEANPOLE_

JORAH SMAHL RAN BLUNT FINGERTIPS OVER THE TOP OF THE console, each tiny chip and imperfection in the housing familiar now. It wasn't quite the curve of a woman's hip, like Sana's when she lay on her side, head buried in the pillows and the rest of her the undulating territory of best dreams.

It was technically illegal to habitate in a tethered ship planetside, but sometimes Jorah could not sleep and took a khibi to the yard on the pretext of overseeing wright repairs. After midnight there was a brief span of deserted time while the shipwrights retreated; shortly afterward the tide of loaders and drones came in so dawn could bring a thunder of rising iron birds into the sky and cold space beyond. It was during that hitch in shipyard breathing that Jorah most often could fall asleep again, spread on a pallet in the hold. This morning the throb and pop of rising ships lunging for freedom hadn't awakened him, but the encrypted ping on his chunky old rister had.

The *Retreat*'s smaller cargo bay was open, and Jorah busied himself with the lifter console as if he was checking it for errors. The wrights had swarmed his ship—though the *Retreat* was Marah's on the papierwork, Jorah could not help but feel proprietary—and he was cleared for maximum jaunt now, not just hops to and from the closest tech graveyard but inter-Anglene starsteal as well.

The haul must have been good, Jorah thought, but he was still uneasy. It wasn't like Marah to stay out so long, or to cram the ship to the gills the way she had.

The true reason for his unease, though, melded out of midafternoon haze on the cargo slope, outline blurred by headwrapping and a long sleeveless artisan's flockershirt under a canvas coat that looked severely worse for wear. Baggy trousers and heavy underboots lacking lowgrav grabbers completed the look of an itinerant wright with a little time to kill wandering among cargo bays, maybe cadging some hot tai and a bit of meandering conversation.

Alladal believed in camouflage. It was probably the only thing she really went to the hull for, despite all her dangerous cant.

"You weren't at home." There was only a faint edge of accusation to the words, not quite a question and definitely not forgiveness.

"You were late." Jorah eyed her narrowly.

"I had to visit your boss." Al began unwrapping her head, probably wanting to resettle sweat-stiff cloth. Platinum hair, returning to its natural darkness at the roots, glowed at the ends. It was going to be another hot day, the glare outside was too fierce for a normal summer morning. The chieweed and Free Network meteorologicals were reminding everyone to hydrate and stay inside, as if you could when there was credit to be raised. "When are you going out again?"

"When the Lady of Madán decides to." Jorah caught himself stroking the curve of the console once more and put his hand away. Sana would have laughed at him behind her cupped fingers, her brown eyes sparkling, and maybe even mime a kiss, one of her favourite little motions when she caught her husband star-gathering. "What the hell, Al?" It wasn't like her to ping his rister before she showed up, and doubly not like her to be so blunt.

"Trouble elsewhere." She glanced over her shoulder and took a few more steps into the hold's comparative dimness. Night chill married to the efficiency of core-fueled climate control would keep the *Retreat* right in the sweet spot for Terran comfort, especially with only two warmblooded beasts present. "I need hold space for Virgo."

"We're not rated to go that far." It was a lie, especially now that the wrights had finished their work. Jorah was glad his bright patterned overshirt was buttoned tight even though he hadn't shaved yet. He was even moderately glad he hadn't been drinking. "And I told you before, don't come to my ship."

"It's registered to Madán. Bet that stings." Alladal graced him with a kulturworker's wide white smile, rubbing bruised fingers through her hair. Fresh skintape was well on its way to turning invisible, holding together thin, bloodless analgesic-soaked lines. A professional's touch had been at work applying medikit to her; she also moved a little stiffly, and her pupils were fractionally bigger than the gloom inside the bay demanded. "You know, the Echelons all deserve airlocking."

"Yeah, when the reckoning comes I'll have a ship of my own, right? Plus an alcazar full of tech too." Jorah snorted, wishing he had a spanner or a wrightsknife to hand. It would give him a reason to move away, cut this stupid conversation short. "Save it. I helped you *once.*" *Because Sana would have wanted it.* His wife had been a Crescent, and a fool for hard-luck stories. That was probably why she'd married *him,* for Discipline's sake; Logic knew Jorah was no prize, but she hadn't seemed to mind. "That doesn't make me your friend."

"A revolutionary doesn't have friends." Alladal said it like she didn't suspect him of having audio capture set up and spread her arms, a gesture as expansive as her grin marred only by her flinch at the end. Looked like she'd been worked over good; she'd really feel the brawl tomorrow. It never stiffened up all the way until forty-eight metric hours later. "But a minstrel has friends everywhere."

"Great Under." He shook his head, his shoulders turtling up. His own grab-boots were heavy oversize mech-loaders, lace them up and forget them. "You'd better be fucking careful. What do you *want?*"

"Just what I left with you." At least she came directly to the point, for once. Alladal finished refolding her headwrap and began the work of coiling platinum strands for coverage. "And since you're not going out Virgo way, do you know anyone who might be?"

Oh, *that* was what she wanted. A recommendation, and probably an introduction. Whoever he pointed her at would hear *Smahl sent me*, and he'd be associated with her if anyone official came along asking questions. The thought left him cold. "There's a departures board in the front office, Al."

"Come on, Jorah." Her smile didn't falter. If it was engineered to remind him of Sana, it was working. "You've got all sorts of reasons to help the cause."

And you'd know all about that, right? A tiny voice that sounded like Sana's was trying to tell him to give Al a chance, but that was a good way to lose everything.

Again.

"I'm not interested in your fucking cause." His growl was only half theatrical. Jorah was used to his bulk making people cautious, but Alladal knew just where to press to get the reflex jump she wanted.

"Not since Mistress Marah picked you out of the gutter and let you fly again, right?" The tips of Al's teeth, bright and gleaming since Sana had paid for an extra bit of medtech in addition to the state-covered transition, showed in an arc. *She wants to sing, Jorah. Can we?* And his own stupid, nodding consent. "You owe her. Or maybe she owns you."

"I am *not* in the mood for this today, Al." His hand on the console had turned into a broad, hairy fist. In a tavern, pub, or drinking hole they would sense the danger and move away, or at least stop needling him. Shaggos were bred for size, strength, and docility, but even the mildest could turn on a Terran too fond of the whip. "You can go check the fucking departures board, and if anyone pings me saying you said I sent you I'll make sure they won't even carry you across a puddle."

Al *tsk-tsk*ed, another reminder of her cousin, as she finished wrapping her hair, knotting and tucking with habitual speed. "You're testy today. Lack of sleep?" Her arms fell back to her sides and her fingers began working again. She couldn't stay still for long; the music was coded in gene-level. *She's got talent, you know,* Sana would say fondly, cradling a fylm- or holocapture of her artistic cousin.

Pure kulturtrash, but who was he to say? Sana thought Al was the next Koah Grezebón or Maitreya Riccat. "Fuck off, Alladal." For a moment Jorah was tempted to use her former name, but Sana would have been disappointed in him. Not that it mattered, but still..."And take your shaggoshit with you."

Al didn't move. "I'll be taking what I left with you, Jorah. Hand it over and I'll be out of your bay."

"What if I told you I dumped it in a graveyard out past Coronis?" It would serve her right if he had, too. Jorah glanced over her shoulder, peering into a wall of bright sunshine. No wrights in view, no loaders walking past on short breaks from their mech-lifting and moving.

"That would be a mistake." Al's smile turned hard, almost predatory. She didn't move, though her fingers kept playing invisible strings. "*I* wouldn't care, but those it's meant for might come looking for you."

Of course that would be the threat. "Let them."

"Come on, Jorah." Now she began wheedling, and sometimes when she did that her voice lightened into something close to Sana's laughing, coaxing lilt. "I won't bother you again."

"That's a lie." Both his hands tingled, and he was a short step through sending a fist through something. Walls didn't hit back, but did he really want to break phalange bones and maybe cause hull damage a wright would have to be called out for?

"Not unless forced to," Alladal amended.

"Another lie." Jorah shook his head. Every minute he spent talking to her upped the risk that someone would drift by and see them together, and there went all the staying-clear-of-trouble he'd promised both Marah and old ghosts. "You never used to be this much of an asshole, Al."

"It must be my hormones." She must've been *really* zoned to say that, especially to him. Alladal didn't quite sway on her boots, but it was close. Her pupils were so wide they almost ate her irises; she wasn't on any OTC analgesic. "I'd really like to go get some sleep. It's been a long night."

The keycard was right on top of the console, of course, since she'd pinged him before showing up. Jorah palmed it up and tossed it like a saucer, getting just the right amount of spin. Alladal plucked it from the air with a quick flicker of her musician's fingers, and a real smile, not just the predatory baring of teeth, bloomed on her sharp, feline face. Each bone, each angle was pared down to its bare essentials, and Sana would call her too thin. *Come in and eat,* his wife would say to her cousin. *You're a beanpole.*

"I knew I could count on you," Al said, breezily. "Sana would be proud."

"Don't you talk about her." The blood was draining from his face. He could *feel* it, juice leaving a sliced fruit, and the unsteady invisible fume in his head was just waiting for a spark to trigger the explosion, like wet kanno. "Don't you *ever* talk about her to me."

"Fine." Al stuffed the cream-colored, oblong keycard in her pocket and turned on her heel. "Which number?"

"24-B."

A faint hot wind breathed past the repellers into the bay; it was time to close up the *Retreat*. He could go up to the bridge and watch the other ships load, sunshine glinting off mechs and heavers.

Al made a small spitting noise of impatience, again very much like Sana. Maybe she practiced her impersonation just to taunt him. "Which *building*, shaggo-brain?"

"Go find out." That would eat her morning up, going from depot to depot checking each 24-B storage pod to see if the keycard worked. Or she'd figure it out from the size and shape of the card. She was smart as Sana.

Just not as unlucky.

Maybe Alladal knew she'd pushed him as far as she could. She stepped out into the glare still laughing, settling her headwrap firmly and tucking any sweat-darkened strays under its anonymous slouch. Jorah let out a long harsh breath, and his large shoulders sagged even further. He'd been looking forward to a hot breakfast from a food-khibi, but good luck getting his stomach to accept even tai now.

He promised Sana he'd look after Al. Had she known what her cousin was involved in, *had* Al been involved before the rebellion lifted its great malformed head and began eating at Anglene?

It didn't matter. Whether Sana knew or not, she was beyond telling anyone. Even her bones were vaporized, worked into the flat rubble of her family's village. *I'll only be gone a tenday,* she'd said.

Jorah could have pointed out that she could file her census papierwork without traveling while things were so uncertain, even though at that point the troubles were no more than widespread riots on a bunch of Aquarian mining moons. But Sana wanted to see her father on Capyra, one of Virgo Secundus's prime moons—and who knew when she'd get another chance, since her birth family was estate-bound and she had travel privilege only by virtue of her marriage to a merchant's son? There had also been Alladal's surgery to consider; she'd wanted to be home for that.

Jorah had just finished a short hop from Capricorn Three to its primary moon—Hirsia, a bitch of a port—when the news arrived.

It was called a terrorist strike, the first real hit of the Insurrection, coordinated across several systems—Aquarius, Capricorn, Virgo, even a couple Sagittarius mining asteroids—by sympathizers within the Crescents who could use the temple fittle system to get messages through half-diplomatic channels over the whole of Anglene. Most of the First Insurrections were crushed within hours, but on the second-class worlds, the small polis forces—"overseers" was the word the insurrectionists used—were quickly overwhelmed by their hereto-fore-silent, sullen charges.

Alladal herself, safe in a hôpital under a pall of narcotics and other meds, had surfaced two days later in a small hôpital room to stare uncomprehending at blurry images of burning on the flat screen of the recreation module. Jorah, as the only living relative on file, had been allowed to collect her from the medical complex; he didn't ask if she'd known about the uprising beforehand.

He wasn't sure he could keep his temper if it turned out she *had*, and he didn't want to give her another chance to lie to him either.

Sana's home village had been right in the path of the Corps roller coming in to "restore order" on Capyra. What the insurrectionists—with their fucking red headrags and kerchiefs, like Saur brats playing at gang life—hadn't knocked down trying to take the polis depositary at the very edge of town, the fresh young Corpsoldat with their uniforms still steam-creased had powderized when they called down artillery strikes.

Better to spend shells instead of soldat blood, right? Cheaper, too.

Jorah stared at his fist. His knuckles were as bloodless as his face felt. He'd been offered state compensation, of course. A pension for the loss of a wife, a citizen's right.

It was only his own damn fault that he drank it all. And that he'd let himself get mixed up in Alladal's shaggoshit.

But he knew that next time Al breezed by with a favour to beg, he'd do it. He'd even mention to Marah something about salvage out near Virgo to see if she'd bite, because each time he saw Alladal's wide dark eyes, they reminded him of Sana's. Al was a jacksnipe swabbie fool, certainly.

But Jorah Smahl was an even bigger one, and he knew it. He hit the door to close the *Retreat*'s hold, and watched the daylight dim.

PEACE AND ORDER_

At least it was dim inside the confessional closet.

The absence of glare was rather restful. Stolid, heavy Bookman Trick eased himself down with a sigh. No matter how gently you lowered your rear, a Bookman's cassock dug in some places and bunched in others. There was a method to arranging its folds, one Trick hadn't thought he would need again. A Crescent in the Corps might minister to the rearward troops in order to avoid lowered morale, but the Discipline's place was among the frontliners, and Trick knew he presented quite a target for redbands anyway by virtue of his girth.

Even on starvation rations his body, wiser than its wearer, refused to drop its padding.

At least on the front lines, there was no room for chapel wear either. Since the war was over and Trick had, incredibly, survived, he was between postings on an Aegis flagship heading for Sagittarius Prime. It should have been somewhat of a vacation.

However, the Discipline did not abide idleness in its Bookmen, so he was scheduled for a confessional shift. His only hope was that it would not be too busy. There was also a slight commotion outside the cabinet, but that wasn't his concern, since his damn cassock was being difficult, again. He had to suppress a most un-Bookmanlike obscenity that would have been right at home in a mining-moon's trench with tracers whining overhead; the entire cabinet was probably rocking back and forth like a kid's funnyholo *Insecto Lapin* short.

The other side of the cabinet opened far too soon, and its occupant wrung a creak from hand-nailed wood. "I search for Logic," the other man said. It was an exceedingly pleasant baritone, well-modulated with a highgrade Echelon's clear diction, and Trick's back began to prickle. Hearing that voice was like the moment after a long-ranger's shot but before the realization that you were unhurt and some other poor bâtard probably was not.

Definitely was not.

The Bookman sank down, wishing he could curse under his breath. "I offer true counsel." The refrain, low or loud, had crossed Trick's lips so many times it didn't need his conscious will to escape. Like a burp or a fart, it just popped out.

"I should hope so." The confessional screen turned any follower of the Narrow Path into an indistinct shadow, but the sound of cloth shifting as another person moved often told a Bookman anything he needed to know. Strange, how when one sense was hooded, the others sharpened. It sometimes made Trick wonder if synthetics had similar compensatory mechanisms.

"What ails you, my son?" A threadbare traditional question, not because Trick was necessarily conservative, but because it was safest to stay on the well-treaded path when dealing with powerful patrons.

There were few more powerful than the Great Helmsman's younger brother, regent instead of regnant but probably not for long since Riccar Planetagen had been gone for a few standards now. The Regnant hadn't bothered to come back for a war; Trick was only wishing he could have signed on with *that* fleet instead of being sent to the Corps.

Even demobilization wasn't the boon it could have been, and

being assigned to a flagship berth wasn't quite the good fortune it appeared at first.

It was always like that.

"The usual." Parl Jun even sounded amused, but then, an Echelon could afford to be. "A long cavalcade of nightly sins, but those don't bother me."

I'm sure they don't. In any case, the bedroom was no place for Discipline, unless one of those concerned was below the age of consent. Then, woe betide the sinner *over* said age; the penalties for such repugnant behavior were severe and lifelong.

Or at least, they *should* have been, but the laws on the sheaves were not always the laws applied. It had been the same on Old Terra, or so the history books said. They also said things were better now, but not according to the insurgents.

"Take your time." Trick searched for an avuncular tone, carefully neutral, and wished his heart would stop pounding. Philosophical or historical conundrums were all very well, except for when they intruded when you needed all your wits to navigate a busy shipping lane instead. Sweat prickled under Trick's hairy, hidden arms.

"I'm a busy man, Bookman. Time is not in great abundance." More cloth shifting; the parl was making himself comfortable indeed. Why was he tormenting a poor plain Bookman? He had to have a private confessor; Logic knew several of the cloth would leap at the chance to serve *there.* "Yet...I wanted to talk."

The fear was all over Trick now, a greasy coating. His testicles had decided to crawl upward for a more congenial home, too, and Bookman Trick faced—not for the first time—his own cowardice. "Yes?" At least he was so used to hiding his lack of fortitude, he didn't have to worry about his voice breaking.

The parl paused, having achieved a comfortable stasis inside the cabinet and perhaps waiting for Trick to add more. When the silence stretched, however, he apparently decided torment was incomplete if the victim wasn't first tenderized. "Have you ever considered fratricide, Bookman?"

Oh, Great Under. Logic guide me. Trick's throat held a warning tickle and he suppressed a cough. A combat habit—*don't give your position away, you shaggoshit simple.*

Thankfully, he had a ready answer, even if it was somewhat cliché. "A Bookman has no family but his fellow Disciples." Nobody would catch *him* treading the edge of a seditious statement, even as a thought experiment. An orphaned noncitizen who had clawed his way into Discipline by dint of sheer hard test-work and the willingness to swallow almost any indignity knew better.

"And the penalty for murdering a fellow Disciple's severe." The parl was finding his victim a moving target, or perhaps he just *did* want to talk. The Helm could afford to say what it liked; such was the prerogative of those called upon to guide and guard. "What is it again?"

"The same as for treason." Trick suspected the parl knew. How could he not? Still, he answered. That was the whole point of this little exercise; maybe the man was a pedant rather than a tormentor. "Crux, or something equally barbaric."

He knew it was unwise; crux was probably one of this man's favourite punishments to contemplate. There were soldats like that, ones who brooded at length over how to punish the faceless bâtards on the other side. Those fantasies, related in graphic detail, were part of the confessional's horrors, and speaking of them was meant to relieve the pressure that might push a soldat into actually committing atrocities.

Supposed to. Trick had his doubts on that point; he had his doubts upon every point, lately. Deep ones he did not confess when he spent his own mandated time inside the conscience-cleanser.

What was the point? Maybe if it was a synthetic inside, instead of a fellow Bookman or Bookmira, he could voice the persistent, nagging, troublesome questions—but synthetics lacked the neural and social flexibility to properly minister, and there would be revolt within the ranks of Discipline itself should such a replacement be seriously debated, let alone instituted as policy.

Parl Regent Jun paused for a brief few moments. When he spoke again, his tone was merely mild, inquiring. "Does not the Discipline hold that capital punishment is allowable in certain situations?"

"The Discipline does, my son." Much was allowable, or even preferable in the name of efficiency or victory. Logic did not mean impracticability, despite many theological debates about the utility or desirability of either. "My own feelings on the matter are allowable as well."

That caused another brief silence, and Trick's palms were as moist as his throat was dry. His cassock wasn't thermaseal; he was going to be damp all day, now. If he wasn't dragged out of the cabinet and brought to trial for daring to voice an unpopular opinion in front of the Helm controlling all Anglene, swabbie to high deck.

That was the trouble with being a coward. It didn't stop you from doing stupid shit, it just let you anticipate the worst outcomes and experience them several times in the course of a conversation.

"You're not an ass-kisser," Parl Jun said finally. "That's good."

Trick decided silence was the safest response to *that* conversational bait. Some followers needed a slow pour-out of sins and omissions, while others wished to empty themselves at once like mechs and drones swarming a new goods transport in a busy hub.

Parl Jun lay somewhere between. "The rebellion is over, Anglene is secure, and order is restored." It sounded as if he was ticking them off on his fingers, a grocery or to-do list recited to a chamber presence's listening circuits in an alcazar tower. "Discipline holds we should long for peace, right?"

"That is correct." Trick wished he could shift and loosen his cassock's neck. This was the man who had sent other men to die in foxholes next to Trick's, sent them on combat drops where Trick was strapped in and praying along with the grunts as a planet's atmosphere buffeted and burned a metal intrusion. Ass-deep in cold mud or bleeding in scorching heat, plenty of them had grumbled in Parl Jun's direction. "Peace is the goal; peace brings order and plenty."

"We had peace before, and order too, before some villeins decided that wasn't enough." The parl's tone was soft, reflective.

Bookman Trick's jaw hardened. His teeth ached.

Parl Jun's a Discipline, ain't he? Go confess him, Bookman! That had been Curridge the bald capitain, a rough and sarcastic comfort to his men and terror to the enemy, whoever they were this tenday. He was dead on PLX-5, a moon with pretensions, substantial rare mineral deposits, and a thin atmosphere as well as a small cell of entrenched redband guerrillas.

Dead in the worst way, gasp-screaming while a double handful of guts splashed out of his wrap-armor, any sign of the mine-layer blurred past recognition by the explosion. It could have been one of the licensed practitioners in the O-house Curridge had finally managed to get away and visit, it could have been one of the hard-bitten, sullen miners; Logic be damned, it could have been any civilian with redband sympathies and a burning hatred of the Corps' heavy hand and the Aegis's polis behind it—any, or all of the above. It didn't matter, because the end result was the same. One moment Curridge had been on patrol with his fellows, the next he was shat-tered as the trap snapped shut, no warning and no shot across a bow.

Where, Bookman Trick had wondered, was the Great Rational when *that* happened? Wrap-armor didn't do any good against a star-burst mine *or* a well-wielded whisp.

"But that's a different matter." Parl Jun's tone softened, became reflective. Did he sound like this when he was deciding where to send the weight of the Corps? Or did the generals decide and present the plan only as a formality? "I came to find Logic. Tell me, Bookman, have you, *personally*, ever considered killing a fellow Disciple?"

Thankfully, Trick had an answer for *that* question. It was even simple, too. "No."

"Are you a liar, or simply unimaginative?" The parl sounded like he didn't care either way.

"Neither." But nothing was sure, Trick could have added. Disci-pline itself came from Old Terra, iron railings to keep wandering children from the worst of sins while the Moon provided hope, release, and intercession. At least, that was the idea. "At least, so I hope."

"Hm." A thoughtful sound, and a creak as the parl moved on the slatted wooden seat. Confessionals were built in the old way, by villein carpenters in Discipline abbeys, their measurements codified long ago on Terra's ancient, exhausted dirt. Abbey-bound servants even had right of travel other noncitizens lacked, another holdover. "Has there ever been an attempt on your life?"

"Other than during the war, you mean?" Trick wished the man would just go *away*. It wasn't a thought worthy of a Bookman, but he'd decided since he was far from the best among Discipline, there was no shame in admitting his own many faults and flaws. "No."

"Ah, you were in the war." It even sounded like the parl was pleased. "Then you understand."

Trick refrained from noting that he had understood absolutely nothing about the fucking war after the chaos of his first battle. It was his turn to make a neutral, thoughtful noise.

Which did not satisfy his royal interlocutor, apparently. Jun shifted yet again, finally allowing his weight to sink fully. Often, Echelons didn't let their back touch the chair; good posture was drilled in during deportment classes beginning almost as soon as one of Anglene's guards and guides could walk. *Their burden is great,* seminary books intoned, *an Echelon must always be conscious of the weight, and every confessor ready to help.*

"A conscience is a terrible burden," the parl said, finally.

That put them on safer theological ground, though Trick might have flinched at hearing one of his own thoughts from an interlocutor's mouth, however garbled. "A necessary one." The fold under his capacious belly was beginning to itch, as well as the creases between tummy and thigh. It was only a matter of time before his balls descended into warmth and began to prickle afresh, trapped uncomfortably in the mandatory unders that were part and parcel of cassock-wearing. He did not have to work very hard to find the necessary severity for his tone. "Discipline exists to guide our conscience, not ease its pressure."

When a follower began mentioning how burdensome a conscience was, severity was called for indeed.

"Sometimes I wonder." Parl Jun's shadow changed shape behind the screen, but not by much. "In any case, I have often thought it would be best if Parl Regnant Riccar remained coursing the starways so I could be sure of peace and order here." Now the trained, flexible baritone was soft, convincing, laying what he no doubt thought was reasonable in the extreme. "Is such a thought illogical? Or sinful?"

"Not necessarily." Trick had to swallow twice and force his throat to work. *I didn't see my flock get their asses shot off to keep this at the Helm.* The logical extension to that thought was never far behind. *Or did I?* "We are fallible flesh, that is why Discipline is needed." And Trick was probably going to come to a bad end somewhere in a polis needle-spire or *chateau-dif*, just for hearing this.

The only thing more frightening than that thought was the sense that somehow, in some way, it would be a relief from the shame of survival.

"I was expecting you to tell me I'm right." The Parl Regent stilled again, his shadow an indistinct blur through the screen. He was examining the thin material as if his gaze could pierce the baffling and discern Trick's expression.

I wish you luck, noble sir. "That is not what the confessional is for, my son." Curridge would have heard the disdain in Trick's calm, avuncular tone; Corps service had gifted the fellow an abiding loathing of, as well as an exquisite sensitivity to detecting, the pure S-grade shaggoshit necessary for dealing with superiors.

Trick was of the opinion that "superior" was, in this case, an entirely fictional construct, but what Bookman could say as much and not be defrocked? The simmering smell of his own ungainly, indelicate body rose to choke him.

Fortunately, the Parl Regent didn't seem to detect the sarcasm. "I was likewise expecting you to point out such a wish treads the edge of treason."

"Only if you have acted upon it." On *that* point, Discipline was clear, and likewise clear was the duty of Trick's next question, although it would no doubt get him sent to brig or stockade in a hurry. "Have you, my son?" *Don't answer. Ask for a penance and leave me alone.*

"No." A soft, thoughtful laugh, all the more chilling for its genuine good nature. "And if I had, I wouldn't tell a Bookman, even in the confessional."

There Trick could have left it, if not for his own cursed conscience, just as wide as his ass or his cassock and significantly more uncomfortable than either. "A sin of omission, my son."

"So we've found a sin after all." Parl Jun's laugh was now a large feline's delight upon discovering ambulatory prey. In all the prop reels, not to mention on credit notes, his profile was thoughtful and somewhat severe even if his chin protruded and his eyes were a trifle close-set under his very sharp widow's peak inherited from old, ruthless Hinri Planetagen. "Should I ask for penance?"

"Would you perform it, if given?" He'd already opened his mouth, Trick supposed he might as well finish digging his own grave. "You came for the absolution of logic. Logically, a wish for peace and order is admirable." *Get out of my confessional and go write an order to arrest me. It won't take long, we're on a ship, you can always find me.*

But then came his cursed cowardice again, and the urge to smooth this over, to say what he suspected his royal visitor wanted to hear. Trick set his jaw, denying himself even the luxury of imagining such a craven act.

The parl leapt to the next rhetorical link in the chain, of course. "Is Discipline merely a matter of semantics, then?"

"It is a guide-rope for us to hold when we begin to lose the way." The trouble wasn't that Trick was mouthing the platitudes. No, the trouble was that despite everything, he still *believed*...and yet, Great

Under and stacked heavens both, how he doubted. Uncertainty was a poison, robbing him of certainty and equanimity, and it started with his own cringing and the suspicion that Curridge was right and Discipline just a bunch of mealymouth scabs with high cassock-collars and fat asses.

"I begin to think that with my brother gone, I have found the way." For the first time, Parl Regent Jun Planetagen sounded almost tentative.

The same stubbornness that had kept Trick from requesting a transfer from Curridge's unit refused to let the Bookman do a half-swabbie job on his own destruction. "You believe you are suited to be Regnant then, Parl Jun?"

"You're not stupid. Good." The parl's shadow swelled as he leaned toward the baffle-screen. "I don't precisely think I'm *suited*, no. But I think I'm better at it than Riccar, and I wish someone, anyone, could tell me if that were true."

"Ah." Now Trick could move, and he loosened his collar fractionally. The relief, instant and shameful, was enough to make him feel faintly charitable as well. Maybe the man wasn't an arrogant fuck-buckle. What was a parl but a Terran, and just as fragile as the rest of them? "High station is also a burden, and there are no guarantees. Even Discipline is merely a guide, not a locked navtrack."

"Very true." The shadow moved in the particular way that meant a disciple was nodding, a burden sliding from his shoulders. "What's your name, Bookman?"

So you can have me put to the crux more quickly? Still, there was no reason to make it too easy, and doctrine was very clear upon the point of *names* in the confessional. "The confessional is not a place for—"

"Fine. I'll get it later. I like you; I could use a confessor who isn't a cringer."

"My son." Trick did his best impression of Captain Curridge in that fellow's rare quiet moments, or when he could be counted upon to argue a commanding officer out of ordering a piece of suicidal shaggoshit. "I'm not trained to be a personal chaplain to a High Echelon, and I have a flock to attend." The last part was a lie, he was between postings, and had just this morning been praying for something, *anything* to do rather than a mind-numbing round of confession and preaching on some backwater mining moon.

"Do you know who the best candidate for a powerful job is?" Parl Jun's laugh was no longer a suppressed exhale but a warm, rich chuckle from a man well used to declaiming for holo-captures and propaganda reels, not to mention the occasional chieweed interview to show he was a man, if not of steerage, then at least of the people. "The man who doesn't want it. Thank you, Bookman. You've given me logic indeed."

The Parl Regent didn't wait for absolution or a closing prayer. He simply opened his side of the confessional and left.

Bookman Trick took the moment to stand, despite the risk of knocking his head on the top of the cabinet. He arranged his cassock and sank down again.

This time his neck was blessedly unpinched, but material wadded under his rear, impersonating a stone. He stifled an extremely pungent curse heard many a time among Corpsoldat and heard the confessional door open again.

"I search for Logic," the next one said. A woman's voice, pleasant contralto with an officer's crispness. You could always tell those born into Echelon instead of raised for merit.

Trick scratched at his jaw. He stubbled early and had worn a beard often on the front lines, but here on a flagship, a Discipline servant must be clean. "I offer true counsel," he said, dismally, and settled himself for a long afternoon.

THE FILTHY BRIDGE_

MILAR MUCHSON DIDN'T EXPECT TO FIND A SEMI-FAMILIAR face in the malodorous depths of the Filthy Bridge, so when he spotted big blond Locke, his smile held equal parts relief and surprise. He shouldered a place at the crowded bar open and signaled for two; Locke arrived next to him, moving through the press of wrights and loaders just off-shift from the closest tether as well as heavies, mecha-mechanics, and unemployed men either morose in dejection or bright-eyed at the prospect of making a connection. Milar's fellow caporal wasn't carrying his ditbag, which meant he'd found a place to rest. Maybe he'd even heard of work.

"You've recovered," Locke said with a half-sour grin, leaning close enough to be heard over the din. He was in the same fatigue jacket, the hood deflating since he'd shoved it back upon entering the pub. His beefy shoulder tapped Milar's, and a hot flush spread like a rosette from the contact. "And you're back at the tap."

"Only way to get rid of a hangover." Milar accepted the two tankards and tapped his chunky state-issue rister, paying for the heavy ale. "Next round's yours."

"Sure." Locke's smile was easy, but didn't reach his dark eyes, one soldat's quick grimace to another. "But I'm here on business."

That was convenient. "Me too. Best place to get a job. At least if you want one quickly."

Locke glanced over the interior, dark eyes not bloodshot anymore. He had a curious stillness, and didn't flinch when someone hammered on a makeshift table across the room, shouting to prove his point. The sound jolted Milar's nerves, still raw from cleanup patrols and the long mess of demobilization; Locke grabbed his elbow, pointing them both at a spindly table and two matchstick stools that were in the process of being vacated by a trio of laze-eyed loaders with big grab-boots and divots from mechstraps on their padded shoulders.

"Know your ground," the older man said with a wink, and Milar felt a burst of relief like a swallow of engine-cleaner before a cold-planet patrol. Plenty of Robard's old friends were total assholes, but this guy seemed all right. And handsome, too.

"Amen to that." Milar took a long pull from his glass. That was another reason the Bridge was popular—heavy unwatered ale at a reasonable price was a glorious thing.

The third reason was the Alley, a row of booths down the long eastern side of the building. Those were reserved for employers both legal and not-so-legal, and a pall of thin mixed hasha and bacca vapor both synthetic and real hanging under the ancient lamps turned every shadowed nook into a dead end. An employer paid a small fee to the Bridge for space in the booths, left once they had their quota, and the next would take their place.

It was better than the streetside temp fairs, but not by much. Drinking while you waited for an introduction or an opening would make you muzzy-headed and waste precious credits, but what else what there to do? At least in here, the gasping heat of late summer drought was drained off by coolant and forced air.

"Lot of assholes back from the war," Milar said, snagging one stool deftly from under the hand of a black-haired man from a neighboring table and showing his teeth when the fellow gave him a snarling glance.

"*Lucky* assholes." Nobody went after Locke's seat; maybe his size and glare dissuaded them. Certainly Milar wouldn't have wanted a frontliner with that peculiar thousand-klick stare to bark at *him*. "You know anyone here?"

"Nope." But just to be sure, Milar scanned the crowd again, hitching a hip on the stool and making a quick habitual movement to keep his weapon clear, arrested when he found out his ryfl was gone. Of course, it was peacetime now. For whatever that was worth. "But someone'll be here this afternoon. Sooner or later."

Locke's sandy eyebrows went up a fraction. "Friend?"

"Of my sister's. Kind of." He examined Locke again, too. He seemed all right, and the way he moved—lithe and catlike—was right up Milar's tether. Only the old-timers moved like that, the ones who had already survived combat and were, therefore, either lucky or less likely to break under fire. Or both. "It, uh, might not be real legal."

"I'm not a polis." Locke's face set against itself like he smelled something bad. Which wasn't entirely out of the question, it was pretty rank in here—labor-sweat, spilled ale, hasha, burnt bacca, and the metallic scurry-smell of Terrans male and female looking for their next meal, their next rent-chip, next drink.

Desperation had an odor, and it was one Milar knew well. A Corps pension was a good thing, but Dad was gone and Mom had lost two sons already. It was up to Mil to take the family forward, and to make sure his younger sister—and Paulo, nobody could forget Paulo—were taken care of. "Good," he said, and took another pull off his ale. He even had new socks, Sylar had tossed them onto Robard's old bed last night. *Because if I know you, there's nothing but holes over your toes.* "I, uh. When I went home I found out about Lamóre."

"Yeah." Locke stared morosely into his own tankard. Despite that, he seemed somehow completely aware of his surroundings, the coiled readiness of a soldat on patrol never leaving him. "Me too."

"Nobody told you?" Maybe he could comfort the guy a little. Milar was a firm believer in the seductive value of a shoulder to cry on. The one-night pickings in the Corps were great, but a buddy could get shot out from under you. Out here there was less danger, but you wanted something a little more long-term.

A shout went up in the back corner where a dice game was going strong, but Locke didn't flinch. "I didn't get a single fittle or bounce-mail the entire time I was in the Corps."

Was that why he looked so down? "Great Under." Milar took a long pull off his ale. His head, freshly shaven for the trip back home to demob, itched. "I know another guy that happened to. Third Echelon guy from Capricorn. Dantes, his name was. Edat Dantes." He was a rangy, pale-copper man with a triangular face and stubborn black hair shaggy even when clipped; Caporal Ed, they called him. He was quiet, but not like Locke; Dantes's silence was a venomous thing coiled and waiting for an unwary footstep, not like this man's colorless, odorless fume of kanno-gassa-waiting-for-a-spark.

Caporal Ed brought all his patrols home, though. One way or another. Now Milar was curious about Locke's war, but it wasn't the sort of thing you asked about.

For one thing, you'd find out soon enough.

"So it wasn't just me." Locke exhaled, harshly, and took another pull. Half the ale vanished, his throat working as he swallowed, and Milar watched the Adam's-apple bob under coppery, shaven skin. When Locke set the tankard down and wiped at his mouth with the back of one golden-haired hand, he glared impersonally at the door. "Anyway, might as well look for work. Can't live off charity or pension."

"Don't you have an estate?" Milar hoped he didn't sound like a terraform washer, hungry to marry or fuck into status. But his interest in the man was fading; he was a looker, sure, but that sullen rage detracted from it.

"It was an administrative position." A single leonine shrug. "And I'm not gonna go into the closest Aegis office and find out. Not personally, anyway."

"Smart." Milar nodded in admiration. Robard hadn't talked about the Lamóre son a lot—it was always best to keep your mouth on a tight leash about Echelons. But they were both soldats, right? The Corps believed in leveling. In approved ways, of course. Not like the fucking redbands, smashing and grabbing instead of just working hard and making do.

The hanging door swung open, letting in a blast of nasty golden glare and swirling road-dust. A slim shape with a swelling on its head slipped through, shoulders rounded and waist narrow; Locke didn't crane his head to see who it was. He didn't have to, he'd chosen an angle that included the door. It was Mil's duty to watch the Alley.

Funny how neither of them had thought about it, just arranged themselves. You could be trained into habit, but breaking it was a lot harder. Especially when your back crawled, knowing a whisp was only a few steps away at any moment.

"Huh." The quality of Locke's stillness changed, and Milar used his peripheral vision to check out the new arrival.

She's tall, blonde, and has a Lunacer turban. You'll know her when you see her.

It was Sylar's friend, the one she said might have good-paying work if Milar mentioned his sister's name. The one who did benefit kulturconcerts at the Camyron, singing Lunacer madrigals and Discipline plainchant as well as bawdy popalong-casso hits made famous by the chieweed of the moment.

"There she is," Milar said, a soldat's mutter not moving his lips too much, pitched just loud enough to reach his companion but not enough to escape the gravwell of their tiny table. "Alladal."

MANY TALENTS_

THE TURBANED WOMAN, LEAN AND LEGGY IN CANVAS WRIGHT'S trousers and her heavy canvas jacket—free of dust and blood; she'd had it cleaned since the morning—slid into one side of the ancient, brown leather booth and indicated the other with a nod, her gaze moving across both of them in short practiced arcs. Hood slid in first, letting Milar take the outside seat. He could slither down the gap between table and seat easily enough for cover, slide his newly made whisp out, and be fairly sure of a few seconds of safety if things went sideways.

Not that he thought they would, but...it paid to be prepared. He'd had to ditch his old Corps whisp; it was nice to have one again.

Almost comforting.

"Slumming?" Alladal gave a bright, fierce smile, teeth glittering in the dimness. Hood didn't see any suspicious bulges in her clothing, but he was certain she was armed. Maybe even with a whisp like Hood's own. "Or babysitting?" She barely glanced at Milar.

The Muchson kid, however, was not ready to be ignored. "My sister Sylar said you'd have work."

"Sylar?" She drummed her fingers on the sticky tabletop once, a flickering arpeggio. Blunt nails, just as brutally short as Marah's. In the dimness her skin was luminous, the exact shade of highgrade blond-bacca dried with vanillin in large airy sheds, filmed for a propaganda reel about abundance in Anglene. "Sylar Muchson?"

"Yeah." Milar didn't add more, which was a blessing. You wanted a patrol partner who could keep his damn mouth shut.

Alladal shifted, leaning against the booth's back, considering them both. "You're...Robard?"

"No." A quick shake of the young caporal's dark head. He glanced nervously at Hood. "Milar."

"Ah, one of the middle brothers." Alladal's fingers shifted to a different pattern, stilled for a moment, and she studied Hood more intently. "All grown up and back from the war."

"Thank Logic." The kid cupped his hands, looking up, the very picture of a young Discipline. Only the looseness at one corner of his mouth gave a clue to the sarcasm; that, and his world-weary tone.

A thin tendril of platinum had slipped free of Al's turban; she stopped tapping the tabletop long enough to tuck it under cloth with a swift, reflexive movement. "And you?"

"I'm with him." Hood indicated Milar with his chin, and didn't miss the kid's tiny, grateful twitch. Great Under, even if he was quiet, how had he survived on patrols? He must have been effective or lucky, you didn't get promoted otherwise. Wasn't there a long-ago Terran general who used to say lucky was better than anything else when it came to getting your ass blown off?

Marah would know. She hadn't asked if he'd be back, just keyed his new rister into the alcazar's security net before retreating to take a shower and ready herself for a day at her clinic; he'd used the chance to make his escape.

It wasn't that she would want to trap him. It was just...too easy, maybe, to fall into the alcazar's regulated quiet, its attempts to assist any Terran graciously allowed in its maw. Marah would be pleased if he stayed. She'd even scold Will if the synthetic started hinting it was time for Second Echelon Locke to find different accommodations.

"Package deal?" Alladal's teeth still glittered, and so did her wide dark eyes. She must have caught a nap; her pupils had stopped swelling. A thin shaggo-hide thong at her neck might have held an ornament; if so, it was tucked under a mech-loader's zipshirt collar. "It so happens I could use a couple nice big Corps bruisers. You ever work security?"

"You could say that." Hood took care to make the words flat and uninflected. His fingers tingled, longing for a ryfl even though the whisp was better for indoor work. "It's all we've been doing for the past few standards."

"Well, I'd call that more *murdering innocent civilians.*" The woman examined him avidly, and her grin had turned nasty. A slit in the booth's back over her shoulder was letting a little discolored stuffing peek out. "Wouldn't you?"

If it was a test, it was a stupid one. Robb's teeth ached, and Milar's face was suddenly much older. Muchson almost, *almost* made a restive movement, a twitch more sensed than seen, but training won out.

That was how he'd survived, then. The roar of conversation receded, a sea leaving its shore, and Hood's whisp at the small of his back could be slid free if he was casual about it. Or he could wait until this conversation was over, follow her, and do it in an alley. The question wasn't *if*, of course, it was merely *how*.

Robb surfaced from Hood with a purely internal effort that nevertheless collected sweat under his arms, behind his knees, and along the side of his dirty neck. The Madán gardener's cottage had a fine shower, but he'd only used the sink for shaving. Taking all his clothes off was an invitation to get whisped, and besides the dirt was familiar. Comforting.

Safe.

"Good," Alladal finally said, very softly. She hadn't shifted, but tension-cables stood out on her neck, and her fingers had slowed their restless tapping. "Neither of you are stupid."

"That was, though." Hood was in the driver's cradle again and turned his head, watching the rest of the Alley and the slice of bar he could see. Three 'tenders pouring foaming ale, taking chits, smiling or silent, moved like a squad in almost-hostile terrain, an efficient dance. One, a lean high-breasted girl in a skin-clinging patchwork dress, stretched her neck while pouring, tipping her head side to side, and the sway of her shoulder-length blue-black hair reminded Robb of Marah.

Had she really written every tenday? Where were those messages? Languishing in digital lockup somewhere? Everyone else in his squads got mail; there were only a few, company-wide, who didn't. All of those few had been Second Echelon.

That was thought-provoking, wasn't it.

Alladal gave a slight, airy shrug. "I can't use hotheads for concert work."

"You want us for concert security?" Milar, a faint sheen on his own morning-shaven cheeks, obviously didn't think much of the idea. Whether he thought much of Alladal herself remained to be seen.

The woman flattened her hands on the sticky tabletop. That took a certain bravery. "I need another hand for backstage and a few for outside the venue. If you do well, there'll be other work. Everyone starts out with sentry duty, though. I'm just like the Corps."

"Not hardly," the kid muttered. He made a sour face, and glanced at Hood, one squad member to another in front of a door that had to be busted. "What do you pay?"

Hood suspected she only needed one of them, and would set them at each other to find out if they were prone to whisping one of their own. He *also* suspected she needed more than a bodyguard or two for her concerts, which were probably low-end kulturtrash if the rest of her was any indication.

In other words, this musical woman smelled to the depths, and Marah was mixed up with her somehow. Of course. If there was trouble or a sad-sack story within a star-system radius, Marah would find both. Maybe *that* was why her mail had been censored.

It would have been nice not have been the reason, Robb thought, safe inside Hood's set face, protective camouflage, and stone-hard shoulders. A real change of pace.

"Per hour for the first three shows." Alladal's fingers went back to work, a single table-riff marching along in doubletime. Maybe she was using the hum of conversation as rhythm backing. "After that, you can go on retainer. *If* you last. I've a show on Tenday."

"That's tomorrow. You gonna give us an advance?" Milar grinned, and the boy's negotiating face was a good one, bright as a new credit-round and charming besides. All he needed was a fetching smear of dirt on one cheek to provide the missing urchin touch. Hood glanced past the kid's nose at the rest of the tavern, scanning unfocused the first time, then hopping from detail to detail the second. Alternating between two states at high speed, like cryon under a nadik beam getting prepped for munitions.

Alladal laughed, a musical tenor rill, very conscious of its modulation and pitch. "Hell no. I'm going to interview a few more prospects and if I settle on you—"

"No," Hood said, the single word slicing the tail off her sentence, a good clean whisp. He even had the pleasure of seeing her tense, though her fingers continued their tabletop dance. "You're not. We won't fight each other for your amusement, *Al*."

Milar twitched as if to elbow his squadmate, but the movement died. At least he had some sense, and was letting Hood play the hardass, good-pol-bad-pol style. It was called a strategy because it worked, and Robb didn't mind people disliking him.

It was safer that way.

Alladal's grin turned normal for the first time. "Good," she said, meditatively. "*Very* good." Her left fingers slid towards her right cuff, and Hood's skin prickled, but she just pulled out two blank-faced credit oblongs and slid them across the table. "Info's on these. There's also a tracer for your risters so I can ping you. If you take the credit and run, you'll never get another job at the Bridge again."

"Duh." Milar actually rolled his eyes. Robb's face felt strange again, and he realized he was half-smiling too, the indulgent expression of an uncle watching a kid piloting a khibiCAT for the first time. The baccasmoke rubbed at his eyes; he lifted his tankard again. This wouldn't take much longer and he didn't want to leave any for the wrights, as the saying went.

"Some things have to be said, even if you're sure everyone knows them. A Corps man should know that." Alladal's mouth turned into a thin line and her wrists lifted, finishing whatever song was playing in her wrapped head. "You're hired, now get the hell out of here. I have other jobs to give today."

"You run a temp agency too?" Robb couldn't resist, though Hood didn't fucking care *what* the woman ran as long as she paid and wasn't likely to whisp them both.

"I'm a woman of many talents." Alladal waved one long hand, a dancer's airy gesture. Nobody batted an eye, she didn't seem to have a trailer in the crowd. Which was interesting as well. "See you tomorrow."

Outside, the hammerblow of past-noon sunshine was only barely mitigated by the narrowness of the street. "I didn't think it'd be that easy." Milar clapped Hood on the shoulder, one-two, light, excited taps. "She pays well, Sylar says."

He wanted to tell the kid to be careful, but suspected it would fall on deaf ears. "You going home?"

"Nah." Milar stepped sideways, taking the standard position for alley sweeps as they passed the mouth of a malodorous crevice between sloping Saur tenements. Shipwhine throbbed in the distance, and everyone on the street hurried while they could. Later in the afternoon, each patch of shade would be used to maximum, and anyone having to move under the weight of direct light would slow, weighed down by atmosphere-filtered radiation. "Gonna check the office at the closest tetheryard, see if they need a loader. I'm rated for anything up to a class V mech, maybe I can pick up day work to go along with this."

"Huh." It was a good idea; Hood should have thought of it himself. All Corps infantry was rated to run a mech or two, and scrambling for a skilled mech position would put off what he had to do about Lamóre. "I'll go with, unless you're tired of me."

"Nah, you're good luck." The kid hop-skipped again; he just couldn't contain himself. What was it like to have that much energy to burn? "I get nervous around civilians, keep waiting for one of them to whisp me."

Which was uncomfortably close to Hood's own feelings, if he could be said to have any. "No wrap-armor out here." But there were probably plenty of whisps. He missed the weight of his ryfl with a sudden vengeance, despite cursing the Logic-be-damned thing on many a hike in training *or* the field.

"Yeah." Milar paused at the corner of Via Bridge, turning sideways as Hood checked the other direction. Khibis rattled, pedestrians scuttled, and the sky was alive with drones and needles as well as lumbering transports and floatboards with bright adverts blinking in stutterflash. It was an assault all its own, and one they couldn't dig in against. "We'll squad up. It's good to have someone to watch your back, you know?"

"Yeah." Hood did, indeed, know. Trust was always provisional, but a buddy had a powerful self-interest in keeping your ass from getting blown sideways, and that helped.

The tethered traffic light began to blink for pedestrian burst and they set off anew, Milar's mouth moving as he uploaded everything he knew about Alladal. Robb listened, made the appropriate noises, and found himself wondering what Marah was doing today.

It was Hood who wondered, almost idly, what she'd say about him working for Alladal.

DOUBTED, WANTED, OR THOUGHT_

"Hand me the tensor." Marah stretched lithely under the tapered tube of the khibiCAT's main body, sliding her shoulders against satin-smooth stone. "And if it *can't* be done, just say so." The alcazar had many a hangar cut into bedrock with honeycomb passages in every direction, just in case—the ancient planners had been much exercised upon Echelons and their villages of dependents needing escape routes in case terraform-stable was a temporary state —but this smaller garage was practically on the surface, and anything short of a grav-transport could fit in its echoing depths. It held the sleek black needle-cruiser Will thought she should use as a matter of course, a junk-looking patchwork needle for when Marah wanted to be anonymous, two khibis in varying stages of cannibalization, and the racing CAT.

Slim, highly maneuverable, and dangerous to driver and pedestrian alike, racer CATs were mostly illegal for personal transport. Proper khibis rattled and wallowed, heavy CATs were used for short-jaunt inventory hauling, but both were an order of magnitude safer than their speeder cousins. Which turned CATs into highly desirable items, forbidden fruit being the sweetest, and also made the Sagittarius Capital CATRace, held in venerable old Sharud, a highly popular spectacle.

This standard—the first race in five, since war frowned upon frivolity—the purse was two million; nobody had crossed the finish line last time. You could enter to place and get a slice of the betting take, or to win and take the purse *and* a slice. Most of the professional drivers entered to place and followed the race circuit; only the proud or desperate even considered entering solely to win.

Which made Marah either arrogant or very desperate indeed, or would to outside observers. There *was* a method to her madness, but it was one she didn't have to share.

For once.

"It is against the rules," Will said instead, mournfully, handing her the sonic spanner as well as the tensor. Anticipating, just like a good skarl.

Marah socketed the tensor and set the dial, settling the spanner between her breasts for temporary safekeeping. "Only technically." A whir, a tightening, and hopefully the bracket wouldn't come loose in tight turns. She was half tempted to take the CAT out and test it in the Blur Canyon complex at the edge of the Flats, but even a First Echelon couldn't go *that* far, especially if that was part of this year's course. The way things were going lately, she'd get nabbed and have to engage a solicitor, not to mention possibly call in a favour from Giz, and goodbye to any chance of competing in any race, let alone *this* one.

Modifications to racing CATs were expected, even ones that stretched the letter or spirit of legality. However, Will was having trouble with the biggest one, and he began to list the objections again. "A secondary consciousness in a CAT is not precisely *illegal*, but—"

"Nobody's ever been caught doing it." Marah tested the bracket, tapping it with the spanner. It gave a reassuring clang and stayed solid. Next came the data cable, which was why they were having this conversation in the first place. She settled the spanner back on her chest and hung the tensor on a handy protuberance, holding out her left hand for the cable. "Think about how many clinic patients that prize purse will save."

Will had anticipated her again, and moved to the left side of the CAT, dragging a snakewhisper of cable. "Your ethical flexibility is somewhat disconcerting."

"*Moral* flexibility, not ethical." The heavy, socketed cable-end dropped into Marah's waiting palm. "The good of funding the clinic outweighs a teensy-tiny bending of the rules."

"If you say so, mistress, I am compelled to agree." Still, Will produced an unhappy and not entirely untheatrical sigh.

The question of just what synthetics actually *felt* was an open one. A hyperalloy chassis holding vat-grown organic matter—muscle, bone, nerve—and highgrade neuron wetware, also vat-grown, inside a largely invulnerable skull might not properly be said to have any feelings at all, their social interactions governed by sophisticated algorithms and cues, heavily anthropomorphized by their owners but not, after all, *Terran.*

Made, not born.

Marah looped the cable, clamped it with a temporary statbuckle. "It won't break any of the core primes, now will it?" *No harm to a Terran through action or inaction, obedience dependent upon the former, self-preservation dependent upon the two former.* She could still remember Will drawing the triangle on a sheet, his stylus tapping each point, and his patient shepherding of her through logic problems exploring the ramifications of each while her father was away on Madán Mizar business, at First Echelon governmental gatherings, or when he was called to the Planetary or Senatus Prime for one reason or another.

Thinking of the Senatus was guaranteed to put her in a bad mood. He'd wanted her to rise through Aegis ranks and arrive at that pinnacle, officers and advisers to the Helm supposedly selected by election and merit. She could have, she supposed; it was well within her capabilities.

And yet she hadn't, and Aethelstan Rotherwood Madán had died knowing the grand architecture of his dreams was in peril. He hadn't lived long enough to see her go into finish Corps training and go into combat, thank the Moon.

At least he was spared that.

Sometimes, when younger, Marah had suspected Will was her real father, like the tale of Hia Genki. The old Terran fable was garbled, but its essential points remained the same—stolen parent, sensitive child, distant android usurper. It was a ridiculous notion, certainly; she had seen Will motionless and frosted with cryo-chill in his upgrade cabinet.

Still, she couldn't help but treat him as a Terran. "Right?" she repeated. If she could logic him into her way of thinking, this would get a lot easier.

Right now, though, Will was more than usually doleful. He circled the CAT, making sure no cables were tangled, his feet shushing in old, very comfortable and consequently battered house-slippers. "I am currently unable to see how it could, which is not the same thing."

"Well, if it does during the race, we'll deal with it then." Marah dug in her hip pocket for a temporary connector. Her own overalls were well broken-in, not to mention filthy with lubricant, dust, and detritus accumulated even upon a religiously cleaned shop floor. She was also in grab-boots with heavy reinforced toes; Will's bones were reinforced, and his feet weren't likely to be smashed into paste if a tether failed or a part plummeted floorward. "Okay. Try that."

Will moved around. He would be hooking himself to the old, hulking data core they were using as a buffer. There was a faint electronic hum. "My field of vision is still limited in the extreme."

Well, yeah. A CAT doesn't have eyes. That wasn't what I need to know, thought. "Is there any static?"

"None I can sense." He wasn't ready to let go of the naysaying yet, though. "Degradation of the consciousness within the small confines of this vehicle is a clear danger, Marah."

"If it goes on for a few tendays, yeah. But a single day?" She stared, unseeing, at the CAT's underside—propulsion, baffles, the nacelles stripped away so the main body could be worked on, the soft pressure of its tether uniform all over her body. If the tether's power supply, backups, and bleed failed, the entire thing would fall on her.

Wouldn't *that* bring all her worries to an end.

Will exhaled, not quite a pitiful sigh but not a sound of enjoyment either. "*Three* days, if you are selected for the random checks."

"I can very easily just race on my own." How many times were they going to have this particular conversation? It was like Giz and his lectures, or Alladal and her needling.

Then again, who else would listen to any of them, if she didn't? Giz would have to find someone else to declaim at, Alladal another patron—and good luck, finding one as patient and highly placed as Madán—and she didn't even want to *think* about Robb right now. He'd left his Corps ditbag, but the rest of him had vanished, and she knew better than to think he wouldn't cut loose even the most cherished of physical objects if he thought he had to in order to make an exit dramatic enough to express his disapproval.

"Not through Beggar's Canyon, mistress." They were betting heavily on that being the last third of the route, a personal wager to match the ones that would sweep through the crowd just before the statflag dropped. Will wasn't satisfied, but had to repeat himself once more in case she hadn't heard. "The risk of—"

"—accident is unacceptable," she quoted, chapter and verse. Just like a Bookmira reciting the Discipline, steady and singsong. Some, like Saint Cathara, had set passages to music; sung in Ald Anglene they were quite soothing. Alladal, with her fine clear alto on the verge of tenor and plenty of lungpower, had adapted more than one.

Marah preferred the ecstatics of the Moon, the full and dark-orb festivals with their crowding, jostling, and crowd's anonymity while shouting, weeping, or singing off-key was perfectly acceptable. So did the redband rebels, apparently. The great white terraform-ancient Lunacer temples were shuttered—temporarily, Parl Jun said.

Marah had her doubts. And she also doubted Riccar, if he was home, would have followed such a policy. Not that it mattered. For all her position as a First Echelon, nobody really cared what Marah doubted, wanted, or thought. They simply wanted to bend her ear or acquire her patronage.

Alladal said Marah had it easy. She was half right, but explaining as much smacked of self-pity a First Echelon wasn't allowed.

"There is no static." Will had obviously decided he had pushed her far enough. "The models for secondary consciousness degradation do have a matter of tendays as the minimum. You are correct, mistress."

At least she could be sure his pride wasn't hurt by such an admission. If it was Giz, or Moon forbid, Robb, she'd have to salve hurt feelings as well as keep her logic sound. She fished the transducer out of yet another pocket. "Hang on for a moment."

The logic transducer was worth a pretty credit or two; she'd found it in the guts of an antique, shredded Aegis cruiser on the last salvage run. It needed a cheap adapter to fit, but the tech was still robust. When something worked and held up to a beating, there was no reason to update it.

She plugged it in. "Try again, Will."

A short pause, another electronic hum. "Oh. *Oh.*" He sounded inordinately pleased, if such a thing was possible for a skarl. "Mistress, that is *ever* so much better."

"Good." She grinned, and wished her hair was longer, so she could tie it back. As it was, it neither cushioned her head from bare stone nor stayed clear of her eyes, so she puffed a quick breath upward to clear a wayward curl and shimmied even further under the CAT. "Start running diagnostics, then. I'm going to recheck that corrosion on the outer couplings."

"Yes, mistress." And, wouldn't you know, Will *still* sounded pleased.

CHEAP SHOW_

DEEP IN THE SAUR THERE WAS NO SHORTAGE OF PRIVATE drinking rooms; some, like the Chokblossom on Via Bowmann, even had pretensions at class. Still, the place did plenty of business because of those very same rooms. Nice enough, Giz supposed, with heavy pseudo-papier on the walls and soundbaffle curtains shaken free of dust once a tenday, even if the smell of desperation and substandard liquor burrowed in from the narrow, heaving streets outside. It was not the best place for a meet.

He was making an exception today, and that always put him in a bad mood. There wasn't even a chance of seeing Marah if he swung by the clinic, either; she wouldn't be there. On every Sixday she was planetside the Lady of Madán was in state at her alcazar hearing tenant cases and making judgments. There would be those hoping for her patronage in attendance as well and Will at her elbow with *précis* of each case, murmuring in her ear, motioning supplicants forward and keeping any dissatisfied with their liege lady's decisions in their place.

Rumor had it the tenants breathed a sigh of relief now that she was back from the war and cases no longer referred to Notheim's appointed Helm magistrates.

Rumor was, in this particular case, undeniably accurate. The regular civil Aegis magistracies would be filled soon now that peace had been declared, but institutional inertia would probably simply transfer the Sharl's Helm appointees over. It wasn't *supposed* to happen, but it would, and Notheim would have clients who remembered the help they were given in the heyday of wartime corruption.

That was a problem for another day, Ged told himself, and in any case, was outside his bailiwick. At least for now.

There was a perfunctory drum-rap on the door, then the partition was pushed aside by a round woman with high-piled dishwater hair and a tai-room uniform, traditional heavy shiprobes belted tight at the waist and long oversleeves pinned carefully back to keep from slopping in table spills. Giz almost winced. He didn't have very much of an Echelon's traditional appreciation of aesthetics, but whatever little he had pained him whenever he visited this fucking place.

Behind the attendant, Wat Krabstaf blinked, a smile of imbecile good nature plastered on his wide, sweating face. He lurched into the room past the round woman's perfunctory bow, and he even swayed for good measure until the partition shut with a decided snap and he straightened, the shambling act shed as easily as water from a diving-bird's back. "Polis Commandant Giz!" A rich, resonant baritone, flexible and full-timbre, vibrated out of his barrel chest. "Long time, long time."

"Sit down." Giz rested his elbow on the fylm-wrapped table; the idea was to tear off a layer whenever the surface got sticky, but anyone could see health codes were only indifferently followed here. He'd chosen the sturdier of the two low, traditional benches; let this fellow rock back and forth on the broken-legged one. "And stop bellowing."

"I can't help it, you just make me so *happy*." Wat fluttered his short, bristling dark eyelashes and settled with a sigh on the bench, ignoring the overburdened wooden groan under his ample, muscular bottom. "And look, you must be happy to see me too. You ordered tai."

Serve you right if I poured poison in, you greedy-gutted bâtard.
Giz smiled, a soft, rather absent expression that would have made
Marah wonder just exactly what mischief he was planning.

He and Locke had been a terror in their younger days, but Robb
was often silly enough to get *caught*. Giz's favourite mischief was the
kind blamed on someone else, or—better yet—passed off as bad luck
or coincidence.

And why was he thinking of that blond bâtard? Oh, no reason.
Except Noth had a tracer on the heir to Lamóre, and had informed
Giz that morning, rather airily, that Old Locke's son had come home
from the war, a real soldat hero.

It could only mean trouble. Robb was just quixotic enough to
decide to dig into the circumstances of his darling father's death.

"None of it's for you." Giz settled himself, catlike, and did not
miss the flicker of Wat's gaze towards his left hand, casually pouring
amber spice tai from a round-bellied pot. It was hard to mess up
amber, but each damn time, the Chokblossom did. This round was
harsh and doused with too much lac. He'd never bring Marah here,
even if she was in a mood for slumming.

He had several places he was waiting to show her, and it was
pleasant to think of each one. Right now, however, there was work to
be done.

Downstairs in the commonroom, a scuffle broke out. Fist thudded
into flesh, bone crunched, and a round of betting rose furiously in the
few minutes it took for someone's pride to be smashed and someone
else's assuaged. The floor was flymsy-thin, and so were the walls
despite the papier and soundbaffle curtains.

Wat's eyes half-lidded. "Couple off-duty polis downstairs," he
murmured, lovingly, but he had paled a shade or two under his
mahogany. "Looks like they didn't agree whose turn it was to pay."

Ged shrugged. "I'm sure they'll figure it out." In other words,
they weren't with him, even unofficially.

"Oh, yes, no doubt you're right, you always are." Wat's bench
groaned afresh as he settled completely. He looked just like a fuzzy

kid's disc illustration of a pre-Shiptime wandering merchant, complete with the wide leather straps forming an X on his broad, soft chest. "Me, I'm just a poor tinker, tinking about. A shallow life, and a brief one."

Giz allowed his smile to widen, strangling his irritation. "You're babbling, Wat. Which makes me think you've wasted my time." He wasn't in a mood to play today, and once again his bad-luck eyes—proof that he was live-born, since nobody in their right mind would have paired the recessives that made blue in a surrogated heir—worked to his advantage.

Pre-Shiptime colonizers were always shown with Robb's hair and Giz's eyes, even in the smallkid paper books with their stiffened pages mimicking proper sheaves. Robb used to joke that between them they made a perfect villain, and it had just enough truth to be funny when you were fifteen and thought nothing could ever hurt you more than the adults in charge.

"Would I dare?" But the Tinker, sensing Gizabón's tension, settled his large capable hands on fylmwrap protecting thin wood underneath and got to the point. "There's rumors, sir. Lots of them, in fact."

When isn't there? Wat meant more than usual, but every moment Giz spent here his skin crawled. "I don't pay you for rumors."

"Oh, I know, I know. You pay me to sift through the ordure and find gold. I have two nuggets and a bar, my lord major Gizabón." The accented syllable sat uneasily in this villein's mouth; the Tinker was here on borrowed flymsies and Giz's official grace, being estate-bound to some extinct alcazar out on Aquarius Secundus. War flotsam couldn't be too choosy about where it landed, and when offered Giz's patronage the man had been almost pathetically grateful—as far as a double-crossing mephitis could be, of course. "Are you sure you won't pour me a cup of that tai?"

"You don't want it." Giz turned the pot so its handle faced the Tinker. He could damn well pour his own; the only person Giz slopped tai for was busy with her own work today. "It's shit."

"Yes, my dear Lord Commandant, but it's shit I don't have to pay for. So." Wat touched the thick porcelain curve of the blue-painted handle. "Your favourite lady offloaded a lot of salvage. Borderline illegal, in some cases, but her middleman's a good one."

"Good." At least Marah wasn't reckless. What little of Madán's resources she could liquidate went into the clinic; the rest was protected by a legal hedge meant to keep a First Echelon's wastrel shoots, not to mention their *noblesse oblige,* from turning an entire House into a threadbare ghost. Selling salvage to fund her charitable endeavors was a fine thumb to the eye to her father's ghost, and Giz suspected that was why she didn't invoke Privilege and dissolve the entire estate. No doubt Parl Jun, ever hungry, would jump at the chance to have Madán revert to the Helm despite the cycles of legal wrangling that would ensue even with Privilege invoked. "Who's she using this time?"

"Nobody will say, though it's likely the same one as last time, and the time before that." The Tinker shrugged, lifted the tai-pot's lid, and sniffed cautiously at the amber. "You didn't spit in it, did you?"

If I had, would I tell you? "What else?" In other words, the Tinker had to take his chances.

Wat's easy smile faded a scant degree. He disliked these little chats almost as much as Giz did, but he did his best not to show it. "Everyone's coming home from the war. You can get prime security for very few credits, it's a buyer's market now. Several of the guilds are buying up all the muscle they can, especially the Miner's Staff and the Wijos."

Not unexpected, and not precisely a gold nugget. Giz waited, allowing his index finger to lift slightly and drop back onto the table-top. The Tinker's son was in a public academy on Sagg Tertius; Tabor's endorsement kept him there—and defrayed the considerable tuition, to boot.

The son gave every indication of being as useful a client as his father, but in the meantime, the Tinker—having escaped both redband pursuit and Corpsoldat service, as well as sunk fine thready tentacles all through Sharud while hiding from the dragoons meant to return estate-bound flotsam—was the tool to hand, so Giz used him.

Wat continued, hastily. "Well, someone else is buying up security. But choosy. One or two of the high-profile picks who just came home have been snapped up. There's also been a spike in the price of cryon *and* finished munitions lately, and a couple people looking to offload skimmed shipments if they can get a freighter going the right way."

The war was *over*, why were cryon thieves still at it? The redbands just didn't know when to quit. Giz wanted to shake his head, stilled. His coat was thermaseal, but the heat outside was unforgiving and even the forced-air cooling in the Chokblossom was wheezing to keep up. "And *our* particular deal?"

"Still negotiating." Wat paled a fraction, and he dropped the pot-lid with a small, fragile sound. Downstairs, the crowd noise returned to its regular dull roar. The fight was over, the loser would be stripped of credits on papier, round, or oblong, and the Chokblossom sailed on. "Price has gone down."

"Down? For what's selling?" *Or what you think we're selling?* Of course he wouldn't let Krabstaf near a *real* business arrangement. That would be unforgivably stupid.

But Giz had a mind to flush one or two other targets, and this was a handy way to do it.

"Yeah. The rumors still say something big is happening, but prices *have* dipped." Now Wat set out to prove his worth, a blunt fingernail scraping invisible figures on the tabletop. "Either they have what they're looking for or they have another supplier. I'm gonna say it's the former, because Figes and Kube the Rattus are *both* sitting on ryfls and gamma mortars."

Gammas weren't as bad as thermal 'nades, but they were still bad enough. What were these idiots planning? "They imported to meet a plummeting demand?"

"Maybe, maybe." Wat kept tracing, scraping at the fylm, a sure sign that he was just as puzzled as his patron. Arcs of well-worked grime nestled under each of his shovel-shaped fingernails. "They're both mad about it, too."

"See if you can't get them to blame each other." The more those two hideous fellows chased each other's tails, the quieter Sharud would be in the meantime. Not to mention a few of Sagg Prime's other cities.

The Tinker's gaze lit up, his thick cheeks bunching. "Finally, a trick worthy of my talents."

Don't get comfortable. "You'll do it for half price unless you impress me by the end of tai, Wat."

Wat didn't look crestfallen at all, which meant he had every intention of doing so. "There's been two false alarms at Helmsman Credit in the last tenday."

Ah. There was the gold bar. Giz leaned back slightly, studying the Tinker's broad face. "Two?"

"Yeah. Rodentia eating the vault wires, who knows?" A shrug like a mountain turning over in its sleep. "But with Kuype Bank and Handa Limited being hit since the surrender, everyone's nervous."

Seventeen security employees dead, some huge electronic accounts crack-drained, and a considerable load of physical credits walking away did tend to make banks, credit co-ops, and financiers a little uneasy. Giz's index finger lifted to tap again and halted, hanging over a ring of spilled amber tai smeared from the bottom of a cheap gilt-sparkling mug. Glittering show to hide any substance, just like real chokblossoms with their frail, floating tentacles.

No wonder the Tinker liked it here.

Giz thought it through once, twice, and arrived at the same place a third time. "Find out when," he said, finally. "If you can. But do *not* trip any tethers." The man was filthy and irritating, but he was effective, and finding another of his caliber—not to mention greed—was a task Giz preferred to avoid.

For now.

The burly man rolled his dark eyes. "You wound me." Wat moved on to his larger objection. "And that'll cost."

"When you have something real, I'll give you what it's worth. As usual, Wat." Great Under, Giz disliked this part of the game. The only consolation was that he was in service to a greater cause, and as usual, that consideration kept him afloat.

And kept him from rolling off-course *too* badly. Or so he hoped.

"Yes, sir-lord-Commandant Gizabón. Congratulations, by the way, on your recent elevation." Shoulders hunched, eyes rolling, he did all but tug an imaginary forelock. Of course he would have found out about Giz's jump from Third to Second; it was in any case standard for a battlefield commission. It was a small matter compared to the impossibility of achieving First, and Giz might have preferred to stay Third for a long damn time rather than see the blood, shit, mud, and death of a galactic war. "Or do you prefer a salute, sir?"

I prefer you to keep your fuckbuckle mouth off my name. Still, it didn't matter. He didn't need First, Second was quite enough to make him an acceptable match. Giz's index finger thumped down. He rose in one motion, enjoying Wat's flinch. "Be careful, *Tinker*. Row MS1, Plot 6 is still waiting."

After all, it was only Giz's patronage that kept Wat Krabstaf from the consequences of a rather severe legal judgment. It was also gratifying to see the big man shrink into himself, scruff-haired cheeks gone ashen. "Yes sir," he mumbled, his chin giving a little jerk.

Giz left, fairly sure that if he glanced over his shoulder he would see the Tinker gazing at his unprotected back, hatred smoking on that bland face, tiny porcine eyes eyes glittering with feverish loathing.

Hate made a man predictable, and predictable was easy to outwit. When Wat was at the end of his usefulness, an accident could be arranged. His son already believed the Tinker dead; Giz fully intended to keep the boy in school unless he proved somehow unfit.

Noblesse oblige wasn't just for First Echelons.

PETITIONS_

MADÁN'S VAULTED GREAT HALL, CHILL BECAUSE THE CLIMATE-control was working overtime, rustled and rang with activity, and the three-step dais at its end held a lone woman, straight-backed, upon a low padded bench. "Now, as to the second matter..." Marah's back-side was already numb, and it wasn't even noon. Her stomach was empty, and she longed for tai and a slice of Kameny's honeybread. Or maybe even a whole Logic-be-damned loaf, if there were any care-fully wrapped in the preservation freeze. "How did the shaggos get into your barn, Hurat?"

"I *tole* you." Big-shouldered Tam Hurat was the picture of injured innocence, from his blushing bald pate to his damp dark eyes. But his large work-hardened hands wrung at each other, a sure sign of both distress *and* more to the story. "They gots spooked. Was a storm that night."

A storm that just happened to escape all meteorological notice? Marah restrained the urge to roll her eyes or sigh. "Really."

"He keeps stealing my shaggos, a couple at a time," Lar Tiefson burst out. He was a stocky, almost endlessly patient man tenanted since her father's time, and he had two matters before her today. One was a request for deferment of tithes yet again, and this was the last. "And lyin' about storms."

Last time Hurat got into trouble, he had said something about a broken fence—as if they weren't well-crafted stone—so maybe the old man was getting creative. "Hurat, you can't have shaggos, you're not rated for them and you don't have grazing rights." She resisted the urge to pinch the bridge of her nose. At least the stasis-spray kept her hair from falling out of the traditional fillet clasping her temples. "You *especially* can't just take your neighbors' shaggos."

"What'm I s'posed to do if they show up on my garden?" Hurat's bottom lip pushed out slightly. "Just let 'em eat?"

"Hurat..." He'd be within his rights to get a fractional return on the shaggos if they were truly in his garden, or he could lodge a complaint with Marah as the liege for both parties. He couldn't just *take* them. She strangled impatience and tried again. "Look, what do you need shaggos for?"

The weathered old fellow dropped his chin, gazing at Marah's toes. He mumbled something, and she leaned forward a little, despite Will's tension. The skarl stood at her right hand, hands crossed at his midriff and his lean face unreadable, switching between aiding Marah's recall and busily collating data for the upcoming petitions. This was the last tenant judgment of the day, and already the tech-laden silver fillet was cutting into her forehead. Her neck ached, and so did her back from the posture required on the low chair serving as her magistracy seat in the alcazar's great hall, open to the public every Sixday she was planetside. During the war, tenant cases had been taken care of by Helm magistrates loyal to Parl Jun—or more properly, to Jun's representative the Sharl—and several of their decisions had been needlessly severe. Marah was almost finished repairing the damage, but it didn't get any easier with Hurat stealing his long-suffering neighbor's livestock.

"I can't hear you, Hurat." It was work to keep her tone even. Plenty of other Firsts would have summarily ended the entire case and moved on to lunch by now. "Please tell me what you need shaggos for."

"I ent need no shaggos," the man mumbled. He had no heirs; when he was gone she'd be looking for another stonewright to take his cottage-workshop and accompanying box-garden. No doubt there would be several ready to jump at the chance, especially in the Saur's deep jostling throat. "I need lac."

He's doing this for tai-cream? "Lac?" She tried to sound encouraging. It was difficult, with her head pounding and her back a solid bar of aching. Her bare back was cold, too.

"Kittos," Hurat finally said. "The poor kittos have nothing to eat."

"*You've* been feedin' 'em?" Lar Tiefson shook his head. "Great Under, Wat, why didn't you say so?"

It turned out there was a colony of feral felines in the fields between them, and poor Hurat didn't know how else to feed the creatures. He *also* didn't know if he was supposed to keep such beasts, so he'd taken what appeared to be the only way out. He was a good stonewright, keeping the fences and walls in repair, but deep or independent thought wasn't his strong suit since the mining accident. Her father would have revoked tenancy, shuffled him off to beg in the Saur, and engaged a younger wright long ago.

But the man did fine work, even if it happened on his own idiosyncratic schedule.

Tiefson rolled his eyes, and it was decided that a minuscule part of Hurat's wright-stipend would go for automatic shipments of cheap pet food, which Tiefson would bring from depot when he fetched his shaggo feed. The ferals served a purpose in keeping both Hurat's gardens and Tiefson's nearby barns free of vermin, and caring for them would give Hurat something to do that wasn't catching his neighbor's shaggos.

All in all, it was a good solution, and Tiefson took Hurat's arm to help the older man from the hall, shuffling past a line of petitioners. Lar was a good sort, even if perennially unlucky and a full cycle behind on his tenant tithe. The benefit of having someone looking after the estate's best stonewright—someone not likely to do something drastic when Hurat got a shaggo-stealing idea into his stubborn greying head—outweighed the cost of carrying a herder tenant with bad luck.

Besides, Lar always made it up eventually, and he had a family.

Marah looked down the line of petitioners, an internal sigh struggling to escape. Most were ragged, dispirited Saur-dwellers, hungry for tenancy. Being estate-bound was preferable to life in the slums, and she knew she had a reputation for being an easy touch. Having to deny petitions never got any easier, especially when they brought their big-eyed, staring children.

Will leaned down to speak in her ear. "Mistress?"

"Hm?" Marah wished she could shift on the padded bench. The entire hall was architecturally focused on this one point, subtly making the occupant of the lone seat before the massive carving of the Great Ship—in stone not native to the Sagittarius system, brought from far-distant Old Terra—look imposing. An ancient trick, probably as old as Terra itself. But it meant a public gaze fastened relentlessly on her, and complete relaxation under that pressure was not her strong suit.

Even if she'd practiced all her life.

Will's murmur was crisp and neutral. "There is an Echelon petition to hear privately."

Oh, Mother Moon, do I have to? Marah suppressed another sigh. Soon she'd be able to power a turbine from tense exhalations alone. "Concerning?"

"A Second Echelon." Will's jaw set stubbornly. Of course he couldn't say here with the hall's steno-recco on, Echelon business wasn't to be recorded by anything so plebeian.

Marah's hands, laid decorously in her lap, tightened. Today she wasn't wearing her signet; she would have fiddled with it endlessly, and that was not proper. "Why wasn't that presented first?" Etiquette was strict upon that point.

"It just arrived, mistress." The synthetic's thin nostrils flared slightly. It wasn't quite the height of bad manners for a lower Echelon to present a petition in the middle of a First's court session, but it was generally frowned upon unless it was potentially a Helm matter. Which meant a great deal of trouble, just the thing to intensify her headache. "Seven minutes ago. The petitioner is in the small east parlor."

Marah rose, and the shuffling line tensed. Near the hall doors, a child sob-snuffled, crying while a parent shush-soothed. A First was not strictly *required* to hear petitions after her tenants' cases and business were done. She could, if she chose, announce the session closed instead of in abeyance, and they would have to khibi-hum or buzzo back to wherever they had journeyed from, a day's worth of wages wasted.

It was unworthy of a First to give thought to the temptation. "Announce a short recess," she said in a clear ringing tone for the steno-recco, "and distribute a cupful of batter for every child and nursing mother." The strong, sweet almost-bread would soothe fractious, hungry little ones, at least for a little while.

"Yes, mistress." Will handed her the tempsheave for the lower Echelon's request and moved away; the speakers threading through the hall chimed their pleasant *attention* sound. The announcement of recess made a tide of whispers and stifled groans flow down the long high light-pierced space. At least the petitioners inside had the benefit of chilly forced air; outside, the sun beat down and Marah had ordered the fountain—normally turned off in deference to summer drought—to play at half strength. It would need cleaning after nightfall, and Marah suspected she'd be at her work until dusk, if not longer.

Maybe the Echelon business was Giz bringing something from Sharl Notheim. That would just complete Marah's day, though it would be nice to see someone she didn't have to play the lady for. Or only had to play halfway.

She gestured to open the small east parlor door, bracing herself for unpleasantness, and strode in. Great Under, she could have worn scrubs or a jumpsuit today instead of this grey dress in the style of Second Landfall, but Will had laid it out for her that morning and she hadn't the heart to order otherwise. At least the heavy silken hem made a soft comforting sound as she walked, and the taps of her borderline-uncomfortable, decorative boots were a delicate reminder that she was armored by tradition as well as subject to it.

"Greetings," she began, very traditionally indeed, but the word died halfway out of her mouth.

Robb Locke, in a scuffed, dirty, mech-padded loader's jacket, stood prow-stiff at the mantel.

UNITE HOUSES_

HE'D NEVER BEEN IN THIS PARTICULAR ROOM BEFORE, AND THE way the spotless bookshelves dotted with priceless antique knickknacks looked at him, he was glad. "So." Fuckbuckle, every time he looked at her, it was hard to keep Hood in the driver's seat. It was Robb who sounded uncertain, Robb's palms that were sweating, and Robb's gut that was a mass of serpentes. "I stopped at a kiosk and looked up Lamóre on a whim."

Marah's grey silk dress—not Old Shiptime style, she usually favoured that—held a rainbow sheen, wrapped around her front to fasten at her nape without shrouding her pretty copper shoulders, and the skirt skimmed from her hips in a long fall the color of a trash-bird's throat. She clasped her hands near the low-dipping V of the waistline, the tempsheave dangling like a flymsy-leaf book, and raised a manicured charcoal eyebrow. "And?"

It didn't help that she matched the room. The same glossy patrician finish, the same easy grace, the same *everything*. The tiny antique writing-desk near the door looked like it had recent use; it was just like her to settle in a smaller room and leave her father's ghost to wander the large ones Aethelstan had brim-filled with quiet authority while alive.

"And it isn't entailed to the Helm," Robb answered. That had been a surprise, but then again, it was a small benefice and not worth swallowing when there was so much other loot around. "Noth still has it embargoed."

"That's odd, but I suppose they have a backlog of...oh. I see." Marah loosened her fingers and glanced at the heavy sheave in her right hand, flicking a fingertip to scroll the legalese. "Huh." The silver fillet of a First clasped her head lovingly, lucky to be next to her skin. It probably didn't even pinch her temples, she was born to wear that sort of thing. "You don't want *droit de majeure*. You want to exercise a Section 9."

"What?" Baffled, he bent forward as if to snatch the sheave's round spicewood handle, but retreated in a hurry when he realized the angle made it seem he was attempting to peer down her neckline. "Shitstacks. Is it the wrong papierwork? It shouldn't be."

Marah smiled and shook her head slightly, her curls moving with sweet soft sounds and the lack of friction at the ends speaking of stasis-spray to keep them corralled. "A Section 9 will mean I can simply return the property to you and your heirs once the treason entailing's done." A patient teacher's voice, her usual homework recital. She'd probably answered serjeants' barked questions in Corps intro-camp the same way. "Then we can file for a—"

"No, Marah." Robb shook his own head, and Hood almost went frantic inside his skin at the unnecessary motion giving away his position. He forced stillness, again, tucked in the angle near the summer-empty fireplace that gave him the most cover. "I want to give up Lamóre."

The dress's subtle color rippled as she breathed. It was *damn* distracting. Even Hood watched that faint iridescence, all but hypno-tized. Marah studied the sheave, then glanced at him again as if she suspected her aural receptors were sparking. "You mean you want to sell?"

"No. I want to *give* you Lamóre, *droit de majeure*." He was sure he had the right term now. He should—he'd paid a chunk of the cash earned by two days' worth of loading work to an accredited streetside secretoire in the financial district to make the tempsheave ready-sign. "I'll let the fucking place rot before I live there." *Or before I let that Sharl piss on it.*

Go figure, now that he was trying to get rid of the place he discovered an Echelon's pride. A mere sliver, certainly, but sharp and stubborn nonetheless.

Even Marah's puzzlement was pretty. "Why not just rent it to—"

There she went again, trying to save him from himself. The Corps hadn't knocked that out of her, or maybe it was just dyed in too deeply to be shaken. "No, Mads." Robb was almost beginning to hope they'd get through this conversation without the biggest, most pressing issue being mentioned at all. "I'd rather it go to you, and it'll increase your holdings. Not like you need it, but still." There were only four tenants, but the mineral rights and transit point anchorage fees, not to mention the easement rentals, were substantial.

His father had made sure of *that*. His father had also told Robb over and over that he had no proper pride; would he be happy now that his loathsome son had discovered a little?

"And you can't be called for active Corps service again unless I release you from security obligation to Madán." She regarded him levelly, those piercing dark eyes so much like her own father's except for the softness lurking in their depths. "Is that what you're after? Because there are easier ways than this. You're drunk, by the way."

Not hardly. Not enough. "I had to work myself up to this. Father would kill me." Robb's mouth settled, bitterly. Here they were, two errant children of iron-hard men, left to make their own way.

At least she didn't dignify the bâtards by asking if the ghost of Old Locke was the reason. Instead, of course, she thought about the downtrodden. "What about your tenants?"

"All four of them?" Just enough to be considered an Echelon, really, but a pittance compared to her own. In brighter days the Lamóres had held more, but two wastrel grandfathers and a suicide without heirs had taken their toll and only the irreducible fragment of shipshare remained. Irreducible, but not non-transferable, and Old Locke had moved in for the kill when requesting his boon for exemplary service. It was a stolen alcazar, which made it more enjoyable for the old man and unbearable for his son. "You know they'll be happier with you than me."

"Robb..." Her throat moved, convulsively, though the rest of her was stock-still, her usual posture when receiving bad news and bracing herself to meet it with icy formality. "We could simply unite Houses."

"Marah..." What a lovely way to put it. His father would have expired of glee, hers of apoplexy. Both were probably watching him fuck this up. *Please. Stop trying to save everyone. Especially me.* "I'd make a shitty husband. Especially for you."

"Yes." Marah's expression didn't change a bit—a set smile just enough to soften her cheeks, her eyes very bright, and the pulse in her throat fluttering right where a whisp could sink in and let out a gout of arterial spray. "You would."

Robb rubbed at his forehead, chin tilted just enough to look raffish, like in the old days when he was sure he could charm his way out of trouble. But his smile felt a little too loose and his own eyes were watering. Hopefully she'd blame it on leftover ale fumes.

Great Under, he couldn't even *look* at her, now. "I wish I could, though," he said, finally, as if she'd asked or protested. It would be easier if she would shout, or slap him. He could, he supposed, even be craven enough to provoke her, then pretend she'd argued him into changing his mind just so he could blame her when she inevitably got tired of his shaggoshit as she had so often.

It would be so easy. Robb knew exactly how to do it, and Hood wouldn't flinch.

The silence thickened. Marah turned, each step the small tap of a tiny nail driven in with a master shipwright's single stroke. Halfway to the door she stopped, her chin almost touching her right shoulder, her lashes lowered. "Robb?" And of course, she went right for the heart of the entire tangle. "What changed?"

Nothing. "Me," he lied, his watering eyes fixed on the small wooden writing desk and its shaggo-hide pad next to the sheave-binder's heavy brass button. "If I was still a selfish brat I'd let you try to fix me." *That* much was true.

It was impossible for Marah's back to get any straighter, or any lovelier. The dress fell in gentle folds, and the antique keyring chained to her low belt—a copy of a Terran artifact, the original rotting under another sun or simply vaporized by time—glittered against soft grey iridescence. The garment was not quite backless but it did swoop low, and without her long-ago fall of dark hair her shoulderblades showed, delicate wings.

Wrap that shit up, soldat! You want to die? His hands shook, so he stuffed them in his pockets. It was a scorcher outside, but he had the padded, secondhand jacket strapped shut. How she could stand to walk around with bare skin showing...it boggled the mind.

If he moved before she reached the door, he could turn this around. He could catch her shoulders, let the words spill out. *Marah, please. I didn't mean it, okay? Just...give me some time.*

Marah took a single step. Paused. She took another, and the tempsheave dangled in her left hand, brushing her skirts. "I'll have Will conduct a full review," she said. "That will give you time to sober up."

Robb was about to move. He was *twitching*, and with his fists in his pockets he probably looked like a recovering dust junkie. It wasn't too late. He'd crossed longer distances than this with a single leap during the war, usually when the pop-thump of mortars began and a foxhole was just out of reach.

Marah. Turn around. Please.

The parlor door slid aside. She stepped out, head held high, and spoke softly, probably to steno-recco a memo for Will into her rister as her shoes tapped out cadence. Of course she wouldn't think of canceling the long afternoon of taking petitions, and hadn't the Corps-trained tactician in Robb calculated as much so he could get in, drop the papierwork, and leave?

If the cut was quick enough, you didn't feel the whisp at all. At least, not immediately. He was still a selfish brat, by any standard. No doubt in a little while he'd start telling himself it was her fault for not turning around once more, for being so willing to let go.

Now he could get out of here. Get to his ditbag in the gardener's cottage and slip through Madán's open gates with the crowd. He'd find a cheap room in the Saur and each time he found himself longing for a little peace and quiet he'd be able to bathe in self-loathing, because if he'd truly been unselfish he wouldn't have left his gear here in the first place. He wouldn't have come near her at all, just handled the whole thing with couriered legal papierwork to Will Skarl as her estate representative. He could have filed Lamóre into escrow and been offplanet before the sheave was ever laid before Marah at all.

If he'd truly changed, if he'd been less of a selfish bâtard, he would have. Beyond a doubt.

"Too bad," Hood muttered to the empty parlor. The side door chucked open, a subtle, very polite reminder that his business was concluded. Probably Will's doing, the synthetic tied into the alcazar's tech and monitoring Hood to make sure he didn't slip something into his sleeve on the way out.

You're trash, boy, his father sneered.

And to prove it, Robbhan Locke sauntered into leaving, instead of scurrying like the penitent thief he was.

SKIN FOR A WHISP_

THE SHIP DISTRICT WAS ALIVE WITH TAKEOFF AND touchdown, mechs and wrights swarming every new arrival, loaders in towering, jolting mechs packing holds with canister and cargo box. The District's busy, thudding, irregular heartbeat permeated the entire eastern half of the Saur, and there were plenty of slummers and poppers hanging around looking for temporary work or, even better, something to lift.

She had a good vantage point, and watched him arrive. He worked the crowd like a born infiltrator, matching his pace to the milling throng, just a tallish man with a battered loader's jacket, the kind you could find in surplus depots if you didn't mind harsh fabric and inelegant lines. The rain-hood was pulled high to camouflage his hair even though the day was a scorcher, heat shimmering over the district along with a colorless edge of flux technology.

It was the way he moved that gave him away, a feline prowl taking every advantage of cover. Finally, Locke vanished from the street. Alladal leaned back in her chair, stretching her legs out, and waited for him to come through the roof door. This cafe's balcony seating wasn't quite a secret, but very few workers wanted to sit outside, especially to eat. A roof over you was a luxury when you only had a half-standard's worth of break to choke your packaged meal down; why stand in the sun at all?

She waited, and waited some more, and was about to throw a partially loaded credit oblong on the table and leave when a shadow fell over her back.

His Corps bruiser's boots also scraped the pebbled rooftop, but only after she'd tensed and shot upright, her chair sliding hard. He stepped past nonchalantly, pulled out the other rickety trashplas seat; his smile was thin, very amused, and not nice at all.

"You're an asshole." Al's heart pounded so hard she almost squeaked the words, which only made his smile a bit wider. Nice even teeth, obviously originals but well cared for. He looked lucky enough not to need budding or implants, the bâtard.

"Never come from the angle they're expecting." Locke dropped into the chair. His chin caught sunlight out of the hood's shadow, and his stubble was gold wire. The smile settled into a hard, not entirely handsome smirk. "I thought you knew that."

"You're going to teach a priestess to sing?" She clicked her tongue, settling back in her own seat gingerly. Now she was sweating, dammit. Locke was a good bouncer, cool-headed and able to intimidate with that hot dark glance, well worth the extra cut for stage protection. The best security was the kind that stopped trouble *before* it began, and young Locke had a gift for the work. Still, the little tickle she got out of using the son in work his father would have countersigned Sharl Notheim's execution order for wasn't worth the wear and tear on her nerves, if said son was going to keep *this* shaggoshit up.

"I doubt you've ever served in a temple, m'dam." He didn't quite sneer, but it was close. A faint haze of metabolizing ale clung to his skin, a thin thread reaching her through the exhaust and simmering of a summer Saur day. "You went to all this trouble to get me here, tell me what you want."

"At least you're not stupid." She eyed him narrowly. It wasn't fair; he was brawny in all the right spots, and even his asshole factor was attractive. Bad boys were an Alladal specialty. "What's with the jacket?"

"I don't like showing skin for a whisp." His chin settled mutinously, and his eyes gleamed in the hood's shadow. Tiny glitters, though she wouldn't have been surprised to see the flat shine of an animal's different rods and cones. "You're no Lunacer. What's with your turban, huh?"

Do you think you're the first one to ask? She had a different answer each time; it was just easier that way. "Same thing."

Locke glanced at the door she'd settled herself to watch, a soldat's ticking off quadrants. "They gonna bring us some tai?"

Hell no. At least the idea was amusing, in its own way. "I'd ask, but I don't think you'd like their blend." Alladal forced herself to relax under the umbrella's thin, rancid shade.

"You don't come here for the tai anyway." He didn't quite relax, but he did go completely still. Something about that quiet was familiar and unnerving at the same time. "You come here for the dampers."

"Yeah." The building's humming dampers, meant to keep the flux from so many ship-tethers under control, *also* meant this conversation could go unrecorded, unless he was wearing a capture. "There's a job."

Now he gazed past her shoulder, either covering her six or bored by her stating the obvious. "So you said." The khibi-rattles from the street began to pick up, lunchtime almost at an end.

Alladal settled her feet, her thighs tensing. It was almost pleasant to sweat when there was a wind to cool you, but this kind of greasy anxiety was nasty at best. "I need a lookout with a ryfl."

"Huh." Locke examined her again, dark gaze unhurried and strangely impersonal. "Does it have to be a ryfl?"

What, like he was going to use a slingshot or a matterbeam repeater? Maybe an old-fashioned lead-slinging projectile repeater, like the old Bovine Boy funnyholos? "You got something else long-range?" Imagining him in *gauch-o* wear was a pleasure she'd save for tonight, if the rest of the day went well.

"I might." He rested his capable, sun-darkened hands on the table's lacework surface. Loader grime worked into his knuckles, black half-moons under his ragged, bitten-down nails—didn't he know how to visit a bathhouse? The Corps was supposed to make a man cleanly. "How long a range are we talking?"

As if he was thinking about bringing artillery. Al had to hide a smile at the thought; wouldn't *that* put a kink in all the Echelons' little plans? She was half tempted to ask for some. "Couple city blocks, at least."

His shrug said that wasn't a long range at all. "What's the payoff?"

"Four for showing up, much more if it goes well." Alladal glanced over his shoulder, seeing if he'd twitch. He didn't. The smart ones were better, but also more dangerous.

"If it goes well, huh?" Now Locke leaned back in the chair, stretching his legs out. Oh, he was good-looking, he wasn't greedy, and her pulse went up a few notches when those broad shoulders swelled, but still, there was something about this veteran she just didn't trust. He didn't look like an Echelon bâtard until you scraped the surface, but the arrogance was there. She might even have thought of pursuing the little flutter low down in her belly, if he hadn't been born into one of their shitsucking clans. Still, Locke got to the point quicker than most. "Is it wetwork?"

"Nope." Advancing the cause in that particular way wasn't on her sheave-binder yet. "And it's nothing dangerous to civilians." The only real danger would be if someone wanted to play hero. There was always one, and you had to stop them hard before they nerved themselves up to it.

Locke's gaze took on a strange sheen, a cooling meteor burning unwary fingertips. "I heard that a lot in the Corps." Soft, his lips barely shaping the words. There was a sore beginning at the right corner of his mouth, stress leaking through a hull.

"This time it's not a lie." She folded her arms. Scant dimness afforded by the tattered, almost rotten umbrella did nothing to cool either of them. Neither did a scorching breeze from the docks, and there was a rattlewhine as a tethered ship somewhere close was pulled along a travel-channel by a straining tug. Flux and tether fought for a moment before settling, the harmonics fading. "You in or not?"

"I want more specifics."

"We all want things." Her father used to say that, usually when drunk and cheerful before the inevitable blackness fell and he got to boiling internally. He never exploded, but he didn't have to—the quiet, static-laden risk was enough to make everyone tiptoe and turn child-Al's stomach into a mining world's acid-pit. The hot breeze touched her turban, laid a cooling finger on her damp neck. "You sign on, you get specifics."

Locke cogitated a few more moments. "Timeframe?"

"Sixday fortnight-ish." That much was a lie, but it paid to be careful. "You gonna get your hands on a ryfl?"

"One better. Anyway, fine." His right shoulder lifted fractionally and dropped, his loader jacket's rough fabric scratching the cheap chair. "I might as well sign on."

Al grimaced slightly. Her pulse was just beginning to come down from its tether, and another thumping whine in the distance was a tug cabling up another ship, preparing to drag it into place for loading. This was a good place for a short meeting she didn't want overheard, but the noise was about to scrape her last nerve off. "Don't do me any favours."

"I'm not." Locke made a short, sharp, dismissive movement. He seemed to hate moving, like certain bufonidae. "I need the credits."

That made no sense at all. "Aren't you Echelon?"

Robb Locke's smile fell away, and a chill touched Alladal's back.

"Not anymore," he said, quietly, and got up. This time he took the roof door, his head down and his shoulders slightly hunched to hide his size. Corps vets were everywhere, some of them with military-grade prosthetics and others with scars, and all of them with that haunted, harried look.

Except Locke didn't look just hunted. He also looked *pissed.*

That was fine. Alladal had a few ideas about where to channel that anger, and in a little while, she'd start coaxing him along for the cause. The prospect was almost enough to put a smile on her face, but she was sweating and her heart kept thump-thudding.

Sneaking up on her like that wasn't a gentlemanly maneuver. He was just getting more interesting all the time, this blond boy.

SURPRISES_

A HOT BREEZE MOUTHED THE SHARL'S NEEDLE, BUT FEW WHO worked in its embrace felt the small singing stress as air parted around a Terran-built structure. It was a good thing the military governeur of Sagittarius Prime's office was soundproof and baffled; outside the floor-to-ceiling windows Sharud lay supine, its streets shimmering with summer heat and the shadows lengthening as afternoon wound its weary way to tai-time.

Sometimes the Sharl worked through even that small, civilizing daily break. He was fond of remarking that crime did not stop for tai, and neither should his polis. At the moment, though, he probably could have used a mug of amber or even a finger-cup of strong, smoky Capricorn Grey.

"*What?*" Noth didn't quite bellow, but it was close. Behind him, a vast window looked over Sharud's well-ordered, bustling heart. The slums lingered on the horizon; they were high up in the Needle. Height was supposed to bring clarity, but Arthe suspected it gave Notheim a completely different feeling.

"Lamóre can't be seized." Head Secretary Arthe bowed his gleaming, shaven head, blinking rapidly. Plenty of people had thought his wide, mild brown stare meant stupid passivity, but there was a gleam far back that dissuaded the observant or intelligent from baiting him or dropping an inadvisable word. "*Droit de majeure*, sir. The papierwork was filed at an accredited secretoire; it all appears in order."

Ged Gizabón, lounging on the long black shaggo-hide sofa tucked in a corner of Noth's office as he was wont to do every tai-time whether Noth imbibed or not, exhaled softly, stirring a cup of amber from the kettle-set in his own office. His eyelids dropped to half-mast. Arthe knew better than to think he wasn't paying very close attention.

It was when Gizabón looked sleepy that he was most dangerous.

"So." Noth settled in his Xomo capitain's chair, pressing his fingertips together. The wall of tinted silica behind him glowed, and the two monitors floating on mini-tethers above his desk bobbed gently. "Little boy Locke has seen his happy home."

It wasn't a question, so Arthe didn't reply. That was his first lesson in working for Sharl Notheim, and he had taken it to heart. He did, however, glance nervously at Gizabón's usual black and blue polis thermaseal. The Tabor Echelon, back from the war himself and bumped up to Second instead of the rapidly diminishing Third, somehow managed to give even standard-issue clothing the air of being tailored, and maybe that was why Arthe disliked him.

Still, you could get along with a man you disliked, and Gizabón even made it easy for Arthe, smoothing over little inconsistencies and smiling in that chacal-like way of his. He hadn't made any overt moves, but should there be an...incident, Arthe was almost certain Gizabón would provide a measure of protection from Notheim's temper.

And that was a very welcome suspicion.

"Who's the receiver?" Noth wanted to know, and Arthe didn't want to tell him. Most especially, he didn't want to with Gizabón sitting right there.

Unfortunately, he had no choice. "A First Echelon, sir; Lady Marah Madán Mizar, sir."

Noth breathed a curse of surpassing and surprising foulness as he spun his chair, looking over Sharud's formicidae seething. Past the Saur's smoke-haze the port shimmered; to the north and west, the green of Sharud Forest—plenty of it set aside as Echelon or Helm preserves—was a dusty green smear. "Is that so."

Again, Arthe kept his mouth sealed. The urge to glance at Gizabón was almost overwhelming, but he stubbornly resisted. It would be better if this office didn't look over the Saur; the spires of northwest Sharud against the forest was a much prettier view. It was even better to the south.

"Well?" Noth's cold-tai gaze swung past his secretary to his intelligence chief. "Anything to say?"

"They've been friends since childhood, and Robb hated his father." Giz's faint smile hadn't altered in the slightest. At least he didn't lift his wrist or his two smallest fingers when drinking his tai, like some Echelon parvenus in old fic-captures. "It's just like him to shove four tenants and a rotting manse onto her, and it's just like her to accept."

"She hasn't accepted yet, sir." Now was the time to place the tempsheave containing the details gingerly before his master, and Arthe did so. His own thermaseal was welcome; Noth kept his office almost cryogen-chilly. "Her representative is conducting a full review. I'm sure we can tie it up in red fylm?" The question lingered, Arthe's eyebrows rising.

"Or make an offer for it." Gizabón set his half-empty tai mug aside and settled into the couch's embrace, all but throwing an arm over his eyes and smirking. He enjoyed when Noth was outplayed by circumstance, and made no secret of it. A dangerous habit, but Arthe had his own habits to attend.

"Why bother?" Noth snarled, staring at the tempsheave. His lip curled magnificently; he could have gone on the penny-stage. Imagining the man as a kulturworker was only mildly amusing, though. "The old man hid it somewhere else, or he was lying."

Arthe winced internally. *I wish he wouldn't say things like that.* It was safer for a secretary not to know some details; Old Locke was proof.

Of course, Old Locke had thought being an Echelon would protect him, and was furthermore a grasping old miser. It wasn't news that his heir hated him. Water was wet, orbits were elliptical, sons disliked their fathers, it had been that way on Old Terra too. Or at least, so the Discipline historians said. Still, if Old Locke's treatment of his tenants had been indicative, the son had reason for more dislike than most.

It took a ladders share of work to become universally despised, but Old Locke had done his best.

"Mh." Gizabón's noise was an affirmative, and a sign of deep thought. It was also an indication that he had more to say, and finally he did. "Either's possible. Yes."

"Unanswered questions." Noth's fingertips were bloodless, but he still kept pressing them together. "I dislike them."

"So you've said." Gizabón's long black coat was a slick puddle-gleam; having settled to his satisfaction, he picked his tai up again and took a mannerly shot. But his bright bad-luck eyes were still half-lidded, and his long nose all but twitching. "We turned the entire place upside down. The old man probably kept everything in his head."

"I sincerely hope not." The Sharl sighed, considering the tempsheave. "If he left it with a tenant..."

"He wouldn't trust a *tenant*." Giz curled up, rested his elbows on his knees, and stared into his tai. Even pitched forward like that, the readiness in him was clearly visible. He attended an old-fashioned salle nearly every day, and was held to be rather deadly with the isabre as well as with antique edged metal pfoils and épfées.

"Not outright." Noth handed the tempsheave back to Arthe with a snort. "Don't tie it up in any red fylm, Arthe. The last thing we need is a First Echelon going running to the Helm or Aegis. If any of the tenants have something from the old bâtard, they'll most likely try to give it to the son. Keep a watch on him, Giz."

"Yes, sir." Giz's expression didn't alter. He took another sip of tai. "Close, or indirect?"

"You know him too, right? Be friendly for old times' sake." Noth waved his right-hand fingers, a wiggling motion that said he was delegating and didn't wish to think about the matter anymore. "If any of those tenants go sniffing around him, intercept."

Gizabón nodded, a slow, reflective movement. His hair was beginning to soften at the edges, the Corps cut losing its crispness. "Of course."

The Sharl's round cheeks gave him a deceptive air of placidity. He stared at the tempsheave in his secretary's hands as if longing to snatch it back and toss it into the grinder. "Any other surprises today?"

"None so far, sir." Arthe devoutly hoped that would continue to be the case. A suspicious dampness at his lower back was not quite fear, but certainly discomfort.

"Good." Notheim made an irritable, dismissive motion; Arthe retreated with a deep, internal sigh of relief. He didn't linger on his way to the door, but Noth was apparently unwilling to waste any time. "Well, what are you waiting for, Giz? Go find young Locke and see what he knows."

"Yes, sir." Gizabón's rising was accompanied by a soft whisper of shaggo-hide and cloth. If he was displeased, he'd probably leave his tai mug on the incidental table, and while it was almost satisfying to see Noth's concomitant irritation, it was still Arthe who would have to clear it away. "And if he knows too much?"

Noth made a small, snorting sound of impatient merriment. "Why do you even ask? Take care of it."

"Yes, sir."

Cold bâtard. Arthe restrained the urge to make the sign of the Discipline Wheel upon his chest—Noth didn't like religion. It took a special kind of ice-veined soldat to do what Gizabón did; hadn't he been in intelligence work during the war?

Maybe he wasn't such a good bet for when the inevitable

happened and Noth came tumbling down from the top of the Needle. It was, like everything else, a wait-and-see phenomenon.

At least Giz scooped up his tai mug and took it with him. Arthe caught himself feeling almost charitable towards the man as he went back to his own desk past the great double doors worked with the thread-thin blue stripes of polis authority.

Almost.

PROPER PLACE_

THE HELM FLAGSHIP *ILEANOR*, NAMED FOR THAT REDOUBTABLE mother of parls, had accepted its highest-ranked passenger just at the edge of the Sagittarius system and now hummed with self-important activity. Stars filled the tinted viewports with greasy glow passed through several layers of fylm since Terran eyes weren't built to handle unfiltered starsteal glow. The great wraparound window behind the fleet abbot's heavy, wooden, silica-topped desk was full of the weird shifting smears, watching his office balefully.

Every fleet traditionally had an Abbot and a Deep Lunacer, but since so many of the Moon's followers had thrown their lot in with the rebellion, the latter's office was often vacant. On Parl Jun's ship, the Deep Lunacer's quarters, chapel, and receiving-rooms were sealed, a bright noro-red stripe across the doors warning the ecstatics that they were suspect at best and treasonous at worst.

It gave Bookman Trick no joy to pass that red stripe, but he suspected the abbot felt otherwise.

Trick, his new cassock just as heavy as—though far more comfortable than—the old, folded his hands over his belly and bent his head. The slick-cushioned seat he perched upon was built to require constant attention on the part of its user, a nagging sensation of sliding under your ass reminding you that visits to an abbot's office were never good news.

"The Helmsman has specifically requested you," Abbot Wat Tilles intoned, his long nose twitching once to clearly denote that he did not understand why such an august personage would be troubling himself with a mere junior Bookman, but questioning was beneath his status. The Abbot's own robes, dark and understated, skirted the very edge of the Sumptuary Recommendations. No doubt he was next in line for confessor duty to the parl, and disliked the interloper on sheer principle. "You will be accompanying His Grace as a personal confessor. I don't need to tell you how much this will benefit both you and the Discipline."

And you personally? Trick dropped his chin even further. "Service is my joy," he said, carefully. This meeting was ostensibly to go over his new duties, but Trick sensed a trap, like a redband mine wrapped in a wooden bloxo and buried at just the right depth so the rattle of a transport khibi would trigger an explosion, sending fragments through metal, sheet silica, cryon cells, bone, flesh.

Tilles even said *Helmsman* instead of *Parl Regent.* No doubt he'd thought it might smooth his own way upward, but a trespasser had somehow managed to clip his takeoff, and consequently must be tethered firmly back into place.

"I won't ask how you managed it," the abbot continued, as if Trick hadn't spoken. "I'll simply point out that this is not how things are usually done. The hierarchy must be observed, Order and Logic maintained."

So that was the reason the abbot had kept Trick waiting in the anteroom for a full metric hour. "It wasn't my idea, my lord abbot." If the other man could be archaic, so could he.

"Oh, certainly. Certainly." The abbot nodded. He was what they called a rank-chewer, a pettifogging little martinet. There were other, more pungent terms soldats used for a man like this, and Trick had been called a few of them in his time, too. Especially by Curridge.

Artificial grav weighed against Trick's arms and legs; he longed for a proper planet's gravity well. Shipboard pull made his stomach uneasy, and so did the new cassock. Trick raised his head slightly, studying the carving on the front of the abbot's desk—the Great Wheel, all things in their proper places, Helm, Echelon, Service, Discipline, Tech, and Steerage represented in high laser-carved relief. "The Discipline could send me elsewhere. I'd welcome that, my lord."

That got the rear-echelon bâtard's attention. Tilles folded his hands inside his sleeves, leaning back in his ergonomic float-chair. "You would turn down the gift of His Grace's patronage?"

"Like you said, the hierarchy must be observed." Trick reached for his high black collar. It wouldn't take much to tear the whole thing open like a solstice festival gift. The new cassock could slide to the floor, and since Trick had pretty much suspected some shaggoshit would occur, he wasn't even wearing the regulation linen shift underneath, just his junk-wrappings.

Captain Curridge would probably injure himself laughing. Trick could all but *hear* the dead man, hunched in a rainsheet on some piss-ass moon, the center of a knot of merrymaking infantry. *So then the Bookman says, no, listen to this, fellows, then the Bookman says, "the hierarchy must be observed," in that prissy little voice, and he begins takin' off his clothes...*

"I do not wish to leave my proper place," he continued, and unbuttoned his velvet collar. Next came the seal down the left side of his chest, fabric parting a fraction at a time. It was a damn shame he couldn't do a little burlesque with it, like a kulturtrash show on a thin-atmosphere moon. "I will return to my quarters and await the orders of High Discipline."

"Now, now, Bookman Trick." The abbot's small, porcine eyes blinked rapidly. Behind him, starsteal smears slowed their random, nauseating slippage. Maybe they were reaching a gate. "Parl Jun has asked for you. We must aid and comfort the Helm, as well as the steerage."

Trick let another fraction of cloth slip. "I am far more comfortable in steerage, Abbot Tilles." Might as well be honest. Maybe a back-planet parish or a spell in stockade would stop the screaming in his dreams, the blood and mud and explosions, men and women calling for their mothers as they died or their bodies were shattered past even modern medical technology's ability to repair. "I don't want this robe any more than you want me to have it." He rose, his knees creaking, and let another slice of his wire-furred chest show. No few of the hairs were holding some grey before their time. "I'll even scourge myself on the way out to prove it."

"Bookman!" The abbot slapped his plump fist, sternly, upon his silica-sealtopped desk. "Button your robe, and sit *down*."

They glared at each other, two servants of Discipline, and Bookman Trick wondered if the Moon was any kinder to her follow-ers. When he took his vows the idea of a universe like clockwork, every cog in its appointed place and the heavens and Great Under with its stratified levels for every sinner or unsinner alike, was comforting. The ecstasies of the Moon Temples, the orgiastic celebra-tions, the off-kilter songs of longing and release, were nothing more than silly abdication of responsibility to young Trick.

Now, though, he wondered. Was there a Lunacer somewhere in Anglene thinking about how his fat ass should have gone into the Discipline and avoided all the messiness of desire and intoxication? At least plenty of Moon-worshippers had stuck with the redbands to the bitter end, refusing to leave their flocks and temples even when given the chance to recant.

Trick stayed where he was, half-unsealed and feeling faintly ridiculous, holding the Abbot's dark gaze.

"All right," Tilles said, finally. "All right. Please, sit down, Book-man." The fellow tried a teeth-baring bureaucrat's smile and made a wheel-sign of blessing with his soft, plump paws. "I should have known Parl Jun would choose such a modest, dedicated brother."

Trick could, he supposed, finish stripping off the new cassock.

Leave it in a pile on the floor, walk out of the office—and go where? You could leave one planet for another, but a ship was a dead end. If he left cloth and Discipline behind and roamed mostly naked through the halls, what would stop him from choosing an escape pod and blasting out into cold space? Ejected during starsteal, he'd turn into into frozen chunks scattered through an anonymous quadrant. Would he feel the shredding of his physical body and arrive in the Great Under clutching at his junk-wrappings, ready to hear what hell he was consigned to?

You could throw your entire life away in half a moment. He'd seen as much during the war, and now there was only the filthy shame of being left alive.

Bookman Trick buttoned his cassock but not his collar. He settled his ample ass upon the slippery seat again, dropping his gaze to his useless hands. It was amazing; the blood never washed off. Oh, *physically* it did, but he could still feel the hot slipperiness against his fingers, and hear the cries of the dying.

None of them called for their fathers. It was always *Mama, Mother, Mère, Moon.* Maybe the Lunacers had only committed the sin of being on the right side, if there was anything approaching a right side in war.

"I don't want to be his confessor," he said, finally. "I did my service in the front lines already."

"Your performance was exemplary." Now the abbot was conciliatory, visibly deciding Trick was either a naïf who would never last in a position of high power, or that rarity, a sincere Terran male. "I'm sure this will be an assignment of short duration."

Me too. Maybe the man meant it as a stinging rebuke, but all Trick felt was the same heavy weight in his gut, a blockage more than physical. "Anything you can do to make it so will be welcome," he said to his clean, traitorous palms, and hoped the bâtard would take it literally. There was something to be said for letting an asshole do exactly what it was intended for.

"Button up, brother." Abbot Tilles began to slather on oily kindness, and Trick obeyed, sealing his collar with clumsy fingers.

He wasn't strong enough to slip this chain and go naked. Maybe Capitain Curridge had it right, and Discipline was a haven for cowards.

Or for one simple coward, at least.

SCHOOLYARD SCRAPPING_

He could have told Noth that it wasn't necessary to go *find* Robb, that the blond bâtard would show up like a bad debt if you just waited long enough, but Ged wanted to get out of the office anyway. Noth believed in sharing trouble, and listening to the Sharl chew himself into yet another lather about Old Locke's missing books was not high on Giz's list of pleasant activities.

So, on impulse, Gizabón quartered the area around a certain clinic at the edge of the Saur, and struck good old-fashioned rare mineral. Half of hunting was knowing where your quarry would rest, and Giz had used this alley before since it held an unobstructed view and wasn't too filthy. He even made some noise as he approached from the six, watching a broad-shouldered figure with a padded loader's jacket and a short, aggressive ruff of golden hair just beginning to shake off the stringent discipline of Corps shavers.

Giz paused a safe distance away and cleared his throat, making it absolutely clear he was a friendly. "I was just thinking about you." His coat-hem flirted with an uneasy breeze, and if his quarry was armed *and* jumpy, Giz might be forced to some quick thinking.

"I'm surprised your brain didn't liquify." Robb Locke didn't bother to turn his shoulders, just his head. He wore loader's dungarees and a wraparound Corps jacket padded for mech work, sealed and buttoned all the way up despite the heat. No thermaseal was apparent; it was just like the man to court heatsickness in a Sagg Prime summer.

"Well, it's unpleasant, but hardly dangerous." That was it for pleasantries, Giz decided. He wouldn't say *so you survived* or *good to see you*; the first was self-evident and the second would be a damn lie. "Why are you here, Robb?"

"I could ask you the same thing." Robb turned, now that he had left his back to Giz just long enough to make the point, and eyed his old friend from top to boots. He looked like a few klicks of bad road, between the dirt on his neck and the rings under his eyes, not to mention the shabby clothing and obviously well-used Corps grab-boots.

"Please." Giz pointed at the clinic, a quick stabbing motion to see if the other man would flinch. "We're a dyad, circling a star."

Locke didn't flinch, and he didn't pretend incomprehension. "That was a long time ago."

Only a couple standards, Robbhan. "And yet, here you are." Giz decided he wasn't going to get upset no matter what the asshole said. His short, uninformative, barely polite letters to Robb—once a metric month, why bother with more—had never received a reply. Still, Giz had kept sending them.

Patience was a habit, and one Robb would exhaust if he could. They were locked into the dance; Giz wanted no complaints about his performance when the music finally, inevitably stopped.

Robb spread his hands slightly, dark eyebrows raised. "Here I am." That slight arrogant smile—oh, when Robb wore that expression, the urge to smash his naturally good teeth and straight handsome nose was overwhelming. Someone in the Corps or on patrol had felt that urge, to judge by the well-healed bump high on the nasal bridge.

The asshole hadn't even bothered to get bone-scrubbing, though. Maybe he thought it made him look better.

Giz glanced at the clinic's front again. He said nothing, letting Robb stew. The constitutional inability to keep his fucking mouth shut had been a Robbhan Locke trademark well before the war.

Looked like it held, too. "Look at you, gainfully employed at last." Robb pulled at his sleeves, his head tilted slightly and his dark eyes shuttered. "You could at least say you're happy to see me."

"You want me to lie, Locke?" But Giz's lips pulled up, a thin, unwelcome smile. "You look good." *For a corpse,* he wanted to say.

"Careful." Robb glanced behind Giz, an infantryman checking his buddy's six. At least there was that. "I'm gonna start thinking you're in love."

"Not in this city." Giz returned the favour. Nothing sneaking up on either of them. He called Locke a friend only because he was puzzled—what *was* the word for someone who wouldn't let anyone else stab you, because they'd reserved that particular pleasure for themselves? "What are you doing?"

"Doing?" Sweat glistened on Robb's forehead, wrung out by a drought-hot day thick with dust and the vibration of flux and tether as well as the faint hint of khibi exhaust. Did he *want* to collapse? "Trying to be a better man."

Better than what? Giz shook his head. "The Corps teach you that?"

"And what did it teach you?" Robb actually looked interested now, dark eyes lighting for a moment. It was a flash of the old secondary-school Locke, ready for mischief at a moment's notice, and to his surprise, Giz found it was welcome.

"Nothing I didn't already know." It was a relief to tell the unvarnished truth to someone, for once and at last. Giz's thermaseal coat kept him cool; the only way he'd sweat in it was with hard exercise. Right now, a prickle touched his lower back, and he disliked it. "How exactly are you going to pull it off, then?"

Robb shrugged, the same old careless movement. "I got rid of Lamóre. That's got to count for something." Despite only a light coating of rubbish it still stank in this alley, but he didn't seem to notice. Had the Corps taught him that, too?

"Shoved it off on Marah's shoulders, you mean." If Giz wanted to provoke, she was the easiest way.

Did he want to, though? The Great Judge of Discipline knew it was the best way to deal with Robb; if you exhausted him with a fist-fight sometimes he'd listen to reason.

"So you know. Of course you do, you're working for Noth." Robb's hot, dark gaze locked with his. At least he didn't look like he blamed Giz for attaining such a position; he probably assumed Giz had been drafted. "It was the best solution."

For you, you mean. Utterly typical, and Giz hadn't had a chance to visit Marah yet to see what *she* thought of the whole thing. She'd be graceful about it, of course...but under that grace her true feelings could be seen, if you attended closely enough. "And now you'll be taking yourself offplanet?" It was a faint hope, Ged couldn't be that lucky.

A rattle-whining khibi pushed past on the street outside the alley; Robb waited until it passed, his shoulders hunched like a grunt nearing the end of patrol, struggling to keep his wits sharp and refrain from spraying ammo at every twitching leaf or dust-swirl. "Can't afford to yet."

"Ah, yes." Of course he couldn't, since he'd shoved his patrimony onto Marah. Giz's hands almost ached with the effort to keep them loose and open. If he gave any indication of ill temper, Robb wouldn't stop until they'd traded blows, whether verbally or otherwise. "You're working loaders?" An easy guess, that jacket had fresh lubra stains above the hips, right where a CV-2's lateral control would press.

Robb's lip curled slightly. "Honest toil makes a man, Giz." He didn't *quite* imitate who must have dinned that old castanea-nut into his skull, but it was impossible not to guess.

The bâtard's first act on touching down was to make Marah's life more difficult; wasn't that always the way? And now he was probably going to blame a dead man for it. "Your progenitor was fond of that one, wasn't he." Ged crossed his arms, not quite defensively. If he didn't keep his hands occupied he was going to take a shot at the man.

Maybe Robb knew as much. "Yeah, let's talk about my father." A slight familiar jerk of his gold-stubbled chin, shaking away the thought. "That'll keep us both calm." His Corps boots probably had blood ground into the treads, along with the dust of other planets. Everything about him screamed *frontliner*, now.

Even the haunted, hunted flatness in his gaze, the same look Giz saw in the mirror every morning. "I'm *perfectly* calm, Robb." Silly Giz, first attached to artillery and thinking that was terrible but survivable before being poached to do intelligence work. Either you shot a few insurgents or you sent other people to get shot, it was the same shaggoshit either way. A man was lucky if there was one small corner of his life where he didn't have to fight *or* lie. "I just don't want you fucking up Marah's harmony anymore."

"Well, you can relax." Robb's grin was a shadow of its former self. A plastiseal lunch wrapper skipped across the alley's mouth, borne on a hot dry static-singing wind. "There's no reason for me to. I'll vanish into the fucking drift like the trash my father always told me I was."

The worst thing was knowing how much Robb believed it. No, even worse was the urge to tell him, once again, that his fucking father didn't know jackswabbie-shit when it came to Robb, and had proved it all his son's life. Maybe Marah could have eventually made that sink in, but Giz was left with wanting to *beat* it into the man's head. For her, though, he'd try it the other way. "You could choose to prove him wrong, you know." Of course Robb wouldn't listen, Giz thought bitterly.

He never had, and he wouldn't start now.

"Now why would I do that?" Robb looked down, kicked at a metal sealbin simmering with refuse. It was a surprising move, making noise. The deep deadly rotting the bin held wasn't nearly as bad as a battlefield. "Was he still hanging there before you came home, or after?"

"I didn't think he deserved cutting down, Robb." *That*, too, was unvarnished truth. It had even given Ged a deep and probably improper sense of satisfaction to see the terror of Robb's childhood hanging lifeless from a fylm-twist. "Not after what he did to you."

"Great Under." Robb paled under his tan. "I'd love to hate you."

"Likewise." And nobody would ever know if that was the truth, since Ged himself was unsure. The trouble with Robb was that he had a core of decency, but it was covered up with so many layers of arrogance and damage you couldn't tell.

Well, that's the flame calling the kettle, isn't it, Gizabón? Right on schedule, the most uncomfortable thought in the world showed up. That was the other trouble with Robb; Ged *understood* him.

So did Marah, in her own way—or did she merely, simply care, empathy replacing comprehension?

Locke glanced away, hunching even more just like he had in secondary school when any teacher called on him. The moment passed. "You still salle at Korovo's?"

Why, you want me to crack you down again? "Every day I can."

"Maybe I'll come by." Robb's lupine grin lacked a few shades of its former self. Well, neither of them were in best condition, really. Not anymore. "Beat you up for old times' sake."

It would be satisfying to smash Locke's face in right now, Ged decided, but in a salle there was safety equipment. Still, the thought held its attractions. He kept his arms crossed so the tension in his hands wouldn't show. "I seem to remember I did most of the beating."

"Human memory's unreliable." Robb ducked his head a fraction, grinning like the fool he was. There was no shelf of golden hair for him to peer through, but the principle remained the same. You couldn't stay angry at him when he used that feckless expression.

Or at least, Marah couldn't. Giz had watched her soften each time, and tried to figure out how, by Moon and Logic both, to deploy the same careless insouciance.

It never worked, so Giz had decided on other methods. His own hair, too long for the Corps now, ruffled under the hot unsanitary breeze. "We could ask Will." The skarl had played sparring-score-keeper more than once before Marah found out and put a stop to *that*.

At least the prospect wiped the smile off Locke's fucking face. "You're an asshole." His scowl was the one usually reserved for teachers and and probably been deployed at Corps drill serjeants, too. Was that why he'd gone into the infantry, that utter incapability to keep his mouth shut or his arrogance camouflaged?

"Takes one to know one. Look, Robb...stay out of trouble, okay?" It wouldn't hurt to give a warning. And if Robb came across any post-humous presents from his old man, he might even bring them to Giz to be buried. It would at least show the ability to learn from the fucking past. "Marah's all I can handle."

"I bet you'd like to handle her." A younger Robb would have grinned, maybe even dug a toe into the alley floor to complete the picture and madden whoever he wanted to fight next.

Giz, however, had no intention of playing that stupid-ass secondary school game. "Why do you always have to go for the cheap shot?"

"That's what trash does, Gizabón. Take care of her, for me." With that, Robb pulled his hood up and swung away, stepping into the shuffle of the sidewalk crowd and vanishing.

He did love a dramatic disappearance, Locke's son. It was how he'd signed up for the Corps, one day here and the next gone, and Marah's absolute quiet on the matter was a warning all its own.

Giz's fingers ached, digging hard into his upper arms. Thin, pale scars crisscrossed his whitened knuckles, remnants of schoolyard scrapping. Locke and Giz, taking on all comers mostly together but also separately, and Marah scolding them. *Pocket credits for candy,* she'd said once, stamping her foot and glaring at them both. *You could get seriously hurt, and why? For no reason at all.*

After a while, nobody bet on their opponents. Had Robb thought they'd be there forever, two bloody-nosed kids in the scuffed dusty flat space downhill past the linkfence just off school grounds, hands sometimes wrapped and eyes always bright with hatred—oh, not of teachers, or school, or of other students, or even of progenitors, but of themselves?

Giz had outgrown his younger self. Or at least, he liked to think he had. But seeing Robb like this...

There wasn't even the prospect of bothering Marah to take the bitter taste from his mouth. She wasn't at the clinic today. Robb, thoughtless as ever, hadn't known, or he wouldn't have been there.

Did you change, or did you just become more of what you already were? It was an uncomfortable question, and not one he wanted answered, so Ged Gizabón shook his head and plunged deeper into the alley. There was yet another exit back here, on Via Kadinat. Robb, of course, would disdain an alternate. If he couldn't make a grand exit, he wouldn't even go.

Robbhan Locke was still the same; Giz was left wondering, uncomfortably, if *he* was, too.

PERSPECTIVE_

SUMMER DROUGHT CONTINUED THOUGH STORMS SAT OVER THE blue smear of Sharud Forest-clad mountains on the far horizon, flicking lazy heat-lightning between their billows and gathering strength enough to rush down onto the city. When they arrived the reservoirs and aquifers would refill, and wrights would curse at the lightning tending to strike wherever tethers were gathered en masse.

It didn't hurt ship, tether, or—thanks to the buffers—Terrans; the energy was even welcome, but the tingling was unpleasant.

That was in the future, though, and Sharud had other business. The Great Awakening marked the day the paired generation ships *Caster* and *Pollux*, close enough to Anglene to scan Terra-like planets and deploy its terraform pods, formally required the Second Echelon to aid the First in preparing for First Landfall. It was also the day those packed in Third and steerage began to be decanted, the ship's vast gestation chambers waking to their task, nurseries cycling through preliminaries. It also marked the day, a full two standards later, that the terraform pods completed their initial work and the first of Anglene's systems was declared borderline habitable.

This cycle, on Sagittarius Prime, the holiday fell on a Sixday; all of Sharud would fill with cheap flymsy masks and children in Old

Shiptime costumes, long and flowing. The First Landfall had been an affair of unisex jumpsuits and shorn hair even for the First Echelons moving into their alcazars; nobody dressed for *that*.

Small bits of candy would be given to children who shouted *"Ship or shore!"* at any doorway, adults smiling indulgently as they passed out sucrose and glucose by the handful or drib-drab. Come evening, costumed revelers would gather in squares or at private celebrations to drink clear fiery *riuma* or bitter, traditional thin-ale and shout when the countdown began, a model of the Great Ship descending a pole in each planetary capital to touch the ground at a synchronized moment. It was a day of feasting and candy, a night of celebration, and the day afterward was famous for two inevitables: hangovers and fresh pregnancies for those who wanted them. Ten lunar divisions after the Awakening was the most auspicious birthday possible, and even in the First Echelon, where breeding an heir was a careful process, applications, inseminations, and decanting went in festival waves.

The streets were crowded, restaurants jammed, those scheduled to work receiving triple pay and a bonus, and every financial centre was closed from Sixday through Tenday.

Which made the afternoon before—Fiveday, Awakening Eve— the best time for what Alladal had in mind. It was a hot, hazy day, with those thick thunderheads over the mountains promising muggy almost-relief once the autumn rains moved in.

Soon, but not soon enough. The rains traditionally arrived after the Race, and that was still tendays away.

Hood, settled on the roof of the Gantry Depot a half-block from the Helmsman Credit building's glow-white facade, pulled his hood up a little further. This knee-length jacket was new, Corps surplus sold cheap at a depot between the Saur and the port facilities, a good base for long-ranger's camouflage. The hood kept his eyes shaded and his hair from gleaming, but he'd rubbed loader-grease into his scalp just in case.

It was like he'd never been away, really, except he didn't have a ryfl. Instead, the ibow, a graceful curve of graphite-colored tensemetal, was inert and untraceable. It was an Echelon weapon, a reminder of Terra's ancient past like the isabre. Where the isabre was a cutting edge, though, the ibow used a konstans-cell to run the string and cycle up the energy bolt. It had slightly less range than a ryfl, but the bolts would cut right through two Terran bodies before lodging in a third and burning like a score-popper. You could even fold its arms in for carrying, and it didn't show on bodyscans.

The comm in his left ear emitted a pleasant tone. He checked the thin circuitry wrapglove on his right hand again; without it to channel and buffer the force, you could slice your own fingers off with the string.

It was a metaphor, but for just what he didn't want to decide yet. You had to save up things to think about while you were waiting for the shooting to start, because if you ran out there was nothing but your nerves stringing tighter and tighter. Plenty of soldats didn't break in battle; it was the waiting that drove them from stable orbit.

The comm emitted another tone, slightly lower than the first. Everything was going as expected. He might not even have to do anything, and could pick up a lookout's portion of the take for just a few hours spent under withering sunshine. He had his retreat mapped out, and had spent two days wandering the area.

Recon was a lot easier when you weren't being shot at or whisped every time you stuck a phalange out of cover.

Marah would be disappointed in him. Or not, if she was patching up Alladal after the pale-haired woman's various not-quite-legal hijinks. Singing kulturtrash-ballad and plaintrash chieweed almost nightly at the Camyron was a helluva cover, though. Who would suspect a dip-brained showgirl with a cloud of teased platinum hair of masterminding a credit heist?

Still, it was a long way from running smuggled goods to this. Robb hadn't asked what Al wanted all this credit for.

It was probably safer that way.

Robb's nape prickled. He thumbed the ibow's scanlock; it verified his gene-and-thumbprint and woke with a slight hum. There was nothing on the comm. All he had was instinct, but *that* bitch was shouting like feedback from one of the Camyron's man-high speakers.

There. He peered at the street, sparing a grim smile as he realized what he was seeing.

The crowd was thinning, people rapidly choosing doorways or other shelter, and it wasn't difficult to figure out why. It wasn't Robb, of course—nobody ever thought to look *up*, especially if it was raining. You had to specifically train soldats to keep track of the high ground if you didn't want them capped right off the combat jump. Modern warfare required three-sixty awareness, the training films drilled it into you endlessly and what they didn't reach your sarje would—by dint of sheer volume, not to mention physical brutality—during introductory camp.

But it was his *other* Corps training, more specialized, that brought Hood up into easy stance, the hood shaken down and a bolt nocked, the ibow string humming as he pulled back and released in one smooth motion, his exhale pausing just before he let fly. The bolt blurred, whining right before it struck the parked khibi just to the right of a beetling black polis bus creeping, lights on but siren hushed, for Helmsman Credit.

That was why the street had magically emptied, and it relieved him of worry about civilian casualties just as he realized the prospect didn't upset him as much as it should.

Robb drew again, the world narrowing to a single small point, and the next bolt punched through the bus's back just as the parked khibi exploded, peppering the street with shrapnel. A glance further up showed another polis bus approaching from the opposite direction, loaded to the gills with red-and-black riot-control fucknuggets. Swift calculations raised the ibow and he let fly a third time, the bolt's arc flattening as gravity sucked hungrily at energy temporarily forced into matter-density. Then he hopped down, doubled over and running, adrenaline coppery against the roof of his mouth and his heartbeat pounding in his ears, the ibow transferred so he could press on the comm in his left ear once, twice, thrice. *Front's watched, get out now.*

He cut across the depot's roof, dodging climate-control and imanec-energy hoods, glancing up to make sure the sky was still clear —it was, but that wasn't going to last now that bolts had been fired. They'd think it was a ryfl; who used an ibow anymore? Some hunting fanatics, maybe, but those Echelons, no matter how high, were ostracized by polite society.

Murder was apparently a matter of perspective. The war required plenty of the same historical skills those fanatics were always whining about practicing. The long-rangers who straight-out liked killing did well in Corps bureaucracy, slithering through papier, fylm, and flymsy. They got whisped regularly in brothels or tai-houses, though.

Idiots. Much better to do something you were good at, maybe even great at, but disliked just enough to keep you alive. Even if you got used to it, and found out the dislike was draining away under hard use like a jacket worn by loader controls.

Robb leapt, his grab-boots leaving stick-pebbled roofing and grav pulling at him just as it did on matterbeams; landed *hard*, the ibow flexing in its carry-mode as he rolled; then he was up again and heading for the vantage point for the alternate exit. He skidded to a stop, snapped another glance overhead—still clear, it was a matter of seconds now before the polis realized they weren't looking at a stop-and-snatch but an actual full-scale robbery—and went to one knee, the jolt clicking his teeth together painfully as he snapped the ibow back out and drew yet again. There was another polis bus heading down Via Seigneur duNord.

You're good at this, Marah had said once during Physical Conditioning in secondary school, her hair pulled in a careless tail and her own shots close but not quite hitting home. They'd used training bows then, just plain lasers instead of matterbeams, Echelon teenagers learning arcane historical skills. *I keep breathing at the wrong time.*

Oh, she'd be disappointed, yes. It was a good thing he wasn't going to see her again.

Right?

In this space, with the ibow string cycling up to a high hum and the bolts flying, one-two-three because the polis were covering this entrance too, he didn't have to think. There was only target, sighting, breathing, release.

Lips skinned back, his breath tied to the ibow's cycling, Robb Locke rained bolts from a clear blue sky.

PART 2
AWAKENING NIGHT_

SILVER LINING_

"Where the *fuck* are you?" Notheim snarled from the floating comm-disc tethered to the Corps surplus desk—just folding legs holding up a reasonably flat surface, there was no need for anything expensive. Calls were bounced a couple times before arriving at this location, a standard precaution for intelligence-gathering Corpsoldat, since this was the closest thing to home Ged allowed himself.

"Getting ready for the Ball." Giz rubbed at his hair with a towel, peering at the projection as he settled behind said desk, on an uncomfortable but supposedly ergonomic kneelchair. The place wasn't much—a walk-up studio, kept bare and anonymous—but its location was central, and in a low-risk slice of Sharud to boot, just west enough of downtown to make the neighborhood quirky, only moderately expensive, and easy to find a midnight meal or supplies within a block or two. "I'm off duty for the next three days, remember?"

"Great. Just great." The Sharl's face, rendered lovingly in three dimensions above the flat disc of the projector, contorted with pixilated fury. The color balance turned his dusky choler a fetching shade of pink, but Giz was pretty sure Notheim wouldn't want to be told as much. "While you're on *vacation*, dancing and dining, someone just stole the polis payroll and reserves from Helmsman Credit."

Ah. "I told you they'd been having false alarms lately, probably as test runs." It wasn't that surprising, but Giz had done his duty. There was nothing to fault *him* for in this, he'd also suggested moving the payroll runs to Torix, which would slow the process but was well-nigh impregnable.

Unfortunately, when Noth was worked up, Giz was a tempting target. "Why didn't you double the guard detail?" he spluttered.

"I *tripled* it, and moved three Rapid Response Teams into the area as well." *You're not pinning this on me.* Giz's formal clothes, carefully laid out on the Corps surplus cot he couldn't seem to stop sleeping on, were a black and white skin, ready to be buttoned, tied, and buckled. There was no *way* Noth was going to have him come in and deal with this, he'd done all he could and tonight, of *all* nights, by Logic. "The roster and the plan were given to Lieutenant Quarl."

Quarl was one of Noth's favourites, it would be interesting to see how that little cloud-haired rodentia-fucker managed *this* event.

Noth's lip twitched, and so did his right eyelid. Between the two, his face was a field sown with thermal 'nades, pebbles popping when a pulse went overhead. "Someone shot up the polis buses."

"Quarl put the RRTs on *buses?*" Giz's eyebrows fought to rise, he forced them back down. It probably wasn't very wise of him to enjoy this call, but he was starting to. "That's...unusual." The word for it was *unprofessional*, with a side helping of *completely stupid*, but he didn't need to say as much.

From the look on Noth's face, he already knew. "Trundled them right for the front door. Even the one coming around the backside of the bank was hit. It's a mess." Now the man visibly remembered who he was talking to, and turned on the charm—what little he possessed, to be sure. "I could use you, you know."

"I'm sorry, sir." In other words, Giz wasn't going to bite. Noth couldn't *demand* a battlefield-commissioned Second Echelon come in, and Giz would probably pay for this intransigence later.

Well enough. The longer this went on, the more he hated this job and longed to be free of it. If not for his overarching objective he could retire to now-hereditary Tabor, but that would put him half a planet away from Sharud. He could probably take quarters in the city and continue handling all the Tabor business remotely, though. He'd done his duty to society, nobody could say he hadn't.

And yet here he was, to the bitter end. Which was looking more bitter all the time, and less likely to arrive within a few standards.

Noth's eyelid kept twitching though a pained, reasonably polite smile forced up the corners of his mouth. His jacket was hastily thermasealed, and the folds would make him look even more rumpled when he stood up. "Well, I can't blame you. This is a storm of shaggoshit and no mistake."

That's putting it mildly. Giz decided to throw the canid a bone. "I'll be in to deal with the papierwork after the festival." Papier and flymsy, the tide that could swallow Terran intelligence—of any class —whole. Giz couldn't complain, though. He hated field work just as much.

Hated, and was good at. Maybe the Great Logic had decided to have some fun with the fifth Third Echelon owner of Tabor, since all the others had been career climbers given a tiny non-hereditary estate for various services to Aegis or Helm. Ged's own progenitor, an Aegis civil climber who also consulted for corporate combines, had never pushed him one way or the other—probably because she knew it wasn't in her son to rest.

Mère had, for all her faults, never stinted on loving her surrogated son, or accepting him.

Giz had finally broken Tabor's long history of being a petty changeabout benefice, but it had meant accepting quite a few tethers —and his mother was a casualty of a redband terrorist's bombing of an Aegis cruiser off Aquarius Tertius's smaller moon during the First Uprising.

And that meant Giz went into the Corps. A man couldn't win for losing, especially if he had any brains and a half-decent set of reflexes, not to mention stirrings of a conscience now and again.

"You lucky bâtard." Noth jabbed a fingertip at him, the phalange cut off outside the disc's edge, a nice clean bloodless slice. "Fucking Quarl. Buses. *Buses*."

One last jab, maybe, to make Noth's fury and Quarl's discomfiture complete. "The tac vehicles were available, I signed the req order myself." All *that* papierwork was in order, too. Attention to such details came naturally, and was probably the only reason he'd gotten promoted.

That, and lucking onto a prime redband cell in his very own battalion. Those fuckers had shown signs of almost-professionalism, but Ged saw his chance and took it. It hadn't taken long, the lawbreakers vanished into the maw of Corrective Enhancement and the battalion was saved from Logic only knew how many ambushes.

Passing intelligence to rebels was a fool's game unless it was done very, very carefully indeed, and attention to detail had served him well *there* too. It had gained him the attention of a certain high-ranking recruiter, as well.

"Yeah, well, they had ryfls and peppered the buses." Noth's eyelid-twitches smoothed out and he looked sour now, which was a sure sign he had decided what to do with the hapless Quarl. If the young officer survived, it would take plenty of work to regain his patron's favour. "Blew up a khibi too. I've got dead officers with pensions to sort out and the payroll's gone."

Parl Jun won't be happy about that. There was nothing Giz could do; to prove it and drive the point home he draped the towel around his neck and spread his hands, an *I surrender* movement that was only true on the surface. He had no intention of going in to clean this mess up. "At least the pensions aren't funded from our particular budget?" They were, in fact, an Aegis concern, and those bureaucrats weren't going to be happy either.

"Silver lining on a shaggoshit sandwich," Noth growled, and, finally resigned to dealing with this by his own merry self, cut the connection.

Ged leaned back in the kneechair, its familiar squeak comforting and unheard. His damp, naked back was cold, but he didn't feel it. He steepled his fingers and stared at the space where Noth's head had sat in empty air, barking its empty rage.

He had to get ready; it wouldn't do to look disheveled next to the Lady of Madán. Maybe Robb could pull off "handsomely rumpled" in black and whites, but Giz knew very well *he* couldn't. If there was any attractiveness to his equine nose, strong chin, and thin lips, it lay in the region of cold precision.

You worked with what you had, ever and always. One of Mère's favourite sayings, and it had done them both well. Had she thought of him those last few moments before the cruiser shredded? Or had depressurization been complete, total, and quick?

He hoped for the latter, but would never know. Except in his nightmares, and those were hideous—but mercifully, completely transient.

Ged shook his head slightly, returning to the matter at hand. It took a special kind of nerve, not to mention inside information, to rob a polis payroll. Credit oblongs—physical, fluid, leaving very little trace—were a necessary evil, even with fittle transfers tying the great web of Anglene commerce together. Helmsman Credit was almost as old as terraforming, and well-respected. They'd bounce back, it was what insurance was for.

Something about it bothered Giz immensely, but the thought lingered just out of mental reach. He finally consigned it to the care of his subconscious, hauled himself up, and returned to dressing, frowning into the mirror over the small bathroom sink. Even his primary in-city quarters were spartan in the extreme; Tabor was stable but not rich and besides, luxury ill befit a polis capitain, even one who had served in the Corps with distinction.

At least when he'd been trapped in battles or breaking redband cells he hadn't had time to brood.

It wasn't until he had sworn twice and restarted his tie each time that the answer came out of the floor of his conscious mind, tiptoeing in like a small, cautious feline.

What if someone wasn't playing two criminals against each other for a bargain? What if, say, Figes and Kube the Rattus were holding onto arms shipments because a buyer was collecting funds?

Ged glanced at the small clock set on his old, familiar white-painted wooden nightstand, the only part of home he'd ever allowed himself to bring to Sharud. Consigning the entire question to the back of his mind for further chewing would impair his enjoyment of the evening, but it couldn't be helped.

A few minutes later, Ged Gizabón picked up his long black formal coat, shrugged into it, gave himself a last glance in the scrap of fuse-mirror hanging on the back of his apartment door, and nodded at the lean, lupine fellow he found there.

Business could wait. There was dancing to be done.

AWAKENING BALL_

THE WAR WAS OVER AND CELEBRATION NO LONGER A SHAMEFUL luxury; the great Community Dome was garlanded with bunting and bright flymsy baubles last seen over five standards ago or made in a splurge of celebration in the past few metric months of demobilization and Peace Parades. Champagne from cultivars brought over uncounted space-gulfs and plasma'd into adapting to their new terraformed terroirs flowed; men and women in costumes of Old Shiptime or newer, more utilitarian fashions thronged. The Great Table was announced this year, as was traditional; during the war standards the Dome had been shuttered and those who wished to celebrate visited Discipline temples and abbeys to pray for peace—or threw private parties that skirted but did not *quite* flaunt the sumptuary laws.

And, of course, this year there didn't appear to be the risk of riots spurred by rationing or security measures. At least, not on Sagg Prime.

It was early yet; the Great Table was behind sealed doors and the dancing at this hour was merely the province of the very young before they were packed into private transports to be taken home to synthetic or Terran nannies. The grand stairway was not quite a bustle yet, moving along at a reasonable clip. Marah, announced by the herald and greeted with a wave of polite applause—plus more than one long speculative glance—was almost relieved when Giz appeared, tall and broad-shouldered in strictly traditional black and white, and bent over her hand like a pre-Shiptime knight.

"You look lovely," he said by way of greeting as Marah flowed into a curtsy. "But you should have waited an hour or so, to be fashionably late."

"Now why would I want to do that?" Marah smiled as he straightened, and her nervousness eased all at once. Sometimes it took a dance or two before she loosened up, but not tonight. It helped that high-waisted Old Shiptime dresses were based on Revivale Grecque designs, part peplos and part Tosca Directoire. They were comfortable, even if heeled shoes left a little to be desired. Her back and calves would ache tomorrow, but it was worth it. "How long were you lying in wait?"

Giz, trim-waisted and well-tailored, looked almost as he had before the war. Even his hair was growing out, stubbornly resisting the iron grip he kept on every part of his grooming. "I just arrived." It could even be true. He indicated the blue ribbon knotted loosely around her left wrist, dangling a simple lead medallion pressed with the formal Madán Mizar seal. "And glad I did. May I have that?"

There was no reason to refuse, and Marah was aware of several gazes on them as she assented gracefully and slipped the favour from her wrist, threading it through the buttonhole on his sleeve. Nowadays, favours were more a conversation piece than actual statements of intent, and she'd long alternated between allowing Robb and Giz to take them at events.

Something pinched high up behind her left ribs and Marah's face hardened, her smile kept afloat only by tether.

"Now we can get to the real business." Ged pretended not to notice, offering his arm and taking her in tow, a warship shepherding a small yacht. "Champagne?"

"Mother Moon, yes." She ran a practiced eye over the gathering-tables—everyone had settled into their pre-war quadrants, First and Second Echelon groups rayed in power and influence, some few of the larger Third at the fringes to attend their betters. The gaps were evident—not everyone had returned, but there were the Panárs and the Medillíns, their circles still hip-to-shoulder. Old Simon Medillín was there, with his youngest son sitting stiffly at the table while his father stood and declaimed some bit of nonsense masquerading as policy to brightly-dressed, politely listening clients. "I thought you'd never ask."

"You look like you're expecting something unpleasant." Giz kept his tone light as he inserted them into the milling at the edge of the central dance floor. Of course he'd know where her table was; he believed in recon. He probably already knew the menu, too, and just how much clients had paid for their tickets. Patrons were supposed to defray that cost, but buying your way in was a time-honoured way to perhaps pick *up* a patron.

"Not exactly." Her own clients were free to celebrate as they pleased, knowing their patron disdained business at such gatherings. Marah let him navigate, taking in the crowd. With her hand resting in the crook of Giz's elbow, she didn't have to watch her step; he'd steer them both around trouble. "I saw Robb." A smattering of First Echelons, a throng of Second, a trickle of Third, a crowd of business and shipping magnates with their trophy spouses and avid stares, corporate combine representatives on expense accounts, Aegis and Helm functionaries, high-ranking Bookmen and Bookmira—it was strange not to see grey-robed or veiled lunar emissaries sprinkled through the crowd.

Parl Jun hadn't lifted the restriction on the Moon's temples yet, and that made Marah even more uneasy. Freedom of religion was a core Anglene right, legally unassailable. There would be court challenges soon.

"I've seen him too." Ged didn't look surprised in the least, which was usual but hardly comforting. He subtracted a tall fluted ship-glass full of bubbly from a passing blue-jacketed swabbie, handing it to Marah with a practiced gesture and inclining his head to the boy, who had turned visibly pale as he recognized Noth's Ryfl. "He came through in one piece."

I'm not so sure about that. Marah tried to catch the swabbie's eye and give an encouraging smile, but the uniformed kid hurried away. "He wants to give me Lamóre, *droit de majeure.*"

"Shoving off a rotted manse and four tenants onto you." Giz indicated a table set at the northern arc of the dance floor, its linens edged with First Echelon piping. Neat place-cards showed where her clients would settle, should they choose to attend. His lip threatened to curl. "Typical."

I will not bolt the entire glass at once. Marah took down half of it instead, and glanced at the neighboring tables. "You know how many tenants he has?" There was Serafina Panár, with her honey hair cropped Corps-short, heading for the bar with a determined step as her youngest brother Federic, just attaining his majority, trailed her anxiously. The absences—classmates, peers, Marah's age or Giz's— were empty tooth-sockets. Younger siblings had grown into adults, orphans stood solemnly next to grandparents, and the black bands of the bereft, whether mourning child, parent, or spouse, ran through bright fabric or lurked at formal cummerbunds.

"Noth had me go through the papierwork." Giz even managed to say it lightly.

To make you complicit, no doubt. "Where is the Sharl, anyway?" The central city-political table held Sharud's Maior and the Aegis's Civilian Commissioner along with their usual keel-cloggers, but there was no sight of round, oil-haired Notheim. It wasn't like him to miss a dance or a chance to widen his net of clients.

"Business called." Giz's mouth curled up on one side. "I'll tell you later, when we've both had more to drink. But only if you save me the last dance."

"Marah!" A cheerful light tenor rang out; a fair-haired, coppery man in a sharp-creased Corps Specialty Pilot dress uniform hurried through the throng. "You've arrived. Splendid."

"Bren." Of course he'd want to waylay her. She tried to sound pleased, and had to slip her hand free to offer it as Giz tensed beside her. "How pleasant to see you again." It was a lie, of course. A complete and total untruth.

Bren Harabón made a show of examining her wrist. "Ah, it appears I'm once again too late."

You were too late in primary school, sir. Two could play at that game, though. "How can that be? They haven't opened the Great Table yet, have they, Ged?" Which rather neatly underscored that he was being rude by not greeting Gizabón.

"Well, the *infantry* always gets their hands on any loot." Bren's teeth had been recently repaired, it looked like, and his left leg was a little stiff. War wounds he would milk with insufferable moaning, of course. He straightened, dropping her hand like it was the wrong end of a live isabre. "We sky-simians have to be content with doing our duty."

"*Duty is the curse of an Echelon*," she quoted. *Did you just compare me to stolen wartime goods?* Marah leaned into Giz's side and replaced her hand on his arm, smiling beatifically and raising her bubbly glass a trifle. Robb would have already bristled at Little Hairy Harabón, but Giz merely stood, straight and sardonic, content to let her handle this. "How is your mother, Bren? The last time I saw her was at Corps induction. That would have been, what, second standard of the war?"

In other words, she was *quite* aware that his uniform was almost a mothball commission, unearned rank bought at the last moment before the surrender in order not to miss out on the glory. It wasn't precisely his fault—his older sister Bryde was the Hero of Secca, and he'd always been held in reserve by their anxious parents while the headstrong Heir made her mark. Little brother had endured one major accident as a pilot, at least—though whether it was combat-related was an open question.

Giz probably knew, but Marah would have to drink far more before she felt like asking.

"Maybe." Bren's smile didn't falter either, but any warmth in his tone promptly fled. "Gizabón."

"Hullo, Officier-Cadet Harabón," Giz purred, giving the boy his proper rank in archaic Corps slang. "Is your sister here? I wouldn't mind her favour too."

Marah downed the other half of her champagne as Bren turned scarlet. Giz outranked him, and had been in combat to boot. It was an unexpectedly satisfying thing to see Harabón taken down a tether or two; he'd been insufferable at Giz all through secondary school.

"Oh, look," she managed, after swallowing hastily. "I think Ama Anadár's over there, and I simply must speak to her. Ged, will you escort me? Bren, do give my best to your mother."

As soon as they were a decent distance away, Ged gave a strangled sound very much like a laugh, and Marah signaled another swabbie bearing a tray. "You shouldn't have done that," she muttered, discharging her empty glass with honours and reloading with practiced speed.

"I know." Ged did not sound remorseful in the least. "But he deserved it."

"Marah!" someone else called, and she smiled, acknowledging. There were a few people here she should sound out, either for the clinic or just to stay informed.

Fortunately, she didn't have to be exactly sober to do either, this cycle. Her practice of discouraging business or policy on Awakening Night was well known, and instituted long ago.

"Don't worry, Lady of Madán." Ged put his free hand over hers. "I'll be a good little soldat for the rest of the evening."

"See that you do," Marah said, and laughed.

MANY DRINK TRAYS had been plundered and her head was pleasantly abuzz, so after several turns paying her respects, extracting clinic subscription promises, and dancing with others she accepted Giz's bow and moved out onto the floor. Robb always danced like he wanted to be somewhere else, frowning slightly as he counted along with the rhythm; Giz, on the other hand, only looked slightly thoughtful and steered her adroitly through the clockwork whirl of step, turn, sway, step again. Antique instruments— stringed, synthesized, or reproduced—in kulturworkers' practiced hands kept a steady beat and played all the traditional valses, reels, trots, tuerks, rondeaus, mazurques, elektraslide, and more.

You could almost believe the war had never happened, except for the scar on Giz's neck, the ache in her left hip, and the Corps dress uniforms sprinkled through the crowd. The massive clock at the southern end of the Dome had black mourning ribbons twined in its carved frame as it counted down to the Awakening, to match the similar ribbons on more than a few sleeves.

The rhythm shifted to a valse, and Giz handled the step-change adroitly. There was no *letting* him steer, he simply *did* it, and it was an unexpected relief to have someone else piloting for once. Marah's shoulders relaxed the last fraction. Time for another tradition, and one she rather liked. "What's your question this standard?"

Giz's brief smile was a reward all its own. "It's a good one." He pushed and she swung free, her skirt belling; when he brought her back she performed an extra tanquo-kick and laughed as he worked it into the rhythm without missing a beat.

But he said nothing else, so she had to prod. "Well?" Was he reserving it for after the countdown? He never had before. It was almost a relief Robb wasn't here, he always looked so patently miserable when the formal wear came out.

Giz, though, could dance all night. Once or twice, growing up, they had—and gone for breakfast afterward, feeling utterly daring like the young always did.

"All right." Electric light glowed in his dark hair. "If you could go anywhere, and do anything, what would you do? And before you say something about the clinic, don't. I'm asking what plain simple Marah would like to do, if she had the chance."

"That's a good one, but you've asked me that before." She could almost smell young green hay again as they lay amid the ripening, Giz on his back with his arms laced under his head, Marah weaving a crown out of broken stalks. How old had they been? Thirteen standards, fourteen? Somewhere around there, and the conversation started then wove down through cycles, returning often and somehow never worn out.

"I have." Ged's grin, for once, held no bitterness or distance. "Never for the Ball."

"I suppose that's true." The pace quickened slightly, musicians signaling a change when the valse finished, but they had a while to go yet.

Giz let her think, the clockwise flow on the parquet floor of Forest Preserve hardwood a river holding their tiny raft. This close, she could smell his soap and a faint edge of live ion-crackle from daily isabre practice.

"Since you ask..." The answer was ridiculously simple, but it wasn't the one she'd given the first time. They were both too old for *that* particular fantasy. "I'd get a ship, and I'd go."

Giz steered them just southward of a tangle of Second Echelons. Someone had cut in, it looked like, and there was a moment of not-so-good-natured shoving. "Where?"

"Anywhere." *Away*, and all the freedom in the galaxy resting in those two little syllables. "Running salvage, passenger jaunts. See all of Anglene, and the outer belt."

"That sounds exciting." He nodded thoughtfully, and that was why this was his game instead of Robb's. He wasn't competitive in the same way—oh, he had his pride, certainly, but not like Robb Locke's prickly, khibiCAT-finicky desire to get there first, best, and quickest in order to avoid a beating.

"It's probably a lot of hunger and drudgery." Marah's ankle threatened to turn; Ged brought her neatly back to center. If it was Robb, he simply would have picked her up and swung her; *his* private Ball tradition was laying private bets on when the first glove would be thrown, and by whom. Robb had an absolute genius for telling when a champagne-fueled temper was going to break. "But if I've to answer, that's it."

"And you have a question for me." Giz lifted his chin, glancing at the musicians. His profile was unexpectedly stern, blue eyes glowing. Those recessives might have given him bad luck, but there was a certain exoticism to his light gaze, unexpected in such a classically severe face.

"I'm going to have to think of a different one." Marah relaxed again, into the warm relief of not having to watch traffic. "Mine was lighthearted."

"And mine wasn't?" But he acknowledged the parry with a wry glance before returning his attention to their route through a constantly moving salvage field. "I could use a lighthearted one, though. Ask what you like, Marah."

And that was the trouble. Ged was too easy, and Robb was too difficult. If only the two of them could somehow be merged...If they could, though she probably wouldn't feel anything for the resultant mediocrity.

I'd make a shitty husband, Marah. Especially for you. It didn't help that Robb was, in that matter, undeniably correct. "Do you ever wish things were different?" She sounded wistful, and it surprised her. She'd meant to ask something else, but maybe the bubbly was loosening more than a few neurons.

A cheer went up on the eastern edge of the Dome. Either someone had thrown the first glove, or there had been a particularly fine bit of dancing. The crowd thickened, more merrymakers pouring in. The gaps weren't so glaring now, but the new faces were everywhere. Even her own table held a knot of clients, people she knew and sometimes liked but didn't want to speak to if she could avoid it.

"In general, or do you mean specific things?" A line appeared between Ged's dark eyebrows. It wasn't quite puzzlement, just a longing for precision. Robb, of course, would have taken the question the wrong way.

"Either." Marah sometimes wished she shared Robb's double gift for holding grudges and taking offense. If she'd been born with a scratch on her circuits like he had, would all this be easier? Would she just not care, the way Robb seemed to? "Both."

"Now what would be the point of that?" Giz shook his dark head, his hand warm and sure at the small of her back. "I deal with things as they are, Marah. It's my coping mechanism."

"Not a bad one." There was a faint buzzing at her belt; the tiny sequined incidentals bag fastened there was waking up. Why had she slipped her rister into its throat?

You never want to have any fun, Robb had said more than once, and she supposed it was true. Ged read her expression and executed a complex turn, aiming them for the outer edge. He would bring them out near her table so she could check whatever priority message had landed and make her appearance among her clients. Before the war he might have made a sarcastic comment about those who came to check their data instead of dance, but if he was tempted, he kept it to himself.

It was one more change, even if a welcome one, and the champagne turned to vinegar in Marah's empty stomach. Nothing was different, and everything was.

She settled into what she hoped was an acceptable expression, denying the urge to bite her lower lip, and dreaded the end of the valse.

AT HOME_

THEY'D SCATTERED AFTER THE HEIST, LAYING LOW WHILE Alladal moved the freight for washing, and now, Awakening Day instead of the Eve, the songbird was making the rounds and Hood found himself suspecting he was her last stop. It didn't matter; the *Admiral's Bliss* on Via 1215 was packed to the gunnels and rolling like an O-house a day after a Corps company comes in from long-range patrol.

"You just get more and more interesting." Alladal's turban for the evening was blue-striped linen, wrapped expertly tight and turning her head into a temple statue's. Somehow, on her, it didn't look like part of a tablecloth pressed into service. "I upped your percentage, in view of your meritorious service."

Some women just had that natural air, like Marah. Or maybe he was getting to know Alladal; familiar topography was more pleasing than the dangerous unknown.

"Split it to the team." Hood hunched, drawing further into the shadowed booth. The bag with his cut of the heist lay between them on the shabby red pleather bench, an anonymous grey satchel used for carrying subscription sheet-flymsies before they were plastered on lamp-posts and unattended fences. "I just did my job."

"Mh. Your line here is *thank you, Al.*" She lifted her drink—a vile blue cherra Rambeau instead of ale, a middling-expensive celebration anyone else would think was in honour of the holiday—but barely wet her lips. Maybe he *wasn't* the last delivery of the day. "Followed closely by *when's the next one?*"

"Is there a next one?" He wasn't going to thank her. What was the point? The money was in return for his services, and they were even, quit-claim the way you couldn't be with a friend. Adding anything else would be superfluous, even if you did like someone's nose.

"You interested?" One of Alladal's dark, freshly manicured eyebrows lifted. Maybe it was an expression she was copying from Marah; it looked Logic-be-damned familiar.

It was strange to be sitting in a Sharud pub drinking instead of poured miserably into formal black-and-white—or hunched in a stinking hide and watching for movement. He restrained the urge to check his rister; he didn't need to be on time for anything tonight. Still, he couldn't help but wonder if the Ball had started yet.

It was after dark, so Marah was probably dancing. "Maybe." Hood decided pretending to stare into his untasted ale was the best course of action. "But I need a few details before I commit."

At least the persistent thoughts of her were safe, and only embarrassing if he admitted to them.

A knot of muscular Corps vets, demobbed but in their ceremonials for the occasion, was at the bar sending up a shout of merriment, the stripes on their uniforms glittering like venomous anurae on some Capricorn moons. Not only that, but there were hard knots of men and women with their haircuts shouting *polis* scattered through the crowd. Alladal was probably testing his nerves, sitting in the same damn bar as a bunch of off-duty polis as well as drunken veterans. Hood kept an eye on them; imbibing heavily and looking for trouble was an Awakening tradition.

Marah *would* be at the Ball by now. She loved dancing, and was in demand every time the music started. The rest of the Echelons would be stuffing their faces at the Dome, pouring down pre-Ship style liquor, and generally behaving like the Terran capitalists they were descended from.

Capitalist, that quasi-obscene word, meaning heedless endemic cruelty instead of the planned inherent malice of *communist*. Both fought over Old Terra like pythonidae, squeeze-suffocating what they couldn't eat outright. Ship society, on the other hand, was supposed to be equal—even steerage had rights—but also focused, everyone doing their job as the inimical outsides pressed upon a thin hull of safety. Science and merit were supposed to have built the ships themselves; hard logic was supposed to have planned the Echelons at the same time, as well as ways to move between them if you had enough talent.

They said all classes had been taken on the generation ships, but Robb had his doubts. It just didn't seem possible, unless Terrans had been vastly different back then. Evolution was supposed to make people better, but from what he'd absorbed in school of Old Terra's history and the centuries of petty parliamentary squabbles after First Landfall, it didn't seem to be sticking.

Then again, those centuries since Landfall hadn't seen flat-out civil war. Polis actions and fractional, factional villein uprisings scattered in odd corners, sure, but it had taken a while for Terrans to start the wholesale slaughter.

And now Riccar Planetagen was out looking for a new galaxy to infest, leaving Anglene to the tender mercies of his brother.

Someone banged on a table, and another shout went up. Live feeds from the Dome hung over the harried bartenders on humming tethers, whisper-thin screens showing the great semicircular steps crowded with a brightly dressed throng celebrating the loosening of the wartime sumptuary laws. If Father was alive he'd be at the Ball too, circulating through the dim rest chambers where policy was discussed, Echelons mixed with their peers, and those there on sufferance—politicians, ranking civil servants, or meritorious clients brought to fill a quota—cast their choknets for patronage.

You never wanted to bring too *few* clients to the Ball. Not if you wanted to claw up the ladder to the open deck, and that was his father's entire purpose.

Did hanging in the free air count? Was he satisfied now, after all his striving?

"You don't seem like the committing type, Locke." Alladal's smile was a thin scrim of ice over churning ocean, almost as fey as Hood felt. Pulling off a criminal act agreed with her, if she was feeling the glow even after a whole planetary revolve. "You're going to need a new name eventually, you know. And ident."

"Only if I keep hanging around you." Nobody cared what Robb Locke did, where he went, or who he saw. He'd made sure of as much. "Which I'm not at all sure I want to."

"You're gonna break my heart." She slid for the end of the booth, but Robb grabbed her closest wrist. She didn't try to immediately tear away, probably because he didn't squeeze, just made a loose tether.

"Wait." He kept his gaze fixed on the screens, letting his peripheral vision do what it was designed for and feed him flickers of information.

Direct looks, no matter the temptation, were a recipe for fixation. If you weren't zeroed on your target, staring only meant you were ignoring your surroundings and just begging for a whisp between the ribs, or a grenade up close and snuggly.

"Well?" Alladal finally twisted for his thumb, a reflex that told him a great deal, but went still when Hood clamped down. "What?"

"Just wait," he muttered. Couldn't she *feel* that? Sometimes the violence circled like selachii, a requin not quite hungry enough to bite, but alcohol loosened Terran inhibition and postwar relief ripped the guard-tethers off completely.

One of the polis drinkers dropped a glass, and a wave of rough laughter swept the room. That was bad enough, but from the dark depths of the tables near the short, malodorous hall leading to the pisser came a snatch of whistling.

Someone else took up the refrain in high, chanting cadence. It was a redband song, a derivative little ditty with a chorus all about earning a spot on the Moon's bright side by whisping your quota of Corps grunters. Some rogue chieweed had turned it into an instahit all over the holos, with only minor word substitutions to get around the anti-incitement ordinances.

"*Shit,*" Alladal breathed, and Hood agreed completely. The head bartender, a lean coppery man in a natty white Festival shirt, shot a glance under the bar, telegraphing either his hiding spot or crowd-control weapon—maybe even both—and the entire place took a deep inhale before the explosion.

"Back door," Hood barked, and let go of Al's wrist.

HE GAVE A PRETTY good account of himself, too, before someone snatched a half-full bottle from the bar's mirrored shelves and tossed it onto his skull. He didn't even feel the cut from one sharp edge; the impact staggered him for a bare few seconds, training sending him into an infantryman's crouch next to the bar's bulk. Alladal had the remains of a barstool and jabbed at a staggering floppy-haired polis, slicing a heavy thermaseal coat and digging a bloody furrow along the man's ribs. It wasn't really a battle—there was no roar of artillery, no pop-pow of mortars, and the screams were mostly baffled anger instead of the desperate throat-tearing cries of soldats holding their own guts and begging for a mother, *any* mother, to rescue them.

But it was a fight nonetheless. Alladal grabbed the back of his jacket and hauled; Hood let her. It wasn't until sticky copper dripped into his eyes that he realized he was wounded, and another flying bottle whizzed past his nose as he hopped backward, trusting the turbaned woman to keep him from landing all a-pratfall.

The back door was blocked by liquor cartons, but fortunately, most of them were empty. Alladal shoved the battered barstool into his hands and began digging to clear a route. It was the battle of Pyr all over again, covering a retreat, except he had no hides and no ryfl, just a collection of metal tubing and half a wooden seat polished by a parade of drunken asses.

He crouched again, shoving a half-full crate of clicking, drained Samban bottles forward with a kick. Alladal cursed, her light tenor breaking, and the whine of an unholstered matterbeam repeater sent Robb diving for cover with thoughtless speed, dragging her down into a jumble of splintering thinwood and crushed cardstock flymsy. His head bounced against a corner, and oddly *that* one hurt, a starry jolt with soft darkness at the edges that was probably a microsecond of losing consciousness.

There was no time for thinking, but if there had been, he would have been amazed at how *familiar* it felt.

For the first time since the surrender, Robb Locke felt completely at home.

A CORPS JOKE_

Bright transient firework-flowers bloomed over the Saur, casting retinal shadows when the streets plunged back into night. Alladal kept her hand clamped over the rough field bandage made of Locke's own filthy loader's zipshirt, her arm aching with the pressure, and checked the side-street between Via Kadinat and Via Orbife again. Her headcover was loosening despite several tether-strong pins, and the headache hatching behind her temples was going to be a killer.

"I'm *fine*," young Locke said again, in a soft vacant tone she didn't much like. She couldn't tell if his pupils were dilated or not, and of course head wounds were messy but honestly, how much blood did he have *in* him? His coat was damn near dyed with claret. Maybe they pumped a double ration of high-pressure plasma into Corps vets, a performance enhancement. "Just fine."

"We're almost there." *I hope she wasn't dancing.* It was the Great Awakening, *everyone* should be dancing; it was just Al's luck to be hauling along a slab of unwashed, button-sealed male instead. Served her right for pulling off a game on a holiday Tenday; her nerves were still raw scoreburns. At least she'd saved Locke for last when it came to delivering the cuts, and at least he'd thrown himself on top of her when someone started firing.

It was downright Echelon-knightly of him, really. And he had his grey bag of shipshare, too.

"Hey, I know this part of town." Locke blinked rapidly, trying to get the blood out of his eyes, and his heavy boots clump-slid in a pool of some liquid it was probably better not to name.

"I'm sure you do," Al replied grimly, and hauled him down the alley. He smelled like sweat, loader grease, and the sourness of a healthy male who didn't believe in bathing, not to mention a copper tang that reminded her of used sanitary plugs.

Alladal wasn't grateful for much, but not having to endure *that* bit of bio was a blessing. Especially since Sana had waxed furious about cramps more than once. Sometimes the vat-grown glands gave Al a hot flash or a few days of irritability and craving sweets, but all in all, she had the better end of a bargain for once.

It was poor recompense for being born into the wrong body, but any payment was better than none.

Fortunately, she and her cargo didn't have to wait long, because a rattling khibi was just disgorging a vision in loose, flowing silvery material with dark shoulder-length hair bound by a fillet and her heels far too dainty for cracked, uneven Saur pavement.

It was a good thing nobody wanted to hang around a closed medical clinic near Via Kadinat on a night like this, or Marah would've been robbed before she went half a block, despite her reputation. Locke's chin fell almost onto his chest, but he seemed to recognize her. At least, he stared at the glittering dress, and a dopey grin spread over his stubbled face.

"Mare," he breathed, and attempted to straighten in Alladal's arms, though they were half a block away. "You look nice."

I don't believe *this,* Al thought, and kept lugging.

. . .

THE CLINIC's smallest examining room was ruthlessly clean as well as windowless; the glare from buzzing ledbars overhead scrubbed at Alladal's burning eyes and tensed her shoulders. In short order, Marah Madán had plunged her hands into the fylm-wrapper and set young Locke on the examining table, his jacket and manky undershirt stripped efficiently from a golden-furred chest. Nice muscle definition, but the ring of dirt around his neck and the yellowing of coppery skin that rarely saw any sun was an uneasy combination at best.

At least he hadn't been stabbed. The claret was all from his head.

"You did the right thing." Marah tweezed aside blood-stiffened hair with delicate, fylm-wrapped fingers. "Ouch. Look at me, Robb... that's good. Follow my finger...okay, now just look straight ahead." A small penlight flicked on, she examined his pupils and their contraction. Normally a synthetic would be doing the preliminary checks, but the clinic could barely afford the homeostasis tables and of course Marah's pet skarl had other duties. "Great. When was the last time you ate, soldat?" She was all business now, moving with a medic's brisk efficiency. You could almost imagine her in a Corps uniform, the object of one or two heated infantry fantasies.

Alladal couldn't quite decide whether to take notes on Locke's frame or Marah's swift grace; either could be distilled into a song. It was an embarrassment of material, she decided.

"Yesterday," Locke mumbled, blinking at Marah with the poleaxed expression of a romantic lead in the holofunnies, like Ayden Turner or Georg Kybirén. "You do look really nice."

"Thank you." Her jaw set, the Lady of Madán laid the penlight gently aside. "Try not to bleed on me."

"Yes, Marah." He blinked several times and tried a lopsided, almost grotesque smile, dried blood crackling on his face. "I'm okay."

"No, you're not." She barely glanced at Alladal, who had already been assessed as unwounded and thus, boring. "Al, that cabinet right there, unflavored glucose tabs...thank you." At least Marah had given her that critical once-over first, as if she suspected the other woman of hiding a more severe injury than the Corps boy-gusher. "You want some tai? The employee lounge has a kettle."

"I'm fine." Al couldn't rest a hip on any of the fylmsheet-wrapped, sterilized counters without feeling like a mass of germs and dirt, so she simply retreated to a corner after tossing the glucose tabs to Marah, trying to make her shoulders relax. They flat-out refused; it was a night of tension, and she didn't even have the prospect of seducing this dirty fellow to take the edge off. She should have just handed him the take and left to visit an O-house instead. "It was just a barfight."

"Should have kept the clinic open." Marah popped a glucose tab into Locke's receptive mouth. He took it; he probably would have even if it was poison. "Chew that, soldat." She sponged away fresh and crusted blood before stitching down a flap of loose scalp with a skinbobbin, biting gently at her lower lip as she concentrated, swabbing at fresh blood with steri-wipes from a bright silver container.

Locke watched her hungrily, not seeming to notice or care the bobbin sinking into flesh.

"What, and miss the dance?" Al folded her arms, sinking her fingers in savagely. The discomfort helped. "Saw it on the screens, by the way. Looked lovely."

"I even managed to get some business concluded before your call arrived." Marah sounded almost prim, and sealed the scalp-flap with skintape over the bobbin-line. She slapped an anodyne patch onto Robb's bare arm, checked his vitals with a quick glance at the homeostat screen, and eyed the bruising spreading down her patient's neck. Healed scars marched up and around Locke's torso, a map of suffering. More bruising across Robb's back—some looked prewar, but there were ugly fresh red marks beginning to congeal over a layer of yellow-greening older ones. "Mother Moon, what did he get hit with?"

"Bottle. Then a barstool, I think. I wasn't exactly taking notes." Al fought the urge to clasp her hands like a schoolkid called to the deck, and settled her buttocks against the only clear space of wall to be found, which just happened to be over a lidded wastebin. "What kind of business on Awakening Night, huh? Eating a record weight in canapés?"

"Convincing a few more rich people to subscribe and keep this very clinic open so I can stay on call for your troublemaking ass." Marah's winged black eyebrows knitted together, and she probed at the second, smaller cut on Locke's scalp while glancing again at the hovering, glowing-blue homeostat screen at the end of its arm. "If you must know, that's what I was doing. Along with dancing."

"Someone pissing you off?" Locke sounded a lot more alert. He blinked, and sharp presence filled his dark gaze again. His shoulders stiffened slightly; muscle moved under bruised skin. "Shaggoshit. Where are we?"

"Just shut up." Marah sponged at skintape and sutures with a dry steri-wipe, this one from a pink-striped container. "When I want you to ask a question, I'll issue you one."

It must have been a Corps joke, because Locke actually smiled—a sour, knowing little curve of thin lips, and Alladal couldn't find a good place to put her hands at *all* so she left them, tingling, where they were.

"Yes m'dam," Locke muttered, and a surprised little cough of a laugh shook him, too.

Marah swore at him in an undertone, but she smiled and ducked her head slightly at the same time, as if to hide it. "Good." Then, bright and impersonal again, she glanced at Al, her dark irises almost matching the pupils. She'd won the genetic lottery all over—old Madán had probably ticked a few extra boxes when going for an heir, unless she'd been live-born. "Are you sure you don't want tai, Al? You're probably going to have an adrenaline crash any moment now."

"That'll be nice." Al couldn't help but sound sarcastic. Her throat was dry, too; she hadn't had a chance to take more than a token sip of her Rambeau before the fisticuffs started. "So how long have you two been an item?"

"All our lives," Robb said, grimly; Marah said, "Never," in the same breath, and Alladal's laughter, for once, was unforced.

"My father wanted us to get married." Locke studied the air over Marah's shoulder. It was uncomfortable, how he so studiously avoided staring at her. "Her father wanted her to go into politics."

That was interesting. Alladal could see Marah standing at the Estates-General—or even the great apiary chamber of a Senatus, planetary or Prime—to make a pretty speech, full of words like *liberty* and *behooves,* that would be ignored when actual policy got made. "And what did Marah want?"

"Not to be discussed like I'm out of the room, for starters." The Lady of Madán ripped open another anodyne patch, this one with the blue stripe that meant antibiotics were added to its skin-transfer gel. The top of her sleeve was artfully slashed, exposing smoothly muscled copper skin—effortlessly beautiful, the bitch.

A thin electronic buzzing tightened all the threads in the room, and she peeled her fylmwrap gloves off before digging in a concealed pocket and pulling out a small clutch that matched the rest of her Old Shiptime silver dress. Even the angle of her wrist while she did so shouted *Echelon*, and Al tried to see how the hell that was possible.

Someday Alladal was going to unlock that secret and glide across the stage to the microphone that way, finally breaking out of the shell of smalltime and hearing a crowd bay her chosen name over and over. All it took was patience and practice, right?

And credits, and a million other things she'd been born without.

The clutch gave up a thin, expensive silver rister, buzzing like there was an emergency broadcast. "Oh, *fuck*," Marah said, softly but with great vehemence. "Listen, you two stay here. Someone else is coming."

"Who?" Locke wanted to know, but Marah shook her head, tossing used fylmwrap into a steri-bin; its top irised shut with a click. Her skirt whispered, a subtle song of feminine movement punctuated by her tapping footsteps. Alladal had heels too; she should practice in them more.

The fuckbucklers made her back hurt, though. Did Marah ever feel anything so plebeian as lumbar pain?

"Patient confidentiality," the Lady of Madán chirped, and headed for the door. "Al, I'm serious, make yourself some tai. There's a small fridge in there too, you should be able to find a snack."

"Hoarding?" Alladal spread her hands in mock-surprise. "Someone call the Sumptuary Commission." The joke fell flat the instant she made it, though, and she remembered a fraction of a second too late that hanging was the penalty for hoarding, and further remembered just what had happened to Old Locke.

Marah halted, one hand on the door, glancing nervously at young Locke, who simply sat, staring at the small metal sink set in a long silica-sealed counter. Alladal waited for a stinging reply. But Marah simply shook her head, squared her slim shoulders under that flowing, rippling fabric, and stepped outside with a flick of her skirt.

"Wow," Robb Locke said, softly, regarding Al as if she was something found crawling under a half-terraformed rock. "You really are a complete fuckbuckle."

"No." Alladal's chest hurt, a sharp lancing. She'd probably pulled something in the mad scramble. "A complete fuckbuckle would have left you there to get trampled, *Locke*."

She tossed the grey shoulder bag carrying his take—and the extra percentage—at the base of the examining table, and swung through the door herself. Halfway down the hall she heard the booming echo of a familiar voice.

Now that was strange. What was *he* doing here?

AVOID COMPLICATIONS_

"That was quick." A cloud of Red Cosmo ale—*a moonshot in each can*, as the advertising jingle went—floated gently around Jorah Smahl's broad shoulders, and his jaw held at least a tenday's worth of stubble. He winced, blinking at a crust of dried blood, and had a hand clamped low on his right side over a wide, spreading stain. His bright purple and orange shirt was never going to recover. "Honestly thought...you wouldn't..."

"Don't you *dare* pass out on me." Marah kicked the clinic's front door closed, palming the pad next to it. "Lockdown, phase three," she snapped, and the hum said the front of the clinic was sealing itself again. You couldn't be too careful at night near the Saur. "There we go. What were you stabbed with?"

"Fuckin' polis," Jorah muttered. They wouldn't leave a man alone, ever. Life was a long series of inconveniences when it wasn't a cavalcade of murderous injustices. He was vaguely surprised he'd been able to remember the clinic address, and further amazed that he didn't have to sit on the front step like a kid waiting for a drunken progenitor to return. "Jus' wanneda drink in peace."

"I'm sure you did." She rolled her dark eyes, kicking her heels off with a deep sigh. Immediately her balance improved, though she was still a tiny tug bossing a very large freighter. If he lost his balance he'd flatten her. "What did they stab you with, Jorah?"

One of his boots was mushy, or so he thought until he looked down. It was unfastened, the tongue flapping. Mother Moon, he hadn't even sealed his *shoes*.

"It was a zuum." He blinked and his cheeks puffed out. The waiting room was worn but clean, from its scraps of threadbare carpet to its much-scrubbed linoleum; its collection of refinished and ill-matched chairs sat patiently in regimented rows. Jorah swallowed a hot, bitter wad of fiery liquid. Vomiting here, no matter how attractive the idea of relief, was *not* allowed. "Uh, long story."

"I'll just bet." Marah hauled him through the door to the left of the darkened, shielded-silica receptionist's desk. "How much have you had to drink?"

"Gre'Under, don't *ask*," he moaned. "Not enough." There was never enough.

"Can you at least tell me *what* you've been drinking, so I can avoid complications?"

Avoid complications, what a neat little phrase. They probably taught her that at Echelon school. "Cosmo," he said, and choked on another wad of bile before grunting out a phrase, off-key, of the ditty. "*Fine and Bright, A Ship Original.*" The jingle delighted him; Jorah laughed, a high, braying titter incongruous in one his size. "*A moon-shot in each caaaaaaan!*"

"Soon you'll be playing the Camyron." Marah pointed them towards the first exam room on the right. It was dark just over the threshold, and Jorah's skin roughened with gooseflesh before motion sensors brought the ledbars on in a buzzing rush. "All right, onto the table. Come on."

He lost the battle with himself, but Marah, sensing as much, had a tiny plastic bucket handy. He heaved into it, a familiar, sour rush.

You great dumb pudding, Sana would say. *Look at you.*

Oh, Great Under, the fireworks were going off again, a rolling rumble all through him like the artillery that pounded his wife's body into the dirt of her village. His guts were full of hot coals and when Marah peeled his big hand away from his side blood slipped hot over his fingers. "Am I dying?" he asked the overhead lights.

"Not if I can help it," Marah snapped, and she sounded like Sana a bit, too. "Oh, it's just a scratch." A glittering of scissors, a dip of her hands into the fylmwrapper, and the slice along his ribs burned with disinfectant. "You said a zuumchair?" The homeostat screen lit with 3D rendering, moving on its armature so Marah could glance to check pulse, pressure, temperature, the chemical composition of his sweat. If he puked on the table—or, Logic forbid, pissed it—she'd probably get a chem profile of *that*, too.

Yeah, the bâtard whose mouth started the fight had tossed a locked zuumchair into the fray, and several carbon filaments had snapped, flying free like shrapnel. "Fuckbuckler hit me with one." Then he realized where he was, and what he was saying. "Sorry, Marah."

She spared him a tight, professional smile. There was a smear of steri-powder on her soft cheek, and her curls were working loose of the fillet. Had she been at a party? Dancing at the Dome? "I've heard worse."

"Did I get any on you?" he croaked, and controlled a flinch as her fingertips probed and she brought out a skinbobbin's spiny, venomous gleam. He *hated* stitches.

"Can't tell yet." She bent to her work and said nothing more, blowing a curl free of her face with a grimace. A touch of cosmetic powder on her cheeks, a touch of matte pink to her lips—she was ready for a night out, Marah Madán, and yet she was here stitching up his stupid steerage ass.

"Ow." The bobbin burned and jabbed, humming to itself. Jorah tried not to flinch each time it pinched, and lost the half the battles outright. "What are you doing, stabbing me again?"

"Shush. When I want your opinion I'll give it to you."

"You sound just like a Corps serjeant." Like every trained pilot, he'd been inducted, and spent his time after initial training ferrying

soldiers around when not doing supply runs. Applying for a griev-
ance exemption hadn't occurred to him until Al had suggested it two
and a half cycles into the war, and to think he'd spent all that time
carrying cargo so the bâtards who killed Sana could kill the ones who
started the whole damn thing.

There was no way to stay clean. Not if you were still breathing.

"You're not the first person to notice that today." Marah blew
another curl out of her face; the silver line clasping her temples was
not meant to stand up to this type of work. "You're in luck, no
muscles are severed. It's messy, but not deep at all."

"Great." He was still breathing, too, and *that* was the worst luck
of all. Jorah couldn't ask her to seal his shoe, that was a step too far,
but it bothered him that it was flopping open. "So it's not gonna
kill me?"

"No." She didn't look at him, concentrating on the bobbin, and
maybe that was why she continued. "But if you keep pouring Cosmo
down like this your liver will go out and you won't be able to fly
anymore."

"Everything's got a price." Jorah lapsed into morose, drunken
silence. Now that he was stationary and under the bright clinic lights,
the world had started to whirl again. Even in stable orbit things were
spinning, you were just too stupid to notice. "Bet you didn't know
that, Lady Madán."

"I'm well aware, Pilot Smahl." Now she was crisp again, every
inch the capitain of the *Retreat*. "Sit still for a moment."

JORAH WAS STILL NOWHERE near sober by the time she said, "I'll get
you a shirt," and was gone out the door in a trice, her skirts making a
low sweet music. She looked damn good in all that material, even if it
was meant to flutter around her in slightly lower grav. The haircut
was all wrong, though—Echelon girls were supposed to have a
real mop.

But Marah had been in the Corps. That meant she wasn't your

usual empty-headed chieweed. She was, however, too soft. Everyone took advantage of her.

Including Jorah, presenting himself—at Alladal's sly recommendation—on Madán's second Sixday back from the Corps and all but begging because word was she was an easy touch. He'd worked for old Lord Aethelstan a few times, carrying cargo for Madán's business concerns, and maybe that was why Marah had brightened visibly and said a few words to Will Skarl. One-a-penny, two-a-penny, and Jorah was put in charge of repairs on the *Retreat*.

Once those were done, he'd copiloted for her a couple times, and on their third trip Marah had changed the *Retreat*'s codes so the iris identsystem had him as prime pilot. *You're good at what you do,* Marah said, *and I like that.*

Bare-chested and wincing as his bandaged side twinged, Jorah levered himself off the table and headed for the door. The hallway was narrow, and when he stepped out he almost collided with someone who very definitely *wasn't* the Lady of Madán.

Instead, it was a brawny blond asshole in an ill-fitting, sealed-up, surplus Corps jacket very obviously not his own, terrific bruising puffing up half his face under neatly bandaged scalp wounds. He had a scowl that Jorah could read a mile away, and a bloodshot gaze that said *trouble* as well.

Everyone had been drinking tonight, some for pleasure but most for escape.

"Who the fuckbuckle are *you*?" Blond Boy snapped.

"Fuck off." Jorah's shoulders rose slightly as he gazed down upon this pissant, using height and bulk for all they were worth. This fellow was almost as tall as he was, but much leaner, and it looked like he'd tangled with a zuumchair or two himself already. "Who the fuckbuckle are *you*?"

"I asked you first." The blond man held himself tense, like he expected a fight, and the alcohol ignited in Jorah's head.

He'd be more than happy to oblige. "Fuck *off*, soldat grease. I'm not in the mood."

"Oh, yeah? Step aside, swabbie," the blond barked, and Jorah couldn't believe his luck. He was going to get another chance at tonight. One of Jorah's grav-heavy fists drew back and the fellow actually *smiled* at him, a rather gentle expression that nevertheless rasped on every frayed nerve and sparking wire in Jorah Smahl's overloaded brain.

"Stop it." Unfortunately, Marah chose that moment to tap Jorah on one shaggo-strong shoulder. She had to stand on tiptoes to do it, too. "Both of you. Can't you go five minutes without trouble?"

"He wouldn't move." The blond didn't quite sulk, and he didn't step back either. He dropped his gaze to Jorah's chest, that was all, and any move the bigger man made would be telegraphed there. Looked like this fellow had seen his share of the frontline. "He got blood on your dress, too."

"That could just as easily be yours," Marah shot back, completely unfazed. "Settle down and go *sit* down. It'll take me a little while to finish cleaning up, and then I'll take you for tai."

Very chummy. Jorah would have been insulted, but Marah had taken *him* to tai as a matter of course before, and several times too. Was this a replacement, or another asshole with a sad story taking advantage of her like Jorah himself? "You know this guy, Marah?" Frankly, all Jorah could see was his chance at a fight ebbing away. Maybe if she threw them both out he'd regain it. "He looks like an asshole to me."

"That's because he *is* one." Now she slid around Jorah, quick as a reconstituted placoderm, and shook her head just like Sana used to do. The silver headband glittered, and so did her crystalline earrings. "And you are too. Come on, I've got a shirt for you."

"Later," the blond promised, retreating down the hall without turning, stepping back but not committing his weight until he was sure. Infantry, then—pilots walked differently, and cavalry or artillery assholes didn't care where their feet or their bombs landed.

Jorah pitched forward, but Marah was there, pushing a violent orange wad of cloth into his furred chest. "Oh, no you don't. Robb, you're finished. Go outside if you can't behave."

"Yes m'dam." The blond—Robb, what a name—tipped a mocking salute and eased around the bend in the hall, out of sight. There was a murmur—so he had friends.

Marah had a full house, and was all dressed up. She should have been dancing somewhere nice instead of putting up with this shaggoshit.

"Poisoned with testosterone," Marah muttered. "Put your shirt on, Jorah. I'm going to call a khibi to take you out to the ship, you can sleep it off there. No more drinking tonight, all right?"

"Sure," he agreed, and they both knew it was a lie. But Marah was distracted; she had more than enough to occupy her at the moment. "Absolutely, Marah. Whatever you say."

Jorah struggled into the orange shirt while Marah folded her arms, all but tapping her foot, newly re-clad in its sturdy dance-heeled shoe. For a man who wanted to stop breathing, he was doing a good job of keeping it up. And why had he come here at all? Was he really that much of a hypocrite?

It looked, Jorah Smahl admitted, like he was. Or, more precisely, like he always had been. It was, as Sana would have giggled, the *habit of a lifetime*, from the old reality-holo show.

Why, after all, change now?

HALF-BUTTONED_

ALLADAL, NO DOUBT NOW SURE HER NEW BRUISER WASN'T GOING
to bleed to death or collapse from brain-swelling, disappeared the
moment they stepped outside. She probably had other business
tonight. Maybe she'd steal something else or had another delivery of
laundered credits to drop off.

Smart girl, not bringing the whole load with her. *Busy* girl.

Robb lurked in the alley near the clinic's side entrance, moving
only enough to keep his muscles from freezing up. The adrenaline
crash was well underway, but glucose and anodyne patches were
keeping it at a distance for at least a little while longer. Still, he had
the unsteady, pavement-slipping feeling he used to have when
coming back from patrol, all his nerves raw and even the sound of
people *breathing* in his vicinity an unbearable rasp.

A khibi rattled into view, and Robb watched as Marah loaded the
giant, blunt-pawed, stubbled giant into it, his orange shirt straining at
shoulder and chest alike. She probably paid his way home too; looked
like the habit of taking advantage of her was well ingrained in every
jackoff swabbie in range. With that done, Marah straightened and
glanced at the deserted street. Fireworks bloom-rattled overhead,
working up to a crescendo. The floating digital counter over Awak-

ening Square would be ticking away hours, minutes, seconds, waiting for a paroxysm of pretty explosions to mark yet another weary standard finishing an orbit around the giant nuclear reactor powering every bit of terraformed life in the Sagittarius system. There was merrymaking all over Anglene tonight—or at least, the parts that weren't scorched into needing fresh terraform or sullenly working off reparations balances.

Hood would have vanished into the shadows, unwilling to be seen waiting for anyone. The man who had returned home as Robb Locke hesitated. Good intentions were exactly what he thought they'd end up being worth; Robb stepped out of the alley, making himself visible. His back prickled, but he was sealed all the way up.

"There you are." Marah beckoned, and her smile was, for once, not the armor-clad grimace of politesse. Instead, it was the weary, grateful grin of a tired soldat seeing a buddy return alive. "There's another khibi on the way. We'll go for tai."

"Bet you think you're paying, too." He hitched the anonymous grey bag higher on his shoulder—it was heavy, and that was good. Credits earned dishonourably, just like his father had always muttered about. He was a criminal now.

So far it was a distinct letdown. Hood hadn't expected it to feel... well, just the same as every other day. And part of the weight was his own blood-splashed jacket; he wasn't about to leave that for Marah to wash *or* walk around unsealed.

"Unless you've got the credits, Robb. Honestly, what's *wrong* with you?" Her hands rested on her hips; the smears on her skirt and the wrapped, draped front of her dress had been dabbed with something that might keep the stain from setting. Marah probably knew how to wash blood out of anything; if not, Will would fret over her laundry. Where the hell *was* the skarl, if not watching over her? "First Lamóre, and now this. You're not yourself."

On the contrary, I think I'm finally getting to what I was supposed to be. "Who else would I be? And where's Will?" He didn't pantomime looking around for the synthetic, but only because he stopped himself just in time. "Shouldn't he be looking out for you?"

Implying she needed nannying was a good way to irritate her, and the way her dark eyes flashed said as much. Her chin rose slightly, too. "I already had accompaniment for the Ball."

"Let me guess." He stuffed his hands in his stained but new jacket's pockets, turtling his head between his shoulders for good measure. There was no ranking officer to tell him to get his goddamn paws out and stand like a soldat. "Giz."

Marah didn't even blink. "You weren't available."

"You didn't ask." Three little words, rapped out like knuckles on a table. When his father taught him to play card games he'd do that, tap the table if he thought Robb was taking too long—or could possibly win if given a moment to think.

For a moment Robb thought he'd finally managed to piss her off past bearing. Marah stood, her hair curling wildly free of silver wire and whatever gel or spray Will had applied to keep it corralled, and simply looked at him.

Finally, abashed, he dropped his gaze to her toes, silver heels peeping from under the hem. The shoes were all right for dancing, but didn't she feel uneasy without a good pair of boots? Didn't the plunging back of the dress, not to mention the low draped neckline, make her cold and vulnerable? How could she just *stand* there?

"Anyone else, Robb," she said, finally, softly. "Anyone else you could pull that shaggoshit with, and they'd get mad. But instead, you choose to do it with me."

It's not the only thing I'd choose to do with you. The old Robb would have said as much, but that bâtard was dead.

Why was he acting like a ghost, then? She was waiting, so Hood said the only thing he could. "I'm sorry." Then, because it wasn't enough, "You shouldn't put up with me. You really shouldn't."

"I know." She spread her arms a little, indicating the street, the sealed clinic front, a piece of flymsy trash skipping down the block, impelled by a stray breeze. "I shouldn't put up with half of what I do, and yet here I am."

Great Under, Marah, get a goddamn coat on. Robb's hands moved independently, unbuttoning the coat-collar like he intended to slip out of the material's safe embrace. "Are you cold? You look cold." It wasn't chilly, not in the least, but goddammit, she was half-naked.

"Don't, Robb." She shook her head again, wearily. A long night, even for a medic. "You were on IP. You probably have related trauma, and—"

"I'm good at killing, Marah. That's why the Corps sent me to do it." Of course he'd been Insurgency Patrol, he had the scars to prove it and obviously didn't want to leave a single edge for a whisp to work its way under. But it wasn't the patrols that slipslithered their way into a man's head and ate all the wiring—at least, not *his* wiring.

It was the *other* work, hides and a custom ryfl and one shot for each life. Hood didn't want to break cover, but he was already committed to the engagement. It was dump your ammo on the target time, maybe helped along by adrenaline aftermath and anodyne.

So he continued, pitilessly. "It's the only thing I'm good at."

"Hardly." Marah's immediate, expected remonstrance was only halfway satisfying. "You're good at climbing trees, too."

There she went, trying to save him. Again. "Not anymore." Maybe someday she'd get tired of it. "Look, we should just get it over with. I'm never going to be worth you."

"Shouldn't I be the judge of that?" Her chin set stubbornly, as if she was eleven again, her hair in a rope-braid and her jeans muddy at the knees, playing bandits in the forest or wandering aimlessly near the Slee. Neither of them flinched at the explosions overhead; there was no whistling that meant a shell was going to land close enough to matter.

And if you *heard* the shot, you hadn't been hit. At least, most of the time.

"No, Marah." Oh, Hood had gotten rid of Lamóre, and he'd aimed himself at the bottom. If he kept hanging around her, though,

Robb was going to try to surface instead of drowning like he should. "Not this time."

He watched the thoughts moving over her face. How had she not learned to be a wall by now? If he left her alone, she'd be a stranger. Maybe not tomorrow, or the next day, but enough time would erase him as completely as he alternately longed for and fought against.

Was there enough time left in his worthless life to do what he should and forget *her*?

"So there's no hope?" Marah's smile was rather gentle, now, a soft, pained curve. She'd redone her lip gloss, too, or maybe he just thought so because he was staring at her mouth. "It's Awakening Night, we might as well be honest with each other."

That wasn't our game. The old Robb might have said it. "Honestly, Marah?" The man who wanted to be alive gulped down traitorous words—*there's always hope where there's breath, right?*

Hood braced himself, and shut the upgrade cabinet on Robb Locke. Locking that door would be best, but he'd probably just have to settle for barricading and keeping anyone with a key at a safe distance. "None," he continued. "None at all."

"Then why do you keep showing up?" Pitiless, with him and with herself. Red and green light bathed the street, fire needing serious adjusting, and vanished in a heartbeat—nothing but tracer.

"This wasn't me." He was a hypocrite, no matter how hard he tried *not* to be. "It was Al."

"Oh, of course." Marah's hands hung beautiful and useless at her sides, her fingers slightly pink from scrubbing away the antiseptic dust fylmwrap trapped close to the skin. Fireworks popped and boomed again. The only good thing about hearing artillery was knowing it wasn't aimed at you. "Blame her."

"I'll see you onto your khibi." Robb's arm dropped too, leaving him ridiculously half-buttoned, sticky night air touching his dirty, crawling neck. He flat-out reeked like he'd just finished a tenday of moon-hunting, a simmerstink of mech lube, ionization from the ibow, sweat both fresh and old, and whatever had been on the barroom floor. "Then we probably shouldn't see each other again."

"If that's what you want." Now she half-turned, looking up the street like she could already hear a rattle of transport under the rolling barrage of bright chemical flowers. "Don't bother staying, if that's how you feel. Anglene is full of wounded Corpsoldat returning home. You'll fit right in anywhere."

He even had the gall to feel *disappointed,* which proved how much of an asshole Robbhan Locke really was. "You can't save them all, Marah." The sooner she learned that, the sooner he'd stop worrying.

As if he had any right to worry about her. As if he had any rights at all.

"Not even the ones I want to." Crisp, clear enunciation, the product of endless deportment and speech-training. She made it sound effortless. The fireworks paused, gathering strength for their next saturation. "If you're not coming to tai, go away."

Robb Locke had been dragged here bloody and half-conscious, but it was Hood who finished resealing his collar. He left before more booming explosions lit the sky or a khibi could arrive and change anything.

Including, of course, what little mind he had left.

MOONSHOT WHEN ZERO HITS_

THE KHIBI RIDE WAS ONLY EIGHT BLOCKS, BARELY ENOUGH TO break free of the clutches of the Saur and halt in front of a brightly lit, two-story tai-house converted from a merchant's decades-old brick domicile. As soon as she alighted she saw him, lounging at one of the wrought-iron outside tables in his formal wear, his long black polis coat carelessly thrown over his shoulders and unsealed despite the hot summer night.

Double-mantled for safety, and he'd insisted on waiting for her after all. *Do what you need to. I'll be at Telum Tai near your clinic.*

And on Awakening Night, too, when any handsome Terran in formal wear could find no shortage of dancing—or other—partners.

"What happened? Are you all right?" Ged glanced at the fare display and tossed a handful of credit oblongs at the sweating khibi driver, far more than such a short ride was worth—but again, it was a festival night, and an Echelon was traditionally generous during those time-ticks. "Marah?"

"Fine." She had to swallow a hot, slick lump that wasn't champagne *or* the light supper Will had badgered her into eating because he knew hunger made her nauseous on formal nights. Her cheeks, scrubbed hastily free of saline or steri-powder, were still damp. "Just clinic business. You know."

"Tonight of all nights." Ged's dark hair, slightly mussed, ruffled under the breeze and glistened when another barrage of colored light exploded overhead. He bent slightly, peering at her face, and Marah leaned back as the khibi rattled away. That made him straighten, hurriedly, giving her enough tether. "I've got a pot of cream tai, but you probably want something stronger instead if we're going to be up all night."

"No, I don't want tai." Marah sniffed, swallowed again, and her hand latched onto his coat-sleeve above the elbow. She had to work to keep the touch light instead of clutching. "I want—"

Another explosion. This time *she* flinched, as if she was back on Galvesto and hearing the battle line creep closer. Eventually she'd stopped hearing the salvos unless they were incoming, but it had taken a long while.

Great Under and the Moon besides, how she hated her own cringing.

Ged's face changed before the night attempted to swallow the city again, the darkness between stars beaten back by streetlamps and the blazing front of the tai-house. Ledbars and neog tubes glowed, and the entire two-story structure was packed with celebrants downing cup after cup of hot sweet strength, munching on tiny cakes, or simply floating from table to table, laughing and squirting vanish-glitter from cheap poppers.

"All right." Ged lifted his free arm, tapped at his rister—he must have put it back on once he left the ball—to pay his tab, and stepped forward, which meant Marah had to move aside or end up being knocked over. He slid his hand under hers, prying it from his coat, and got an arm around her, setting them both on a course down the sidewalk. "Come on. Tell me what you want."

Marah's stomach revolved. The champagne had deserted her, leaving only sour heat and rolling, floating queasiness. "I'm fine," she said, desperately. "Just...the noise."

"Yeah." His arm tensed, but he kept their pace nice and slow, as if he could tell that her feet were swelling. Dancing was one thing, but bandaging up a pair of assholes, resealing the clinic, and enduring a hit like a heavyball to the gut in secondary school Physical Conditioning was quite another.

Jorah, despite his promise, was probably going to find another watering hole and try once more to drink himself into oblivion; Marah didn't quite blame him. He didn't talk about what had happened to his wife, but the grief was all over him, a clinging cloud. And Robb?

No. I'm not going to think about that right now. Any of it, at all. "I don't want tai," Marah repeated, more firmly. "I want to get drunk. It's almost countdown, I want to be moonshot when zero hits."

"That'll take some doing." Giz's jaw firmed and he looked straight ahead. Seen in profile, his nose was even more of a prow, a Grecque statue from Old Terra come to life. "But it's possible."

"You don't have to, Ged." Of course he'd start solving the problem instead of asking useless questions. You could set a ship's chrono by Ged, really. Marah's stomach cramped again; she took a deep breath, attempting to force it back to its various, usual tasks. "I can go home and drink there."

"Now why would you want to drink alone on Awakening Night?" If he kept the same tone, light and amused, she might be able to match it. "Besides, it'll be fun. A test of my talents." His left arm was over her shoulders; he held his wrist almost in front of her face to tap at his rister with a knuckle. His fingers were warm but not sweating, and his coat brushed at her skirts. "I think I know just the place."

"You always do." Marah's ankle threatened to turn. What was she doing? She should have just popped him a rister message—*don't wait for me*—and gone home. Will would be fretting until she was safely back in the alcazar, too. "Doesn't anything ever upset you, Giz?"

"Oh, lots of things." He dropped his rister, his arm tensing again to guide them both around a crack-heaving piece of paving probably as old as terraform. "But not tonight. Look out, the pavement's uneven."

"Everything is." And now she was getting philosophical. She could have stayed at the clinic, made some tai, and gone through papierwork, filling up sheaves by the case. Discipline knew there was always plenty of *that* to go around. "I should be working."

"You work too much." He gave her a sly sideways glance, acknowledging the theft of one of her favourite scoldings for him. "I've got a needle coming, we'll go up a street to meet it."

Of course he would arrange for transport; Marah couldn't tell whether his practicality was comforting or maddening. "Always prepared."

"It's part of my charm." Another soft, sipping, sidelong glance, blue eyes bright, his strides shortened to hers. "There's blood on your dress, Marah."

So he was going to ask a question after all, but obliquely. Marah decided that was acceptable enough, especially from him. "People don't take vacations from getting injured, even on Awakening Night." She could even close her eyes, if she wanted to.

His arm was warm, and comforting, but also a yoke dropped over a shaggo to keep it pulling forward. "In other words, it's not yours?"

"Not a drop." Mother Moon, how she hated to keep the calculator in her head, gauging the distance needed to keep everyone else in their proper orbit.

"Good." Giz's tone was just the same—soft, polite, untroubled. "I'd hate to have to kill someone tonight."

That did it. Her stomach turned sideways inside her and Marah doubled over. *Mother Moon, no, please don't let me throw up on my dress, please.* It was fine for other people to bleed on her, but by high and deep, she *hated* vomiting.

"Shaggoshit. I was joking, *mon-trésor.*" Ged steadied her, and the endearment passed almost unnoticed. "Marah?"

She closed her eyes, throat working and belly cramping. If she stayed very still for the next few moments, she might not spray champagne and Will's tiny, exquisite pre-Ball supper all over the sidewalk.

Assuming there was any of either left to escape.

Giz freed the silver fillet and stroked her tangled curls back. He said nothing, letting her collect herself, and when she straightened he tapped at his rister again. A few moments later a sleek black polis-needle dropped out of the traffic pattern overhead, and Giz muttered something to the uniformed driver. It was a borderline unethical use of institutional transport, but Marah climbed in gratefully none-theless. When the needle rose from the ground and heeled in a grand curve away from the Saur, fireworks splattered streets and buildings below with venomous multicolored light.

It was only an hour to countdown; the needle dropped them off at the edge of the northern residential district. Giz was as good as his word—there was a neighborhood pub with mahogany paneling and red velvet booths; Marah ordered six tandu shots to begin with, ranging them on the tiny table Giz's glare and polis thermaseal had cleared for them. She knocked the first two back methodically, Ged sighed and matched her, and when countdown hit she was well past caring about anything other than singing along with the Helmsman Anthem.

Ten. Nine. Eight.

She slung an arm around Giz's neck. He smiled, alcohol soft-ening both his expression and those strange, cold, pale eyes.

Seven. Six. Five.

The entire bar was counting along, voices and heartbeats synchronized, pleasant tension rising.

Four. Three. Two.

Marah's elbow knocked over a tiny shotglass, and the sound of its shattering was lost.

One.

Giz kissed her for the first time since that warm summer night in secondary school, and she let him. He was careful, and thorough; he smelled of leather and tasted of spicy tandu, and for a few blessed moments Marah didn't have to think about the clinic, Robb, or anything else.

It was a relief to have the machine in her head finally halt, no matter how short the duration. Right after that the sheer amount of tandu she'd poured down hit, and she didn't have to care about anything ever again.

Or at least, until the hangover arrived. But for the remainder of Awakening Night, Marah Madán was reasonably free.

And it felt *good*.

PART 3
INTERDEPENDENCIES_

MERELY MILITARY_

"You look very natty." Parl Jun's smile was wide and extraordinarily white, his teeth probably scrubbed and re-enameled every half-standard. Today his dark hair was combed straight back and, added to his high-prow nose, receding chin, and widow's peak, made him look like the illustration of Parl Domno in the old 3D *Ship-fast* series. Maybe it was even intentional, since Domno was a perennial steerage favourite. Behind the sweep of his wide, silica-topped desk modeled after a navbay, a wide screen showed blur-smeared lines of starsteal moving now clockwise, now widdershins, while characters showing heading, gates, grav percentages, and other necessary information slid down the left side in tasteful blue instead of noro-red. "It suits you."

Bookman Trick clasped his sweating hands behind his back. "Thank you, sir." What was the proper form of address? He'd been thinking about it all the way here, trying to put off the inevitable and yet move with a Bookman's firm, measured step. "I mean, Your Grace."

"*Sir* will do." Sheaves both temporary and perma-loc stacked Jun's desk, and no few of them carried the noro-red banding of urgency. Three also bore the gilded sign of the Great Helmsman himself—probably messages or leftover directives from Parl Riccar, boldly advancing across the gulf between galaxies. How much did Riccar know of his little brother's rebel-hunting? "Abbot Tilles has explained your duties?"

Not so much. "I believe the abbot didn't wish to presume." There. That was a reasonable understatement.

"You mean that fat, lazy tick-humper didn't bother, he was too busy being jealous." One half of Jun's mouth curled up, a lazy expression that didn't quite qualify as a smile. "But you have some tact. Good. You'll need it."

"I wasn't aware a confessor required such a quality. Even a personal one." It was relatively easy, Trick decided. You just had to not-care, and everything else followed. During conscious hours, the flagship's hallways and working spaces drenched with ledbar glow approximating planetary daylight, he could manage that very well.

It was when he returned to the new, spacious quarters allotted Parl Jun's confessor, dialed down the ledbars to simulate dusk, and tried to snatch a few hours' worth of rest that he could not manage at all. Trick's eyes were grainy, his shoulders ached, and his new cassock, while thermasealed, was heavy as fuckbuckle. The collar was an irritant, his unders rasped, all heavy rich material a silent shame.

Parl Jun laughed. Thick carpeting swallowed the sound; silica-sealed shelves full of sheave-spines and the prissy fine-grained faces of heavy old-fashioned papier books lining the room gleamed with ledbar reflections.

Captain Curridge would have mocked this shit mercilessly. Trick wasn't quite up to the task.

"You can consider yourself in excess of requirements upon that particular point. That's your desk." Jun pointed to a smaller but still luxurious amanuensis to the left of his massive workstation. Bookmen were in high demand as personal secretaries; there went all of Trick's non-hopes for this being an empty benefice. "You'll sort correspondence, take dictation, advise me, and look after my Discipline. No doubt with you at the helm, my ship will avoid many storms."

A thankless task, just like anything else. Hopefully the Parl Regent would tire of his meek and mild confessor before long and tap Abbot Tilles for the position. Still, Trick bowed his head, making the sign of the Wheel upon his chest. "We are fallible, sir, but Logic and Reason are strong."

"Let's hope." Jun's expression didn't change. "I'll give you today and tomorrow to familiarize yourself with the flow. The amanuensis is already keyed to your biometrics." Which meant every keystroke would be logged.

Out on the front lines, or patrolling, there was no need for papierwork, a fact the good captain often either bemoaned or sounded vaguely gleeful over. And why was Trick thinking of Curridge again?

The man was dead. Let him rest.

"Yes, sir." Trick restrained the urge to salute. Parl Jun didn't look like he'd enjoy that, even if he was stuck back in Old Shiptime etiquette. Then again, insisting on traditional deference was probably useful for a parl whose right to rule depended on his brother's succession statement.

The seat at the smaller desk was—for once—large enough for an amply padded pair of buttocks. Maybe it was a mark of the parl's attention to detail, a small signal that loyalty was rewarded with comfort.

A Bookman, of course, would naturally understand the reverse of that flymsycredit: disloyalty meant discomfort. It wasn't particularly subtle, or even unexpected. A parl didn't have to threaten. It was almost a compliment that he'd taken the trouble to do so, even indirectly.

Trick palmed the lock on the amenuensis's glossy, oleophobic surface and spent a few minutes looking through the glowing text and scrolling data. There was a tablet, a collection of pens and varying styli, a sheave-blanque—he'd gone into the Discipline as a coward, been turned into a poor excuse for a soldat, and was now a fucking stylus-licker again.

"Do you drink, Bookman Trick?" Parl Jun halted before the

starsteal window. Some of the Moon's ecstatics said there were patterns to be found in the greasy slipslide-swirling lights, secrets of the great principles, scientific and irrational, that moved the universe.

I could lie. Trick cleared his throat, an uncomfortable half-cough swallowed by luxurious surroundings. "No more than the next soldat."

"That's right, you're a veteran." Jun nodded like he'd expected as much. "Aren't all Bookmen soldats, though?"

Trick refrained from pointing out that a soldat was a soldat, a Bookman was a Bookman, and a parl should know the difference. Sooner or later his tongue would slip too far for recovery, wouldn't it? Except it never had, so far, and he was almost getting tired of waiting.

Maybe a sharp tongue was a sign of bravery, and one more thing Trick lacked. "Discipline isn't merely military, sir."

"Indeed it is not." Parl Jun clasped his hands behind his back, probably conscious of the picture he made standing before a blurred starsteal window. It was right out of a propaganda reel. "Take down a message, Trick. I rather like your name, by the way."

You and everyone else. Whatever ancestor had put the family moniker on a generation ship manifest had a sense of humor, or of the absurd. Or it could have been a villein-name; the genealogical listings only went back a century and a half for noncitizens. "Yes, sir." Trick palmed up the steno program, grabbed the tablet, and fumbled with a stylus. The tiny thing almost squirted between his fingers. You used audio capture for emergency casualty and incident reports, any other command papierwork was stylus or keyboard-driven; he'd done no few of Curridge's reports for him. It was almost familiar, except he wasn't in a tent or a pop-bubble listening to Curridge growl a steady series of obscenities, blasphemies, and situation reports while Trick scratched them into fluent military-speak.

The captain laboriously filled out the family notifications for families by hand, though. Each and every one in his crabbed, slant-wise swabbie primary-school scribble.

"*Jekkut*," Bookman Trick said, the traditional invitation meaning

I'm listening in one of Old Terra's long-dead tongues. Sure, he could listen, but he didn't have to care, did he?

Parl Jun was silent for a long moment, so long Trick looked up and found the man had turned from the the display and was regarding him with a faint frown.

Had he expected any other answer?

The regent of Anglene's gaze was cold and dark as leftover moon-shot, the cheap version with only enough synthetic lac to cloud its deep brown. His smile was back, though, bright and hard. "To the Military Governeur of Capricorn Secundus, as follows—"

Trick hunched his shoulders, the stylus responded willingly. Maybe if he did this well enough, subsuming thought in the exigencies of service, he'd find out the great, grand reason for all the blood, mud, shit, and pain. There would be a moment of clarity, and maybe then the dead would leave him alone.

It was a comforting fiction, but being without one was worse. Or at least, so Trick told himself, over and over again, while his ear funneled words down his arm to his fingers without letting any lodge in his aching, overcrowded brain.

KOROVO SALLE_

KOROVO SALLE DIDN'T LOOK LIKE MUCH, TUCKED BETWEEN TWO
huge brooding hulks that had been graceful Second Echelon dormito-
ries during Landfall, their outer walls of stone turned plastic while
terraforming wracked the planet and bearing characteristic ripple-
marks. Subdivided several times into a warren of passages, tiny suites,
smaller rent-rooms, and arthritic, wheezing climate control fueled by
ledjuice instead of cryon, they now housed small swabbie families
and young kulturworkers, many of whom took fencing instruction in
the dingy shell-shaped building ducked turtle-head between giant
stone shoulders.

No matter how stained the exterior was, the front steps were
always swept and sprinkled with water in summer and deicer in
winter. Before the war, First and Second Echelon parents in Sharud
thought it best to send their heirs to Korovo's, and their subsidiary
children if they could afford it. Since the Corps had temporarily
taken over the practice of training the young during recent hostilities
the salle's business had somewhat fallen, but it was whispered Korovo's current director had a powerful patron who kept the place open.

Nobody seemed to know quite *who*, and it wasn't considered
healthy to probe the question. Soon enough, the Echelons would

return to sending their children here for a form of antiquarian prestige.

The salle's great central well was full of skylight glow and ledbars shining weakly to take over when dusk or cloud intervened, ozone from the regulators, the hair-crisping smell of live isabres, a tang of metal and the clashing, slithering clatter of the basic forms drilled into new muscle and flesh light-years from the rocky cradle of Old Terra.

In the middle of a work day, there were no schoolchildren or young toughs from the edge of the Saur scraping together credits to pay for instruction in the ancient art of skewering an opponent. Korovo's students consistently placed high in divisional, continental, and planetary trials, but what the bravos came for was the third-and fourth-cycle curriculum, which covered basic Corpsoldat hand-to-hand as well as rough but effective barroom brawl tactics. The instructors, a mix of square-cropped former soldat, kultur-professionals with their lives dedicated to thrust and parry, and lean, blank-eyed Wi8 defense-training models dual-programmed for combat instruction and medical work, held a surplus of combat experience; advanced classes were expensive but well worth it.

A Korovo-trained duelist, even one shackled by the formalized rules of pfoil and points, was held to have a distinct advantage over others, especially from less noble systems. The classes were unforgiving, brutal in the higher reaches, and indispensable.

"*Next*," Ged Gizabón called, shaking sweat-soaked hair out of his eyes—a Corps cut was an insult to any aesthetics, true, but at least it didn't drop stinging into the gaze. His last opponent, an Echelon brat too young for the pfoil he was swinging, swore and surged forward, but two instructors had his arms and hauled him away. Whoever was on medical duty would skintape the two razor-thin slashes on the boy's cheeks. Back on Old Terra they would have been marks of caste and privilege, but here they would simply be taped shut and vanish.

It was a pity, Giz thought as he settled his helm again, the fylm-woven visor clearing as it adjusted to the humidity of trapped breath.

If the young asinus had to bear a stripe or two, it might teach him discretion.

His next opponent was far too broad-shouldered to be a youth, masked in a rented helm, and swung his pfoil with a professional's graceful economy. The whole point of this round-robin was to push Giz past endurance and into mastery; this fellow had waited until a batch of younglings was disposed of before moving in. Or maybe he had just arrived, but the end result was the same.

Giz took a cautious guard. His arms burned; his quads and hamstrings trembled. Once the match actually started he'd be fine, but at the moment, his lungs were full of fire and the sweat in his eyes and trickling down his back was an irritant. This was nowhere near as brutal as full Corps kit and training marches, and several systems away from the screaming chaos of real combat—but it was what he had.

He knew as soon as his opponent gave the salute, of course. There was a certain twist of the wrist, the pfoil singing as it clove air, and the size was right. A little trimmer in the waist, a little heavier on the heels, but it was definitely, unavoidably *him*.

Of course.

So Giz saluted in turn and moved in without preparation or footwork, a straight rush. Clash-slither-chiming, metal with flex tolerances held to a rigid margin whipped and scraped. First point went to Giz, a touch to his opponent's throat-bib.

Pfoils were a fool's game; his opponent had simply never been fast enough. Another touch, this one on the wrist. The patterns of formal combat were just as strict and unforgiving as polis procedures and legal process—and just as easy to subvert.

Once you had allowed them to fill even your dreams, seeing the weak spots in the patterns was ridiculously easy.

The third touch was a trifle showy, batting aside his opponent's slug-slow point and lunging, blades ringing as edge slid against edge, and the match was called. Giz tore his helm off, his opponent did likewise, and the two men stared at each other for a long moment.

Robb Locke's hazel eyes burned above semicircles of bruise-dark insomnia, and his jaw was tight. The same banked fury as ever rippled out from him, a heat-haze like summer atmospherics above the Saur. Giz recognized that mute, hopeless rage.

How could he not? It lived in his own veins. "Quit playing around." His throat was dry. A cry of victory echoed from one corner of the salle; the racket of metal against metal was a constant thrum. "You don't want pfoils. Why bother?"

A single shrug, one beefy shoulder lifting, dropping under the padded, rented jacket. Sweat and grime crawled along Robb's stubble, turned his hair dark at the temples. Traces of loader grease lingered on his scalp, stiffening his growing-out hair.

"Fine." Giz glanced at the match caller, a hovering Wi2a with several long flexible multitool arms whose nametag said *Toaster*. Below it, in smaller letters, was the unit's formal anthropomorphic handle, *BriBri*. "Bri! Isabre authorization. Go get my armor."

BriBri beeped, cocking his round, bald head, and scurried off on his tentacles, forgetting—again—that he had grav-repel.

That was why he was called *Toaster*.

Robb still said nothing. What had fellow soldats made of his stubborn silence when he'd decided there was nothing to do but beat the shit out of something? The serjeants probably thought he was a dream come true until one of them put a foot over one of Robb's only-visible-in-retrospect borders. They wouldn't have to watch for him, though, Robb had always disdained striking from cover. He'd probably been stuffed into stockade more times than Giz had written up a sitrep that said *nothing actionable* at the bottom.

"Gizabón!" It was Jill Ouseide, the resident épfée mistress, her helm tucked under one arm and her braided chestnut coronet losing only a few strands so early in the day. "What in Logic are you playing at? You've got a line of dancing partners, move it along!"

"I found an old friend." Giz indicated Robb with a jerk of his chin. "We're gonna have some fun. Get the cage ready."

"Oh, for the love of..." Ouseide glanced at Robb, taking him in from crown to boot-toe, and recognition bloomed on her sharp mahogany-carved face. "Locke? When did *you* get home?" At least she knew them both well enough not to expect an answer. "Fine. Both of you better have waivers on file, or I'll run you through myself."

BriBri clattered up with his arms full of gear, swaying drunkenly since his primary tentacles were occupied.

"Mother Moon." Ouseide looked up at the ceiling, natural light falling over her in a cascade. Seen in profile, she looked a little like Marah, or that could be because every attractive woman did to Ged Gizabón. "Toaster, turn your damn hover on."

The Wi2a unit beeped, its hover activated, and it rose with a short chiming sound of wonder. It also dropped Giz's sleek black isabre helm, and dove for it with a whining of gyroscopes.

A thin ripple of laughter eddied through the onlookers. Giz's sparring line hadn't shortened, but now everyone in it was unbuckling helms and putting their pfoils in walking-ready.

Looked like they were going to have an audience.

A DEAD ISABRE didn't *look* like much—just a cylindrical hilt with a power crystal at one end and a flat cryon disc at the other. When live, though, a bar of vicious, venomous light extended for almost a meter from the disc, plasma corralled by a konstans-cell and mag-pull. It made a low, terrible thrumming that cycled up with activity and sparked when touching another bar; isabre duels were, as a rule, generally short and somewhat dramatic.

Onlooker safety was the primary consideration, and the cage—baffle-bars humming with their own semi-malignant glow—reflected as much. The armor was baffled too, but mobility demanded the sacrifice of absolute safety. You could, if you were nasty enough, subtract a limb from your opponent. The cauterization made re-attachment more difficult and less successful than, say, an industrial accident. You had to replace with bud-grown.

Giz had lost weight since his last isabre practice, but not a lot. The mag-buckles on his armor needed another person to tighten them and BriBri sufficed, his multitools clicking and a steady stream of boops and low whistles falling from his dome as he went through the pre-fight checklist. He'd remembered his hover again, a break from routine jarring ancient synaptic circuits into high-functioning.

Jill, stripped of her padded jacket and with dark half-moons under her arms, checked when he was done. "Baby Locke back from the war," she said to Giz's shoulder, her touch impersonal and efficient as she tested each buckle. "And all grown up."

"Knock yourself out." Giz shook his head slightly. The isabre helm had no fylm-backed visor; speed and peripheral vision both too crucial for compromise.

"Not enough chromosome to be my type." Now Ouseide sounded amused. On the opposite side of the cage, BriBri was checking Robb's armor. Robb, of course, glared at Giz across the mat flooring, fixated. "Does he have a girlfriend?"

"Used to." Now Giz tasted tandu, citrus and alcohol kick married to a long finish of synthclove. He'd tipped an extremely drunk and almost somnolent Marah into Will's arms at the alcazar while a polis needle hummed near Madán's dry courtyard fountain the morning after the Ball, and come to the salle for a tenday straight afterward to burn off healthy frustration. A kiss was nice, a series of them even better, and there was no reason to jeopardize what he already had by being an asshole.

Robb probably wouldn't find that parable instructive at all.

"Is that why he's here?" Ouseide was an inveterate romantic; once you got her drunk she'd invent tragic pasts for everyone at the table. And she loved comforting, in her own inimitable way, any girls with broken hearts.

Giz knew the feeling by now. "I don't know if *he* even knows why he's here. Check him up and let's get this over with."

As soon as the cage slammed shut behind Jill, Robb's isabre burst into humming life, a viridian bar. Giz's was crimson, polis-issue, several shades away from noro-red despite its glow.

It was just like scrapping in the schoolyard, fellow students' faces pressed to a twisted rectangle of spunlink fencing. By common consent, behind the school fence was the viewing gallery; step out, and you were likely to be taken for a combatant.

Giz was no longer smiling. The salute with isabres was not a pfoil-slash or even a single lift, it was considered sufficient to give your opponent a few moments before attacking.

No such luck here. Robb was already on him.

INTERDEPENDENCIES
AND IRRELEVANCIES_

HE WAS UNDER THE KHIBICAT, THE PRESSURE OF THE TETHER well within tolerances all along his bipedal chassis. The humans had been unable to find the problem, so now it was the synthetic's job, and Will Skarl's only comment—of course, he would not have said it aloud—was that they should have asked him first.

But to be a synthetic was to be used to the order of logical operations being overruled by *il*-logical Terrans. It was the way of the universe, and standing before such a juggernaut of convention and usage served no purpose. So Will ran the diagnostics while he listened, almost pitying the two fragile, inconsistent beings he was performing this necessary duty for.

"Can't find a damn thing wrong with it." Jorah Smahl hunched his broad shoulders and suppressed a rancid burp. His bloodshot eyes were dry, by the way he kept rubbing at them, and he had—unusual when he was trapped planetside—a scruff of three-day beard.

Awakening Night was traditionally hard for him, it seemed, and the tenday afterward even worse. Marah intuitively understood as much, which was perhaps why she had invited her employee to *come take a look at this damn CAT, if you're not doing anything else?*

And who would refuse an invitation from the Lady of Madán?

Certainly not the steerage fellow who already took more than his fair share of the mistress's forbearance.

It was quite a habit, the taking advantage. Lord Aethelstan had not been so burdened, but his daughter was of a more tender nature. Will did what he could to insulate her and the estate from those with grasping fingers, but again...it was not a skarl's place to decide.

Only to perform.

"Well, that's what I expected." Marah's frown was also genuine and quite uncharacteristic; she'd scraped her hair into a wispy, stubbornly short ponytail. There were easy treatments that could give her back a pre-Corps appearance, at least where the keratin straw atop her head was concerned, but she disdained them. "There's a burr in the higher registers; I wish I could just take it out on the estate and figure it out."

"*I'm* not gonna." Jorah *hated* CATs. According to him, a proper ship was one that pierced atmo; otherwise, it was just a glorified rattle-taxi. Will did not disagree, but he *would* have to make an objection if Marah decided to take the CAT outside this particular garage space before the race transport date.

"Of course not." Marah elbowed the large man, but gently. She had largely recovered from Awakening Night's alcohol. Terrans were odd, drinking, injecting, or snorting things that overloaded their systems and enjoying the resultant pre-poisoning; Will had the idea something emotionally taxing had occurred at the Ball, outside the range of his sensors. At least Ged Gizabón had not...well, Will's estimation of the new Second Echelon was rising. "I didn't ask you here for that."

Will's sensors also picked up the concomitant spike in Jorah's pulse. The man was not immune to his mistress's charms. Well, really, who was?

"Then what?" Jorah almost snarled, as if offended by his own body's quite proper response. "I'm a busy man, Lady of Madán."

"Busy pouring more Cosmo down your throat?" Marah kept her tone light, but her own vitals showed the stress of worry. She had far too much empathy; it was not something that could be planned for in genetic manifests when choosing an heir's collection of traits and skin-hair-eye shades. Nurture and nature both affected the complex creature that was a Terran.

It was another thing to pity—their bewildering array of choices, both those they took without question and those they thought themselves barred from. Even a synthetic would have trouble with that much freedom; how much more did those under their care suffer?

Jorah folded his large arms across his barrel chest and indifferently laundered jumpsuit. Under its unsealed front, a violently patterned orange shirt peered out, also none too fresh. "My private life's my own."

"Indeed it is," Marah agreed equably, touching her ponytail to make sure it still held. "But if you're drunk you can't take the *Retreat* up."

Ah. So that was his mistress's aim. Will scanned the underside of the CAT again, giving the Terrans time for their parlay. Lord Aethelstan would never have engaged a drunkard as a pilot, even for a personal project like the *Retreat*. And last time, the artificial grav had been troublesome; the ship was not elderly but it was well past its youth. A bright, shiny new craft would be at risk from other salvage-diggers; there was safety in anonymity, balanced against the risk of aging tech.

Jorah digested this. "We're going on another run?" He didn't sound as pleased by the prospect as usual.

"I'd love to, but I can't." Marah sighed, her regret palpable and aesthetically compelling at once. "I was going to ask you to get a couple hands and make the run for me."

"You'd trust me with the ship?" The pilot sounded outright baffled, now. "Alone?"

Marah's tone had finally hardened, a perhaps-unconscious imitation of her sire's usual brusque refusal to countenance any familiarity. "Not if you're going to keep drinking like this, Jorah."

A long silence descended. Normally, Terrans disliked quiet and couldn't wait to fill it with verbiage.

Finally, Jorah moved, taking a single, restless step away from Will's mistress. "Is this the carrot or the stick?"

"I've about had it with mouthy Corpsoldat lately." Marah folded her arms too, examining the khibiCAT like it had made some kind of impolite noise. Will had found the problem, but it was probably best to let his mistress finish this conversation before he said as much. Consequently, he busied himself with smaller checks—the CAT was coming along, but it was far from flyable in this condition. "You can say you're not interested and I'll find another pilot, but stop being a swabbie."

Will switched his optics to another angle. The poor humans couldn't do as much; they were locked into one body, one temporal point. He, on the other hand, had the entire tech-starred alcazar to peer through, his attention upon several beating pulses like those Terrans who conducted masses of musicians, tweaking here, marking time there, listening to the whole instead of to one or two parts at most.

"Good luck getting anyone else to fly the belts." Jorah's chin settled on his chest as he glared from under his bushy eyebrows, and he visibly remembered who he was speaking to and what he stood to lose from her displeasure. Perhaps there was even a trace of sympathy lurking in his large frame. "Sorry, Marah. I'm...it's a bad time."

"I know." Her face eased, degree by degree, and she pulled a thermaspanner from her work belt, clicking it on and taking a reading from her palm, a child's fascination with the toy to hand or merely something to keep her digits occupied. "It's universally bad. You'd think the end of the war would make everyone happy."

"Didn't know you were so much of an optimist." Jorah's brows beetled afresh and ferociously; he shifted a fraction, catching even more of Will's interest. The pilot had something on his mind. "Who was that guy at the clinic? The blond one?"

"A friend brought him in." Marah weighed the statement, visibly found it wanting. She clicked the thermaspanner again, playing with it like a fidgetdisc. "I grew up with him."

Jorah let out a short, breathy sound of comprehension. "Ah."

Blond and *grew up with him* could only mean one particular person, and any mention of *him* was to be avoided for his mistress's peace of mind. Something had indeed happened during the Ball, and Marah hadn't said a word. Well, that was her prerogative, even if it made performing his core functions more difficult.

Will shimmied from under the CAT, his greying hair wildly disarranged and his jumpsuit full of shopdust. "I have found the problem," he announced. "The primary thermal trans-coupler, mistress. There is significant corrosion on the hood's topside; it couldn't be seen from underneath."

"Great." Marah sighed. "That'll be fun to fix."

"Well, the race is a while away." Jorah's tone shifted from combative to practical, perhaps because Will's presence activated memories of his proper place. "Maybe I can find something nice out in the salvage fields."

Marah grinned, spinning the thermaspanner's handle on her palm. Natural grace and good reflexes turned it into a kultur-juggler's trick. "That means you're taking the job?"

"What, miss a chance to get off this rock? Besides, I can't refuse my dear patron." Jorah's sudden ease was no doubt meant to spread to her, but his pulse was still a bit too high. "How far do you want me to go, by the way? I kind of thought of going Virgo way."

Marah gave him a very odd sideways glance. That was interesting; did his mistress suspect something? "That's a long ride, Jorah. But we just did refitting, so do what you think best."

"I could probably get a thermal coupling hood for cheap on Virgo Secundus, if I can't find one in the belts." Jorah scratched at his stubble. "The Alley there is probably full of them."

"If you think you can." Marah's shoulders dropped; she rolled the thermaspanner over the back of her hand and caught it again. At least she hadn't demurred at the program of proper hydration and healthy foodstuffs Will had prepared after the Ball. "I wish I was going up with you."

"Why don't you? Leave all this." But Jorah's tone suggested he knew Marah wouldn't.

"Responsibilities. And getting this thing ready for the race." Her dissatisfaction was palpable. She would be happier without the burden of the alcazar, or so she thought—old Lord Aethelstan had often sounded a similar note, though not nearly as softly. It was probably a blessing Will's mistress didn't know how much like her progenitor she actually was.

A synthetic did not have the capacity to be truly dissatisfied with its lot. Terrans would be much happier if they lacked it, but there was no confluence of genes responsible. Like a synthetic itself—or any other complex system—they were more than the sum of its parts; strange interdependencies and irrelevancies were to be expected.

They simply couldn't reprogram with the ease a synthetic could. Will was no longer a reflection of old Aethelstan's tastes and priorities but his daughter's—and the skarl protection Lord Aethelstan had taken as a matter of course must be more subtly performed to avoid impinging upon said daughter's sensitivities.

"Why are you racing, again?" Jorah cocked his bushy head. His vitals smoothed out as they always did when piloting the *Retreat* was mentioned. Besides, he had what he'd come for.

"Prize purse can buy a lot of skintape." Marah's tone was light and laughing, but her pulse had quickened and a faint colorless fume of stress hung around her. Why? She had invited her employee here, and apparently wanted him to go on another salvage mission. At least she wasn't planning on accompanying him.

Will could do without *that*. A synthetic did not have true dislikes, but antipathies were normal, and he had one centering upon interplanetary, let alone interstellar, travel.

"The clinic, huh?" Jorah crossed his beefy arms. "For a moment I thought it was 'cause you have a deathwish."

"Who, me?" Marah spread her hands and imitated a current chieweed star, a Second Echelon with the habit of using the rattle of a khibi and a cheerful ding-ding bell at random moments during her show.

Their shared laughter was pleasant, but Jorah's vitals held a few interesting inconsistencies. So did Marah's. Neither of them were being exactly truthful, and Will wondered, as he did so often, why that would be. While he rested in his upgrade cabinet, he would have much to process.

Terrans were always interesting.

KISSING GAME_

THE SOUND WAS JUNGLE-PLANET INSECTS BUZZING, DARTING, splattering static-laden luminescence; sweat stinging his eyes and the armor not quite fitting right, working into his underarm when he slashed. Of course he could blame it on the armor, but the fact remained Robb Locke, and therefore Hood, was sadly out of practice.

Isabres were not part of Corps drill.

Hard zinc adrenaline against his tongue, the isabres crackling as he held corps-a-corps with Giz, the blank shield of the other man's mouthpiece reflecting only the blankness of his own. Sparks spat, winking out before they reached the ground, a shower of heatless light. Digging in, his calf aching, both power cells screaming as they sought to override the other—there were ancient pictures of isabres and their wielders from Old Terra, full of digital snow but still thrilling. At some point there had been many schools of isabre-wielding, but nowadays there was only the one style: flexible, fierce, and brutal.

Giz broke contact almost contemptuously, shoving him away, and Robb was sure the fucker was using that iron-clad little smile behind the mouthguard. The way the corners of his pale eyes crinkled up all but shouted it. Hood grinned fiercely back from inside Robb's own helm, the world contracting and suddenly very simple.

If only everything was always this clear-cut. Disengage, slide forward in a sloppy thrust not to actually make contact but to give himself room for the next few moves, muscle memory and physics dancing as his wrist faded to the side, batting aside Giz's own answering cut. They circled, the hum of isabres almost drowning the crowd-noise.

It was taking too long for an isabre duel, and Hood suspected that was because Giz knew Robb was out of practice and was dragging the game to wear his opponent down. Normally Giz believed in efficiency, but maybe he wanted to show off today.

In other words, he was stealing Robb Locke's own strategy, and the realization filled Hood with the cold clarity of a target in the crosshairs and his finger easy on the ryfl trigger. He used to think it was shameful to take a shot from cover, before he realized that pride was just another way to get killed.

It wasn't that he wanted to live. It was that death was an indignity, and he'd swallowed enough of those to fill him from toes to sinuses, as the saying went.

He surged forward, choosing battering over finesse, a flurry of blows that drove Giz back almost to the cage bars. There was shouting now, open mouths and wide avid eyes; the freeze-rush poured over him, nothing but the next move and the next. Giz quarter-turned, letting Hood's momentum push him past, and the quick, jabbing shot to Hood's face by Giz's left gauntlet was enough to turn the rage into clear cold Discipline, the *flow* Lunacer ecstatics always talked about.

How many of the white temples were smoking ruins by now? How many had Hood himself seen burning? The shapes sihouetted screaming against the flames, ryfls cracking to put living Terran torches out of their misery...

Giz now had the open expanse of the cage to his back and pressed in, isabre crackling as he batted aside Hood's lunge. The only way out was to duck, the cage's baffle-bars flushing as his armored hip touched one and went numb, his leg almost buckling.

You sonofaswabbie fuckwit bâtard. Hood pitched forward, green light flaring as his blade slid down Giz's, and drove his shoulder against the other man's. Close contact, balance lost, toppling, a scream from the crowd as the combatants went down in a tangle of arms and legs. The borrowed green isabre clattered away, blade losing its glow as feedback through the hilt halted, and Giz's faceshield rang under Hood's fists. The gauntlet wouldn't fit through the empty visor-space, but it would still daze an opponent.

Rolling, Giz's hilt clattering away too, and the man brought a knee up into Hood's eggs and rasher with the accuracy of a lucky, well-practiced brawler. Even *that* didn't halt the fury; Giz had his other knee on the thinly padded floor and was punching in return, gauntleted fist smashing Hood's helm over and over.

Hood yelled, a short bile-scented yelp wrung out of lungs struggling to strip usable oxygen from the stale hot plastigel trapped inside his mouthpiece instead of air; he overruled the desire to curl up like a marine crustacean and stamped his right heel down hard to give himself something solid to push against, timing the hip-raise for when Giz was drawing back to strike again. The other man went sprawling, Hood rolled desperately and thrust out a hand, seeking a hilt, any hilt.

There. Too far away, but he still scrambled for it. Giz fell on his back halfway there, dragging him away and locking an arm around Hood's throat. A moment's worth of thought paid dividends for the lean dark-haired bâtard, as usual; Giz had his foot and knee braced and reared back, Hood's hand questing a good armlength from the nearest dead isabre hilt, gloved fingers feline-scratching tough canvas pad-covers.

More shouting. Giz yelling something, hoarsely. Maybe he was asking for concession; the thought ignited Hood's rage again. He convulsed, arching his back, but Giz had his opponent's helmet worked free of the collar and applied pressure to the windpipe.

"—*off!*" Giz yelled. "*Keep that door closed!*"

Hood was trapped. Nowhere to go, nothing to do but thrash while the rage burned through every nerve and pore. The weight on his back was an oppressive safety, and the faint, flying thought that some part of him hoped Ged wouldn't let go infuriated him even further.

It felt like forever but was probably only a few moments before Hood went limp, receding with a sound like atmo parting around a dropped troop-needle. Robb Locke took his place again, tasting copper adrenaline, soaked with combat-sweat, and with a deep drilling hopeless agony in his crotch. It was too early to tell if he'd pissed himself like some soldiers inevitably did during a fight.

If it didn't smell of dirty trou it was only a kissing game, as Corps serjeants said dismissively. Usually with a heavy load of spat obscenities between each word.

Giz's ribs heaved in tandem with Robb's own. "Just give it a metric minute," he said over his shoulder, but his arms didn't slacken. He suspected Robb had a wriggle or two left in him. "He's a veteran, just *give* him a second."

Oh, fuck it *all*, first Marah tried to save him from himself, and now even Gizabón was getting in on the act.

"You gonna be reasonable, Locke?" Giz's voice crept through the knocked-ajar helm; his breath full of morning tai and the faint copper of hard physical effort. He must have lost his own helmet in the scramble; a rasp of stubble touched Robb's padded shoulder. "You smell awful, by the way."

"Bâtard," Robb hissed. "I'll fucking show you *smell*."

"Nope, not all right yet." Giz choked up on him a little tighter. The helm's face-shield, knocked awry, also held a spiderweb of cracking. "You could have just sent me a sheave, you know."

That was how duel requests arrived. Well, Giz probably thought Robb hated him; it would serve both of them right. "Don't have your address," he rasped.

Giz immediately let go, slithered to the side, and rolled up into an easy crouch, safely between Robb and the scattered isabre hilts. Wise of him, but Robb was back in the driver's cradle now.

Right where he hated to be.

"Anything broken?" Giz was now businesslike and cold despite his wildly mussed dark hair and the flowering of an ugly bruise on the right side of his neck. Those bad-luck eyes were narrowed, fine lavender lines in the iris glowing.

"Nothing but the fucking helm." Robb got halfway up, coughed rackingly, and controlled the urge to spit. He'd swallowed worse in the Corps, frankly, and Ouseide was going to be pissed at him already. He shouldn't upset her.

At least he had *not*, after all, unloaded his own stupid bladder. He blinked, Hood trying to rise through the letdown at the end of a fight, but he was safely Robb again, at least for a little while. "Let's go again."

"I'm not sure you're up for it." Giz heel-and-toed back, moving in the easy crouch of a trench soldat under fire. He got the first hilt, carefully didn't turn his back to Robb, gathered the other. Then he rose, a careful, coordinated, lithe movement, just like Marah. They both sailed through deportment classes, while Robb puffed elbow-awkward in their wake.

He hadn't thought of her for the entire fight. It was a Lunacer's miracle.

"Give me a hilt and we'll see." Robb held his hand out, conscious of the staring eyes, the solemn faces. No few of the audience had melted away, probably veterans themselves. Or easily nauseated. "No armor, Gizzy. You and me." *I'll even let you wrap your hands.*

"*Definitely* not sure you're up for it." Giz handed the hilts through the baffled bars, gingerly, to a white-lipped Ouseide. Then, of all things, he paced to Robb, set his practice-boots, and offered a hand. "Come on up."

It would be so *easy*, Hood thought. Kick Ged's legs out from under, get the thumbs in the eyes. Get a good purchase on the throat, crush the trachea before help could arrive, and the job was done.

Hood's whisp at the small of his back was an option, too. Would Giz be surprised when the blade slid in?

No. From the look on Ged's face, he wouldn't be surprised at all. Still, the man just *stood* there, hand held stupidly in midair, knowing perfectly well the wild animal might bite.

Locke took the hand, let Giz haul him upright. It was also Locke who smoothed it over with Ouseide and promised to pay for the cracked helm, who joked with Giz and even went a few pfoil rounds with some interested and foolhardy kids who had missed the war.

But it was cold necessary Hood who watched from the back of his brain, and it was Hood's credit oblongs spread upon the salle's counter for Gros Jahn the club secretary to issue a hardfylm membership receipt—not to mention the additional receipt for repair of a rented helm—and it was Hood who pocketed both slips with a quiet nod and turned down Giz's half-serious offer of tai and breakfast.

And of course, because Giz was Giz, he had to say *practice a little before next time, Robb,* and it was Hood who copied his childhood friend's lupine grin and sketched salute.

He hadn't killed Ged Gizabón. That was a relief.

It was, to his shame, a temporary one, because not even Hood could be sure he'd tried hard enough.

OPENING GAMBIT_

IT WASN'T THE FIRST TIME A FIGHT HAD BROKEN OUT DURING one of her sets. It wasn't even the first time the unrest had spilled out of the Camyron's front doors and into the streets. It wasn't her first time in a holding cell, either, but it *was* the first time she'd been bailed or comped out *before* a magistrate hearing. Alladal straightened her turban—in holding, they only wand-scanned headcovers instead of issuing you a square of manky material and a stonefaced matron to watch while you wrapped your locks—and hoped this wasn't even worse luck than getting dragged from the stage in the first place.

If Locke had been on bouncer duty, it probably wouldn't have happened. But he was off on post-Awakening Night holiday, maybe drinking his cut, maybe not. She'd been forced to use the Camyron's part-timers, and they were *not* worth the percentage taken from the door.

The blackcoat polis who motioned her out of the holding cell's chaos also didn't clip Alladal into restraints. Either she was not considered a flight risk, or...

"I understand that," a man said, as Al was ushered into a tiny, cluttered, soundproofed magistrate's office at the end of the hall. "This is a kultur asset; artists do tend to mix with all types."

The young, snub-nosed under-magistrate responsible for initial screening, sweating in the required buff robe of Aegis civil authority, looked like he'd swallowed some kind of mud-smeared amphibian. Which was pretty much the way you'd expect a palm-greasing syco-phant to look when faced by the black-haired man who lounged in a hastily cleared office chair among stacks of flymsy, papier, and temp-sheaves, a blot of black with bright blue polis piping reflected in his eyes.

"Highly irregular," the under-magistrate said, faintly. "Highly... uh..." He couldn't look away from Alladal's lean frame, long strings of sequins dripping from angles and curves. She loved this dress, but the glitter onstage had made it impossible to hide when the fighting started. The young man liked what he saw, evidently, and Al tipped him a wink before arranging her face when the black-haired polis glanced at her.

You didn't want to be caught grinning when Noth's Ryfl had decided the occasion did not call for levity.

He was taller than he looked in fylm captures, soldat-wiry instead of heroically built but with a good set of shoulders. Word was he did live isabre drills daily at a salle stuffed full of Echelon bravos, and his polis work *definitely* wasn't the desk-bound type.

His lazy half-smile looked like armor, and was as cold as leftover tai. "Thanks, Clowson." He nodded at the officer who had brought Al out, and *that* worthy saluted before hurrying to make himself scarce. "We'll get going. There's bound to be a great deal of magis-trate work waiting."

The Aegis magistrate gulped and waved a hand; Ged Gizabón shepherded Al into the ledbar-lit hall and past a line of erstwhile rioters clipped into humming restraints. One or two of them recog-nized her and a mutter ran down the line; Al realized why she wasn't clipped.

They wanted it to look like she'd flipped, or like she was about to.

Well, the people who really mattered knew she was no turncoat, and in any case, this fit her plans as neatly as if she'd arranged it herself.

"My lady kultur-asset, please." Gizabón, now that he'd sown suspicion, indicated what had to be an interrogation-room door, the capture board next to its blank metal face glowing softly as processed lawbreakers were cycled through. "Do you want some tai?"

How would Marah respond? "No, thank you." Alladal sailed through, touched her turban once to make sure it was still secure, and discovered the chair he indicated was bolted to the floor. The table was too heavy to shove, so she simply left it. Marah would fold her hands in her lap like a good, demure little Echelon girl, but Al didn't have that luxury, so she laid her palms awkwardly on the table's sticky surface. It stretched her arms just a fraction too much, but she'd already done it, so she settled for watching him.

"They can't decide if you're a hardcore Lunacer or a dilettante songbird with a gimmick." Gizabón settled in the chair across the table. He probably had a nice smile, but the one he was wearing now was definitely *not* it. "Half of Sharud goes around with a head-covering, and three-quarters of the Saur too."

As an opening gambit, it wasn't bad, but Al wasn't an easy target. Or at least, she didn't intend to be for a short while yet. "It's illegal to question me about my worship affiliation."

"I haven't asked you a question yet." The Ryfl's smile didn't alter. "When I do, you'll know."

The sweat had started under her arms, at the small of her back. So she settled back in her chair, looked down at her fingers, and waited for the music.

"Allada Dalette," he said, opening the fylm folder. Her old name was gone, thank the Moon; the one Sana had chosen for her was on every bit of papierwork and hardcode, a ghost of her cousin's kindness trapped in bureaucracy. "Stage name Alladal. There's also some doubt as to whether you're here just to escape your home planet, but honestly, I can't blame you. The Corps re-terraformed out there."

So far, pretty standard bureaucratic piss-swinging. Even the dig at her home. "They did a service." She'd even practiced the right tone —bored, but with a prickly edge. Even if you hated your farm, you had to defend it. "Place stank."

Come on, Al! Sana with her hands on her hips. *You won't get anywhere by dreaming.*

Except she had. The price for such dreams was high, and she'd paid. Moon and Discipline both knew how much she'd paid.

"So, here illegally, but a kultur-asset nonetheless, since your shows at the Camyron are recurring. Chake wouldn't keep on a show that didn't pack the place, so you must be quite the burlesque." That same non-smile, a pleasant expression unless you missed the way his eyes never thawed. "All in good taste, I'm sure."

You'd be wrong. The big thing was to keep track of her hands. She began playing her usual piece, an antique mathematical fugue from Old Terra. It sharpened the mind, gave her fingers something to do, and made her look distracted, all valuable things.

Gizabón glanced at her fingers, returned to his perusal of the papier folder. "I'm told you're reliable." He sounded like he doubted the notion. "You can drop the act now."

"Act?" She tried an un-smile of her own, letting just the tips of her teeth show. "I'm a kultur-asset, my entire life is a perform—"

"Don't insult my intelligence." He turned somber, those bad-luck eyes narrowed just a touch. "I can simply shoot you now."

"An extrajudicial killing? Well, that's pretty standard for Noth's Ryfl." Letting him know *she* knew just who he was. Toss out the bait, see if the chokfish would bite. They couldn't help it, instinct and survival forced them to snap at anything in range.

Gizabón, however, made no sign of rising. He simply studied Alladal for a few moments and closed the folder. "It's strange," he finally remarked. "The level of protection you've hired, and still you get dragged off the stage."

"My best bouncers were on vacation." Besides, this was all part of the plan. She'd been dangling herself through the dark waters for a while, now it was paying off with black-market interest.

Gizabón affected slight astonishment, another signal by his mouth that didn't reach his eyes. "You're a generous employer."

"Almost an Echelon." Al decided on another test, just to see if this fellow was really all she'd heard. "That's right, you've just been promoted, too. A battlefield commission, right?"

Even a simple *none of your business* would have been a crack in his armor, but he *still* didn't rise. "So there just *happens* to be a riot the night your bruisers are dabbling their toes on a vacay moon. How very strange." His gaze rose, pinned her to the chair, and Al's fingers stammered on a particularly difficult passage.

"The Camyron's known for its ebullient clientele. Every performer engages extra security." She started over again without missing a beat, cocking her head thoughtfully. "Why don't you just ask me what you want to know and we'll be done with this? I'm sure you have better things to do."

"Bartolet said you were annoying. He also intimated you were useful enough to balance that out, but I suppose he was wrong." Gizabón swept up the folder and stood, his chair giving a high whining scrape. The single ledbar illuminating this hole was doing its best, but shadows still gathered in the corners—and she could be sure the steno-recco was running.

Very sure.

So. It's Barty. Or maybe not, it could be a double-blind. Either way, the name was valuable. She let him get to the door before speaking, pitching the words a little high to show anxiety she didn't quite feel. "You want to know about the credit heists, right? And what that money's going for? It's not for some deckhand's holiday, that's for sure."

For a moment she was sure she'd cut it too close and lost him. His head turned slightly, the folder dangling one one had—was there anything really in it, or was it stuffed with scrap flymsy? He didn't seem the theatrical sort, but then again, people could surprise you.

They did it all the time.

"You have two ticks of a navsat to convince me you're not a chie-

weed yappie, *Al.*" His hand rested on the doorknob; a quick turn and
a step through would consign her to spacetrash.

Or so he wanted her to think.

"Nobody knows where they're hitting next, but they're not after
the credits. Those are just a means to an end." A mathematical fugue
didn't change its tempo; she forced herself to slow down and play in
time. She had to speed up her words so she sounded anxious, though,
and chose to triple-time *them*. "I don't know what for, really, but it's
big, and it has something to do with cryon. Not only that..."

"Not only that?" He didn't move.

"Look, if I tell you my life's not worth a lot. I'm just a kulturtrash
songbird, I don't want to be involved in this any more than I wanted
to be born without Rey Aludat's voice, okay?" Was that the right note
to strike? A thin finger of sweat traced down her spine-channel, colors
standing out sharp and clear. Even the cracks in the walls—poured
concrete, not terraformed rock, but just as durable—were in glaring
map-relief. It was like knowing you had the audience, hearing the rise
of cheers and whistles when you started what could be a hit if you got
enough of them interested enough to hum it after they left.

"Then stop with the tabletop-tapping and tell me something
actionable." Gizabón's entire posture didn't alter. He was a good thes-
pian, but she must have the tether locked on, because he was still in
the room. "One tick left, Alladal."

Good. She brought the fugue to an end, dropped her wrists, let
her hands lay limp on the table. It would take some harsh Saur soap
to get the sticky feel off her skin, but she was used to it.

Scrubbing until you bled was, after all, a family tradition. *Oh, Al,*
Sana would say, her large dark eyes soft and wounded. *What was it
this time?*

Same damn thing it was every other time. But now she was in the
right body, she was doing the right work, and Alladal moved in for the
kill. "A tinker," she said, staring at her hands like she was betraying a
confidence. "A tinker named Wat. He's putting together something
big with cryon. That's all I know."

Gizabón was silent for a long enough measure Al thought she'd missed her jump. Then he turned from the door and regarded her, a level blue gaze—even his *eyes* were polis-colored—fixed on her expression.

A born performer, Sana called her, and Alladal hoped like hell she was right.

DIRECT HIT_

IT WAS A BUSY MORNING AT THE CLINIC. NOT BECAUSE OF THE patients—it was, during mid-tenday and despite the weather, one of those odd lulls in the Terran business of stabbing, shooting, and misadventure. Besides, a new batch of citizenship markers had just gone out, the Aegis processing applications in doubletime to make up for the freeze during the war; new marker-holders could visit state hôpitals and clinic networks instead. That meant records requests were flooding in.

Bureaucracy and papierwork expanded to fill every spare corner, like ink in water. "I just can't get it to match," Sibby said mournfully, staring at the papier report. Today her hair was molecule-treated a very fetching pink, and the tender undersides of her dark eyes looked almost bruised from lack of sleep. Thankfully, the latter was because she was young, and liked ale-fueled dancing in nightclubs. "I'm sorry, Marah. I'm useless today."

"Hardly." Marah ran her gaze down the columns, her eyebrows coming together. *Oh, those swabbie bâtards.* "I don't think it's you. I think the Aegis is trying to short our stipend again. Just attach an appeal codicil." It wasn't enough that they took only indifferent care of non-citizens, the civil administration had to continually try to short them any grant money they were entitled to for it.

"Huh." Sibby took the papier sheets back, her nose wrinkling. Her fastidiousness wasn't just administrative; she didn't want to learn any med, even to check the stasis readouts. "Swabbies. You'd think they'd be grateful."

"Wouldn't you?" But Marah had a different reason for peeking into the receptionist's silica-sealed, repeater-proof domain. "I'm going to get sandwiches, you want the usual?"

"Sure." The prospect of lunch perked Sibby right up. "The usual, please. I'll generate a *raison d'informe* for this, too." She was beginning to get a handle on Aegis bureaucracy, and when she left for fresh fields it would be a sad day for the clinic. Marah already had a reference sheave with Madán's Greater Seal prominently featured, ready for that eventuality. It would get Sibby good work anywhere in the Sagittarius system, and quite probably on any other first-rate world in Anglene.

"Perfect. Don't forget the hash at the bottom." Not like Sibby would, but Marah had to say *something* or the receptionist would agonize over whether she'd forgotten a critical part.

Orienting on the details was an anxiety-making way to be built.

"Yes, my lady," Sibby intoned just like a swain in an Old Shiptime drama, and Marah laughed as the door swung closed.

Her next stop was just down the hall where Dr Tamarl, her sleek black bowl-cut gleaming atop a crisp white lab coat, poked at a touchscreen at Medstation One.

Marah hid a smile. "Heading to the sandwich khibi, Doctor. You want something?"

"Sonofabâtarding flymsy," Tamarl muttered as she jabbed. She hated charting with a passion though she wouldn't let the clinic steno-recco AI do it; Tam's records were works of art. She should have been a story-spinner. "Uh, yeah, I'll take a red shipstack on secale, please. Extra capitata." As per usual, but Tamarl wouldn't dream of just saying so. Precision was inherent in her every utterance. Losing her to a better clinic was going to be a blow, too; she'd already stayed far past the end of her residency. Maybe she simply hadn't found a position she liked yet, or maybe she was determined to see this through.

The last to give an order was Pannelore, who looked just as pleased with the prospect of lunch as Sibby. "You spoil us," he rumbled, and rubbed his big hands together. "Two Burunos, please. And some lager if they have it. In a bottle, I know, I'm not drinking on duty, but it'll be nice to take home."

"Aye-then." Marah sketched a salute. She already had Doctor Quinín's order and her own. Tomorrow was Sixday, she might as well treat herself before *that*.

Pann laughed and opened the door for her; Marah stepped out into the hot yellowgreen overcast swallowing Sharud, already regretting not taking the thermaseal coat Will had laid out that morning.

Her skarl, in the dun and grey of a synthetic's usual jumpsuit uniform, was waiting for her in front of the clinic, his grey head gleaming and his straight, stiff posture a rock for the thinning crowd to divide around. He brightened as he saw Marah, and hurried forward to offer his arm.

"Have you hydrated?" He let her set the pace, gliding beside her with a synthetic's grace, each movement calculated for maximum efficiency. "It is very warm."

She might almost suspect him of indirectly scolding her, except that was beneath a synthetic's dignity. "I'm fine. I'll even have tai when we get back, just to make sure. What do you want?"

"I am content, mistress." His chin dipped a little as he realized that wouldn't save him from having to order a sandwich. "Perhaps a shipstack? If there is one without harmful bacteria, that is."

His nutritional needs were inconsiderable, but synthetics liked tastes and textures as much as Terrans did and developed preferences in that area too. Marah had to hide a smile; Will sounded like an old captain bemoaning planetsiders' lack of hygiene. "You can watch them make it, you know."

"My attention is better spent upon the crowd, mistress." Still, he looked pleased. Marah recited the order inside her head, from Quinín's to Will's, start to finish as if it was a memory game. "You are quite happy today."

"I am." Light patient days at the clinic put her in a good mood, and citizenship markers going out were a reason to celebrate. "Tomorrow's Sixday, though."

Of course he was eager to plan and prepare. "I have collated all the—"

"Tomorrow, Will." Her heart was light, and she even skipped a step or two while holding his arm. His smile mirrored her own, and for once she didn't wonder if it was real or just a synthetic copying its owner's expression, mirroring to enhance Terran comfort and trust. "It can wait."

Later, she would think she should have known, that nothing good in the Saur ever came without a measure of horror. As it was, they joined the line near her favourite Fiveday food-khibi. The owner, a square-hipped, square-jawed woman with hair as golden as Robb's pulled high and piled atop her head like an emergency tether, squinted at the line in front of her big silver cart and smiled, a reflexive baring of teeth as her hands moved with practiced efficiency to layer protein, solidified lac, and other toppings in third-meter breadrolls.

That was when a massive, tearing artillery noise boomed up Via Kadinat, giving birth to a burst of black smoke. The pavement rocked slightly underfoot and Marah clutched at Will's arm, going limp and dragging them both down in case of shrapnel or ryfl-fire. Will, his reflexes quicker than a Terran or feline, managed to get his hand under her head, but Marah's skull still bounced hard enough to ring every klaxon and alarum on her brain-ship.

Direct hit, she thought first, then, *no, no please, don't tell me, have to get to the tent and scrub for the casualties...*

The screaming had begun, but she was in a bubble of silence. Nobody was yelling *"Medic!"* yet, it was merely the first crop of shocked or stunned yells, the shapeless noises that rise before Corp-soldat realize their well-ordered camp is under attack and training takes over. Habit triangulated the impact site as she lay, dazed, in Will's arms.

It can't. Not there. Please, not there, Mother Moon, not there. Let me be wrong.

But she wasn't.

WHERE THE MADÁN FREE CLINIC had stood there was only a ragged crater scarred with broken pipes, the surrounding buildings—Plegacír Credit, two tenements, the empty graffiti-robed storefront that used to house a Kaladin bodega—leaning drunkentooth around the cavity.

To be continued...

ABOUT THE AUTHOR_

Lili Saintcrow resides in the rainy Pacific Northwest with her children, dog, cat, and assorted other strays.

www.lilithsaintcrow.com

www.ingramcontent.com/pod-product-compliance
Lightning Source LLC
Chambersburg PA
CBHW051536260626
47170CB00003B/962